Banks of Green Willow

Banks of
Green Willow
Kevin Myers

SCRIBNER
TownHouse

London . New York . Sydney . Tokyo . Singapore . Toronto . Dublin

A VIACOM COMPANY

First published in Great Britain by Scribner/TownHouse, 2001
An imprint of Simon and Schuster UK Ltd and
TownHouse and CountryHouse Ltd, Dublin
A Viacom Company

1 3 5 7 9 10 8 6 4 2

Simon and Schuster UK Ltd
Africa House
64–78 Kingsway
London WC2B 6AH

Simon & Schuster Australia
Sydney

TownHouse and CountryHouse Ltd
Trinity House
Charleston Road
Ranelagh
Dublin 6

www.simonsays.co.uk

A CIP catalogue record for this book is available from the
British Library

ISBN 1-903650-12-7

Typeset by SX Composing DTP, Rayleigh, Essex
Printed and bound in Great Britain by
Omnia Books Limited, Glasgow

To Rachel, who makes everything possible.

Part One

CHAPTER ONE

Seth and Osiris: alpha and omega

The elderly man lay in the bed, white and trembling. Sheen covered his face, and a web of saliva connected his lips, tremulous in the shaft of sunlight shining through the hospital window.

'Worse, worse, than ever I seen him,' intoned the elder of his two visitors. 'Worse begod be far.'

The speaker, a man in his seventies, shook his head at the girl by his side. A soft rattle rose from the lungs of the patient, as if he were testing for the possibilities of speech, then he shaped some sounds with his lips: Vog-ush-ka.

'What was that?' asked the male visitor.

The girl shook her head. She was about twenty, handsome if you cared to examine her more closely – though people were generally not inclined to. She said nothing, but her eyes spoke volumes as she looked at her companion and, in return, the old man's eyes glittered at her under twin thatches of eyebrow, before he turned his attention back to the man on the bed.

'Drinkers,' he said. 'Crafty as a barrel load of monkeys. How else would a fellow in his condition in a place like this get a whole bloomin' bottle of whiskey? Probably downed it in one. Not long for this world, I'd say.'

Another sound emerged from the patient, guttural, confused: Vog-ush-ka.

'Vodka. He wants vodka, the cheek of him.'

'My,' murmured the girl. 'My oh my.'

Prompted suddenly by an instinct that surprised even her, she moved towards the dying man and took him in her arms. He sighed. Reaching with her hand to stroke his temples, her

fingers met a cold, waxy skin, greasy with sweat. She began
to murmur those ancient, wordless noises of compassion
which we turn to when speech no longer serves. He uttered
the sound again: Vog-ush-ka, before sleep slowly embraced
him, as it would with a child, and she released him.

'Tell me, me dear, have you a boyfriend at all, at all?'

'No,' she smiled, 'I'm not lucky in that line. Why do you
ask?'

'Why do I ask? What sane man wouldn't ask? Are young
men today so blind that they don't see beauty when it smacks
them in the eyes? Begod, is this what the world has come to?'
He raised his hand and touched her cheek, and she placed her
hand on his. 'What a lovely young woman you are, me dear,
and me an old rogue.'

'Well, the last bit sure is true.'

'Rory got a better deal, though it didn't seem so at the
time,' he observed as they began to leave. 'Better be a bullet
than be the booze. That's the worst I've seen him. I'd better
have a word with the doctor. You wait in reception.'

The figure in the bed awoke and made the same
meaningless noise, a small whimper of approaching death.

'And that,' said the male visitor, gesturing sadly, 'was
Rory's friend, the best friend me poor bloody brother ever
had.'

*

'Me tea,' the voice had boomed incredulously as Mrs
Ryan ushered Gina into the dining room of the Ryan bed and
breakfast. 'You appear to have forgotten me bloomin' tea!'

The radio in the background was detailing the likely consequences of the recent re-election of President Nixon, even as
US forces intensified the bombing war in Vietnam. This was
Gina Cambell's first morning in Dublin; she felt shy,
uncertain, her stomach uneasy.

'I have done no such thing,' Mrs Ryan replied forcefully to
the only other person present. 'What you need, Mr O'Reilly,
is a touch of the Pentagon medicine. Sure, a bit of a
clobbering with a few of those B52s would teach you
manners, you old whelp, you.'

She sniffed in triumph before turning back to Gina, 'Now, my dear, what would you prefer to have before your fry – cornflakes or porridge, what you Americans call oats?'

'On a day like today,' declared Mr O'Reilly, 'I'll go bail she plumps for the porridge. A fiver she says the porridge.'

Mrs Ryan scowled and then gave Gina a smile.

'I'll just have the fry,' replied Gina, quietly. A lash of sleet hit the window and the entire room shuddered in sympathy.

'It's on the pan already, and pay no heed to that Mr O'Reilly there,' Mrs Ryan tutted, exiting busily.

'Is it the south of Americay you're from,' he asked, 'where they have all the darkies?'

Gina felt her irritation rise but she stayed silent. She realised she should have gone to the bathroom before she came downstairs.

'No doubt, being an American, you're a student of that phenomenon known as Anglo-Irish lit-er-ra-ture.' He nibbled around the syllables like a horse picking grain from gravel. 'Sure I know it all, ignore a giant like Swift – Swift, have you heard of him? – and then revel, begod, in minnows like Sheridan, Farquhar.'

Mrs Ryan appeared at the door. 'Ah!' he cried. 'Here's me tea.'

Their host sailed past him and placed the plate of fried food before Gina. Mr O'Reilly let out a little yelp of disbelief, 'Where's me tea?'

Mrs Ryan performed a show of exasperation. 'Now will you give our young guest a bit of peace, Mr O'Reilly. Gina, dear, eat it while it's nice and warm.'

When she had gone, Gina glanced up from her meal. He caught her look.

'Anglo-Irish literature indeed,' he declared. 'Wilde. A fine writer, but couldn't be left with the boys for a minute. Mind you, nor could Mr Behan, and him only an average writer. He made a little go a long way. Sure he was a housepainter; isn't that the way of all them fellas, spreading it nice and thin? THE TEA, MRS RYAN,' he suddenly bawled. 'ME BLESSED TEA.'

Gina's irritation finally overcame her shyness and she

heard herself declare tartly, 'Yes, I have heard of Swift. But no, I'm not here to study Anglo-Irish literature. Which doesn't mean I'm not getting any lectures on the subject, whether I want them or not.'

Even as Gina bit her tongue, Mr O'Reilly slapped his leg. 'Begod I like a girl who speaks her mind, and in such an enchanting accent as well. If I had any bloomin' tea, I'd toast you in it.'

Gina, reddening, explained more gently, 'I'm just here on a three-month college placement in county Mayo, to look at Irish life. I got Ireland. Some of my class are in Germany, France, Italy, you know?'

'And you got Mayo? You poor misfortunate creature. Begod you drew the short straw there and no mistake.' He smiled at her and, feeling guilty at her earlier tone, she smiled back.

'The short straw? Never! I drew the best one. I just love Ireland. And Mayo too. It's beautiful.'

'Ah. Which only proves that you don't know it,' said Mr O'Reilly. 'What has you in Dublin?'

'A weekend visit, that's all.' She looked up at him again. His face glowed with a warm smile, and she felt even more apologetic for her earlier manner.

'Look . . .' she began.

'Pay no attention to me and the phenomenon of Anglo-Irish-lit-era-ture,' his dentures stepping from syllable to syllable like rocks in a stream. 'I'm in fierce bad form this morning. Anno Domini, you know, and I have many onerous duties to perform today. Forgive me for being such a tiresome old bore.'

'Do you mind me asking something?' she said. 'Please, do not say darkies. It's kind of disrespectful, don't you think?'

'Is it? Sure lookit, what would I know? Nothing! Just bewitched be the eyes, I am, like many a younger man.' His own dark eyes twinkled across the cold room.

'Oh Mr O'Reilly, are you flirting with me?'

'It's Mr O'Reilly to those I do business with and do me best to rob blind, but Con to me friends. Will you make it Con, will you?'

'Why I'd be only too delighted. And I'm Gina, Gina

Cambell, and yes sir, since you did mention it, I sure would love to be studying Anglo-Irish literature, Swift especially.'

'And why might that be?'

'Well a lot of things. Not many writers write with so much passion and so much honesty. Real honesty.' She paused, thinking. 'You know his verse about Celia, you know, about going to the bathroom and stuff?'

'Begod you're right there. Swift the scatologist. Tell me, how are the rashers, what you Americans call the bacon? Best covered with hair, always the sign of health. Me own head is me pride and joy, and me past seventy.'

'I guess Swift knew things about us all, and hey, the *rashers* are both fine and bald, which is the way I like them, Mr O'Reilly. But I'm not sure about this thing.' She prodded a dark object on her plate.

'Black pudding,' he pronounced. 'The north face of the Eiger of Irish Cuisine. And it's Con.'

'Sure, Con.'

'Painless when you know how. Con. C-O-N. As in cheat. You know Swift founded a hospital for the insane?'

'Did he? That's amazing. I thought way back then that they just locked the mentally ill up in prisons – in what, bedlams?'

'They were. Young lady, I liked you the moment I met you, yet here you are, still rising in my estimation.'

'What happened to Swift's hospital?'

'Sure amn't I going there myself this very morning? Would you like to see it? Swift's hospital?'

'I sure would, only . . .'

'Only you've got sight-seeing to do, places to visit, of course. Anno Domini again. Me wits is all over the place, like a madwoman's knickers.'

Gina pointed to the wind-rattled window. 'Sight-seeing? On a day like today? I would just hate to impose, I surely would.'

'Impose, is it? Impose, me arse. Oh where, oh where, is me bloomin' tea?'

*

'Why are you called Gina?' he asked half an hour later as he peered through the rain-lashed windscreen.

'Short for Georgina. Except nobody calls me that, just Gina. You mind me asking what you do?'

'Sell medical supplies. Linctus for one end and suppositories for the other. I live in Wicklow, but I stay with the bould Mrs Ryan when I've a lot of jobs in town. *Gerronoura'at*, you blithering eejit!' Their car lurched to the wrong side of the road, there was a sharp bang and Gina leapt in terror. She looked back and saw a caped cyclist struggling in a kerbside lake.

'We hit him,' she whispered.

'Only clipped him. Be right as rain in a couple of days. Sure it happens to us all. Me mother hit one only th'other day.'

'*Your mother?*'

'Ninety-four, a widow for nearly sixty years, me poor daddy drownded when I was a gossoon, and up every morning at seven to make me and Madge breakfast, even though she's that blind she can't see the stove.'

Gina scarcely managed to murmur, 'What's a goss—' before the car again wandered across the road.

'Gossoon. Little boy,' Con replied nonchalantly, as a truck braked sharply to avoid them. He tapped his forehead meaningfully. 'Madge is me sister. A bit backward, but devil of a problem with her since the little incident with Canon Fahey and the electric hedge-trimmer, though the ould urges seem to trouble her still, and her the age she is. Temptations of the flesh and all that. Sure you being young would know what I mean.'

Gina opened her mouth to disclaim any such knowledge, but instead another small noise of terror escaped her as they veered in front of a hurtling bus. The faces of astonished passengers flashed by.

'Nothing personal,' said Mr O'Reilly, waving his pipe and turning to grin broadly at her. Gina shut her eyes. He continued, 'Human nature, but little enough I'd know of that. Kissed a girl in Belmullet once. That's in Mayo, you know. Maybe not such a bad place after all. But then that was a while ago. My brother, now, he was one for the girls.' He fell silent and Gina opened her eyes. They were alive, and had stopped at traffic lights.

'Families,' he resumed, sounding baffled. 'Fierce quare things. Me now, I was in the IRA in the ould days during the Tan War. You know the Tan War with the British, fifty years ago? Never fired a shot, thank God, but proud to serve me country when the call come. But what did me baby brother Rory do when Hitler's war come along? Only run off to join the British army, the very crowd I'd been fighting. Families. Madder than Mick McMadd, families.' Suddenly, he stopped talking and began to dab at his eyes. The lights were green.

'What happened to him?' asked Gina.

'Killed. This Harry fellow we're visiting was his best friend, in the same regiment. The Royal Ulster Rifles. Harry never talked about what happened to poor Rory, just that he died. Me poor boy, born after me father died, and nearly young enough to be me son. The years go by, but a younger brother is a younger brother to the grave and beyond.'

Behind them, horns were sounding. Con brightened. 'Still, he was spared a life with that ould bitch Eileen Boylan. One of them stuck-up, mind-your-manners Boylans of Montenotte. What are them fellas sounding their horns for?'

'I think because the lights are green.'

'Jesus Mary and Joseph, why didn't you say?'

The car lurched forward, Gina shut her eyes again and Con resumed his tale. 'After the war, she went off to Americay, taking Rory's little son with her. To her uncle in Texas, I think, and I seen hide nor hair of neither since. So poor Harry's me only link with me baby brother, and sure he never got over the war neither. Or the drink. Worse than them bloody Nazis, the drink. And I'm all he has. His family – northerners, sermonizers, teetotal, whited sepulchres – don't want to know.'

*

'Is anybody sitting here?'

Gina looked up. A woman with a little girl stood before her.

'No, well, not at the moment, but I do have a friend coming back.'

'Good, my feet are fucking killing me.'

Gina blinked, startled by yet another display of Irish familiarity.

'This brat'll be the death of me. You're American, yes?' her companion continued gaily. 'I'm here with my mother. She's visiting her brother who's got . . . well fuck me.' Her child was crawling over to Gina's lap. 'That is only fucking *amazing*. This hospital's full of babysitters of mine. And *she*' – she pointed accusingly at the child – 'put them here. You must be special. Howrya, I'm Josey O'Flaherty, and the reptile from the black lagoon is Clare.'

While Clare clambered up her body, Gina introduced herself.

'Con O'Reilly, as I live and breathe,' said Josey, looking past her. 'Good morning to you, Mr O'Reilly.'

Mr O'Reilly blinked. 'Josey O'Flaherty, is it? Begod it is. And I suppose the infant's yours too, with no sign of a husband, I'll be bound. No more than could be expected either. Agh well.' He stroked his moustache and chuckled, as Gina absorbed this other truth about Ireland: everybody knew one another.

''Tis a long time since I saw you,' said Con affably to Josey. 'Was it with your father Seamus, God rest his soul, in the National Gallery?'

'It was indeed, in the National Gallery, with my father, God rest his soul.'

'I thought so. Poor Seamus. My condolences. Sure he loved the gallery. A place of real art. None of our modernist daubings. Jackson Pollock? Jesus Mary and Joseph.'

Clare put a finger in Gina's eye and Josey grabbed her, hissing, 'Viper.'

'Viper, is it? Viper? Josey O'Flaherty, I seen you in infancy, and you were something begot be the devil, be the devil himself.'

'What side of the bed did you get out of, Con dear?' replied Josey, putting a soother in Clare's mouth.

'Matter a damn what side I got out of, puts me in bad form thinking about modern art. Sure there's been no art to speak of, nor music neither, nor writing either come to that, by anyone born since the Edwardian times. 'Twas the old certainties which made great art possible, not this modern mishmash. Babies' nappies next, you mark my words.'

'Speaking of which,' said Josey, and raised Clare to her nose and sniffed. 'Oh fuck! I changed you only an hour ago to the sound of the Angelus bloody bell, you shitty little bitch.'

'Delightful talk in front of a child,' declared Mr O'Reilly, 'delightful talk entirely. But it was never to the Angelus, sure it's not even noon yet.' He consulted his fob watch and started: 'Jesus Mary and Joseph, all this talking has me wits astray. 'Twas in Lucan I was meant to be five minutes ago. Linctus be the gallon and suppositories be the score is promised there, with me here and me poor bloody patients dying like flies the length and breadth of the town! Gina, my dear, can I leave you with Josey here? If she gives you a begging bowl, don't be surprised, she being an O'Flaherty.'

'God forgive you, Con, and you a mere O'Reilly,' sniffed Josey.

'I'll see you back at the fair Mrs Ryan's, Gina, my dear; we might together essay the foothills of her black pudding, but till then will you forgive me?'

He doffed his sodden trilby with a graceful flourish, turned, and scuttled out. Gina had barely a moment to consider before Josey said, 'Providence, sweet Jesus, providence. Thank you, God, I might even give up sex. Gina, my dear, you're the very excuse I need not to have lunch with Mother. We're keeping the wrong one in here. My uncle is sound as a bell, my mother is barking. Listen, will you have lunch with me? A humble pasta? Please. Fuck, here she comes. Say yes, say yes.'

*

Still slightly shocked by the speed of events, and confused by the way the Irish transform acquaintance into intimate friendship, Gina went to Josey's home, a small house near the Grand Canal. Her host toyed with the primary ingredients of a spaghetti bolognese until a bottle of wine brought those preliminaries to an end. Soon Josey was drunk, aggressively, arguing over the spelling of Gina's name.

'There's no such name as Cambell without a p,' she sneered.

'There is,' declared Gina, producing her student ID. 'Ta-daaaaa.'

'That means fuck all,' said Josey. Gina was frantically thinking up an excuse to leave when the phone rang.

Josey answered it and listened briefly before shrieking, 'You fucking what? You fucking cunt. You fucking wanker. You fucking arsehole!'

She slammed the phone down. 'The fucking babysitter's cried off, and I gave the little bitch a quid tip on Friday! I fucking well don't believe it. And I've got to be in work in twenty minutes.' She sat glaring at her glass of wine.

Appalled, Gina heard her own small voice offer: 'I could mind Clare.'

'Brilliant,' said Josey with evil alacrity, rising, grabbing her coat and her keys, then declaring airily, 'Any problem, go next door to Eileen Bardwell. I'd have asked her to babysit for me, but she drinks like a fish. And anyway she's got her hands full with her Mickey, the wee brat. Oops,' she muttered as she caught sight of her wine glass. She downed the last of its contents, smacked her lips, waved to people who weren't there, and was gone.

'But . . .' Gina cried to the still-echoing door.

Incredulous at the chaos which seemed to ambush the unwary at every turn in Irish life, Gina sat down alongside Clare on the settee. How was it possible that her day had gone so uncontrollably awry? A discussion about Swift had taken her to the bedside of a dying man, and now here she was, alone and minding a child whose mother had been a complete stranger to her barely an hour before.

What next?

The doorbell rang.

CHAPTER TWO

The train carrying Gina back to Mayo and the Bracken family howled across the mudplains of the midlands, grey birds rising in flurries from brown bogs and bleak sedgeflats. Gina sat gazing through the rain-streaked windows, thinking of the stranger she had met the day before.

Her memory danced to the rhythm of the train. *Click-clickety-click*. Shorry, he had said. I wash ekshpecting Joshey. She remembered seeing a slender young man, built like a dancer, fine-faced, high cheekbones, slightly Roman nose. *Click-clickety-click*. And as she listened to him, she had realized that his lisp wasn't caused by drink, but by a small speech impediment. *Click-clickety-click*.

My name is Stefan, he had said. Stefan. Josey was gone, she'd explained but she'd invited him in, thinking, *What am I doing?* as he followed her into the kitchen. Ireland: the endless triumph of the unexpected. Swaying in her seat in the train, she smiled to herself. He had lifted her student card from the table and looked at it. 'Georgina,' he had said. 'Yes,' she had replied, and that was what she remained: Georgina. The memory warmed her. Georgina. She liked it. A new name, an old name, a new person. Two new persons.

A sour-faced inspector checked her ticket. She smiled at him, and in full measure he returned the smile. *Clickety-click*.

She turned the memory over, feeling it, caressing it. Something good had happened. Every part of her body told her that. Even the rhythm of the train agreed with her.

Stefan had sat down over coffee and a cigarette, which he smoked with earnest elegance; he had told her about himself. A Yugoslav father now dead, an Irish mother, he a student of Yugoslav affairs. He was working with the Community Relations Commission in Belfast.

'You've been mighty successful there, right?' she'd joked. She smiled again, this time at the memory of her jest.

'Brought peace and brotherhood my first day.' He grinned.

She'd told him about herself – like him, fatherless – and when there was silence it had been companionable. She had felt emotions adjusting, an ease calming the natural doubts of a woman alone with a stranger.

One doubt had remained. Why was he visiting Josey? Was he a boyfriend of hers? He was younger than her, but still . . .

'Are you a friend of Josey's?'

'Only sort of. She's too unreliable to call a friend. No, my mother owns the house here and she asked me to drop by and collect the rent. Which I hate. Some chance anyway. Getting money from Josey is like pulling teeth from a hen. Normally we talk and agree, next month.'

He'd smiled at her again. Things inside her had moved. 'You want to go for a walk?' he'd asked. 'I've got my car outside. I'd love to take you to Wicklow. Can you spare the time?'

She'd nodded.

In the train, she recalled the pronunciation, *outshide*. Their eyes had met. They'd said nothing for a while. Then he had stood up and said, 'Let's go. The three of us. You, me and Lucretia Borgia here.'

Gina had laughed. He'd leant forward to kiss her gently. She'd kissed him instead.

'Oh,' he'd said.

'Walk,' she'd replied.

'Yes,' he'd agreed as their hands met. 'Walk.'

*

They drove to Wicklow, south of Dublin, where the hills rose steeply, their sides russet with the winter bracken, silver streams falling and cascading towards a distant sea. As they walked he hoisted Clare on his shoulders and sang:

By banks of green willow, a maiden once strayed.
A soldier waylaid her, a compliment paid.
Young maiden I know you, and I will be true.
By banks of green willow I'll give you your due.

Later, after they returned Clare to Josey, who was both sober and apologetic, Stefan drove Gina to her bed and breakfast. Had he made a serious move on her, she might have distrusted him, but still said yes. He didn't. He simply kissed her. She kissed him in return, and each felt the draw of their bodies, their hips. She told him that she was returning the next day to the Bracken family in Mayo, with whom she had been staying for the past three months, but she would be back in Dublin, she said. Soon.

'Promise?' *Promish.*

'Oh believe me, I promise.'

'I'll come on down from that northern hell-hole.'

'Do.'

*

At the station in Mayo, Matt Bracken, red-faced and beaming, grasped her as if she had escaped on the last flight from the Congo. 'Lost without you, we've been,' he roared heartily at her. 'Lost entirely.' He grabbed her bag with one hand and put his other to her face. 'Child, you're freezing. Come.' He turned. 'Maureen's made the mother and father of a soup, that'll put some life in you. I've felt warmer corpses.'

Gina followed his broad shoulders with deep gratitude. How lucky she was – the girl who originally got the placement with the Brackens had cancelled after her brother's death in Vietnam. They were approaching their car when Matt shouted, 'There's Noelly! Noelly! Noelly!' Across the road a young boy wheeled from his companions and ran to join them. 'Da, Gina.' He put a hand on his father's arm, but kissed her.

'Gina, Gina, never leave me again, sure they've been flogging me every night, sure th'ould thug here has me beaten black and blue, the brute. Alliteration.'

Gina laughed as Noelly got into the car, and he cried, 'It's true. They had me sweeping the chimney last night, them watching telly and me with my toothbrush going scrub scrub scrub. They're making a bloody hell of my life.'

'You'll be back up the chimney tonight with your

toothbrush if you don't watch your tongue,' said Matt
jovially. 'Lamb chops for tea.'

Noelly winked at Gina. 'Forgive me, aged P. The hades I
was referring to was sanguinary.'

Matt groaned. 'The Brothers have got you reading Dickens
again.'

'The Brothers? Decent Christians who only hit you with a
decent shovel with a decent Christian blade on it. You know
where you stand with the Christian Brothers. There's Paula!
Run her down, Dad, run her down! Curses! Missed her.
AGAIN!'

The car drew up alongside Paula, Noelly's older sister, and
she got in, all lump and knee and scarlet cheek. 'Gina,' she
said. 'Oh Gina, I thought you'd never come back.' She looked
as if she were going to lean forward and kiss her, but
awkwardness intervened, and she waved a hand, her face
glowing with joy and embarrassment.

At the Brackens', Maureen fed them all soup. 'Tell me
about Dublin, so,' she said to Gina, with that steady look
which suggested she knew everything anyway.

'Well, I did some sight-seeing, went to a gallery or two, did
a lot of window-shopping, visited St Patrick's Hospital, and I
took a long walk in the Wicklow mountains.'

'Mountains? Lumps,' said Noelly. 'Wee lumps. Not like
Nephin.'

'Tell us about the fashions,' urged Paula.

'The fashions, the fashions,' murmured Noelly into his
soup. 'The hemlock, the hemlock.'

'You're skating on thin ice here, my boy, and there'll be no
US cavalry coming to your rescue,' said Matt sternly.

'Nope. They'd drown,' said Noelly over his spoon. He
sniffed. 'Mixed metaphors always end in disaster. Is that
what did for Custer, mixing his metaphors? Little Big Horn,
I ask you.'

'Where in the name of the divine Jesus, God forgive me for
blaspheming, did we get you from and all this talk at all?'
asked Maureen, the soup ladle poised enquiringly as she
scanned the table for more takers.

'Brother Thomas,' said Matt. 'The things he's got you

learning. Gray's "Elegy", P.G. Wodehouse, Joyce, Frank O'Connor.'

'*Playboy*, compulsory nudes, agony,' added Noelly.

'What do you know about nudes?' asked Matt, a little severely.

'Nothing,' said Noelly, 'and more's the pity, with me a norphan an' all.'

'You bloody well will be the way you go on,' said Maureen. 'Now. Chops.'

The main course was served with potatoes and cabbage and gravy. Though Gina had been hungry, her appetite began to diminish as she thought again of Stefan. She decided she would ring him at his office. She knew he sometimes worked late. She pushed her plate aside, feeling Noelly's eyes following it.

'Gina, fair Gina, you wouldn't ever take pity on a famished orphan and give him your uneaten, unwanted little chop? Pleeeeease?'

'Here, now don't you go stealing food from off the plates of guests,' said Maureen sternly. 'You can clear up the plates, young glutton and master-know-all.'

'Me? Clear up the plates? What about Paula? What about the twins, they never do anything. Never. Ever. It's just not fair.' Noelly, now his age again, glowered at the table. The twins meanwhile were lost in a private exchange at the end of the table. He examined his plate furiously, and suddenly looked up, smiling. 'Pray let me clear the dishes *and* do the washing up, Mummy dearest. It will be my pleasure.'

'If you'll excuse me,' said Matt, rising and shaking his head, 'I have a son to slay.'

'And I have a phone call to make,' said Gina. 'May I have the torch?'

'You can of course,' replied Maureen, looking at Gina meaningfully. 'Where is it now?'

'On the sideboard there,' replied Gina pointing, ignoring the implied *Who are you calling at this hour?*

'Clever girl,' said Maureen, still studying her closely. Gina felt her colour rise. Unaware of the moment's tension, Noelly took the dishes to the kitchen from where he could soon be

heard singing along with the clattering of crockery, while his
voice accompanied in shrill mimicry of a guitar riff. 'Crazy
horses, yeeeeoooowwwww.'

'Oh for God's sake,' bellowed Matt's despairing voice from
his study.

'Back in a minute,' whispered Gina to the carpet as she
edged towards the door.

'Noelly! Stop that racket or I'll come and crown you,' cried
Maureen, raising her eyes to heaven as she passed the torch to
Gina.

'Living in terror, Ma, oh bejasus living in terror.
Yeeeeoooowwwww,' Gina heard from behind her as she stole
out of the front door and up the hill.

*

Gina stood in the telephone kiosk, her torch illuminating the
instructions. The Brackens had been waiting for a phone for
over a year. Matt had one in his office in the town, but at
home they had to make do with using the public telephone up
the road. The wind hunted through the broken windows of
the cubicle, and she was bitterly cold.

She learnt from the torchlit card that she could not call
Belfast direct. As instructed, she dialled 10 for the operator,
who came on the line so quickly that she might have been
watching Gina from behind a hedge. Her voice was cheerful,
and sounded as if she smoked fifty cigarettes a day. She
wheezed with jaunty regret that lines to Belfast were virtually
non-existent, but Gina was to have two ten-penny pieces ready.

'Sorry about this, but the system's stone-age here,' she said
proudly. 'Don't I know you? Are you staying with Matt
Bracken above in the new bungalow? He must be doing fierce
well building a grand place like that, and him not inheriting a
single blessed field, never mind a farm.'

The kiosk shook in the wind and the temperature dropped
even further. Gina had a sense of being in a holed spacecraft.

'What's your name?' asked the operator.

'Gina Cambell,' she said through chattering teeth. 'Gina for
Georgina. You think my call to Belfast might be ready soon?'

'Soon or never, begod it could be any time. Generally I say

half an hour, that way people are not too disappointed when they're kept waiting, and delighted when they're not.'

'I'd love to be delighted.'

'Sure wouldn't I love to delight you, but these things are not in my power. 'Tis the operator above in Castlebar itself has the power of life and death over the pair of us, over the pair of us no less.'

A shudder erupted from Gina. 'I hope you're not cold,' said the voice in her ear.

'I'm *freezing*,' she gasped.

'Well of course you are, you're in the bloody old box on the Belmullet Road, sure that'd make the North Pole seem like Benidorm. I was in Benidorm once. Nice. A bit cheap. The lower class of English, if you take my meaning. We can't have an American perishing of cold in Mayo, now can we? I'll make up some lie about this and that. Hold on there, hold on.'

Gina waited for what seemed like a frozen eternity, worrying about what she would say to Stefan. Would he be interested? Why was she standing in this freezing cold booth while he was up there in Belfast, which seemed to stagger from one unspeakable atrocity to another? Why? . . .

Finally the operator came back to her. 'Sorry for keeping you. Me lies were of no avail,' she lamented. 'No avail at all at all. Done it once too often. The good news is that there'll be a line ready quite soon. Ah! Here it is, on its way now. Hold on, hold on, oh glory be, glory be, hold on there, hold on there . . .'

Gina heard cogs mesh and marry distantly in some telephone exchange, and her pulse began to quicken. Then there was a sharp bang, followed by a long electrical yawning noise.

'Jesus Mary and Joseph, we've fucking lost it, I don't fucking believe it!' the operator shrieked into Gina's ear. There was another bang and the operator snarled, 'Oh fuck that, we've lost the fucking lot! These fucking phones will be the death of me, the fucking death of me, and there's you, standing there in that great big freezing cunt of a phone box on the Belmullet Road. Christ alive.'

In the silence that followed, the wind moaned through the dark night, and Gina, nonplussed, said nothing.

'It was working in England during the war what done it,' the operator explained with sudden nonchalance. 'In Coventry. My uncle's place, Gallaghers'. I was in the site office, just seventeen, barely out of school, never heard a curse in my life, and everywhere there was eff-this and cee-that, the blitz all around me young head, and sometimes it all comes back to me in times of stress, and there's no controlling it until I calm down. Hold on! I think we're getting a line!'

'Community Relations Night Service,' said a voice in Gina's ear. *Night shervish.* Her heart plummeted and her throat seized shut. 'Wrong number,' she tried to say.

'You're through, you're through, modom,' said the operator in a new and oddly English accent. 'Hold on there, Belfast, you have a call from a Miss Cambell from Mayo, and her only freezing to death there. One second. I'm putting the caller through now. Bye Georgina!'

In panic, Gina reached to cut the phone off, sure she was investing too much faith in their brief relationship. As her finger touched the button, she heard Stefan's voice say, 'Georgina, I've been trying to contact you all day, through Josey, Mrs Ryan, everywhere I could think of.'

'Stefan!'

'I thought I'd missed you or something. Christ, I'm glad you got through.'

'That's nice,' commented the operator in her polite voice. *Thot's nase.*

'What?' said Stefan.

'And her in the box on the Belmullet Road, and you there in a nice warm office,' she declared as if he were responsible for the weather, before adding, 'What's it like in Belfast?'

'The usual. Rain, sleet, snow.'

'Well of course it would be. Georgina, are you still there?'

'Yes,' said a little voice, shivering.

'God love us, it's frozen to the marrow you must be, poor creature. No more charges. On the house, as they say. Nice talking to you, Stefan.'

'And you, operator. What's your name?'

'Bernie.'

'Thanks, Bernie. Look after yourself.'

'Look after yourself, sure that's only a madhouse you're living in, a madhouse. I'm off now. Bye.'

Click and finally they were alone together, she on a windswept boggy hillside in Mayo, he in a warm and brightly lit office in the drearily brutal city of Belfast, where glum soldiers patrolled in the rain.

*

Bosnia, 1992

See them, these other soldiers, a generation later. They make their advance in skirmishing order through the waves of hot air which fill the vault between mountain slopes, their legs moving through this ocean of sweat as leadenly as deep-sea divers.

Can you hear the cuckoos chanting over these upland meadows? Glorious, is it not? Observe the banks of wild flowers, toadflax, yellow rattle, field gentian, orchids and an infinity of tiny irises flourishing on this alpine prairie of grasses. Please. Examine each grass head, a miracle of snowflake elegance. Is this existence not a wondrous thing?

The men are silent as they move forward carefully. Insects rise like hand-flung seeds before their feet, but their eyes do not see them. They wait for the first of their number to be hit by a sniper. They have rehearsed this in countless dreams, the moment when a bullet, moving at a speed of two kilometres every three seconds, impacts on a human skull. The head cracks open and spills its contents, the body collapsing, sighing, as around the falling man his companions drop, just as they have risen, wide-eyed and scrambling from their dreams to escape this moment.

Behind them a boy walks and dances, uttering little jokes. A tall blond machine-gunner moves with a languid gait on the left flank, a loose belt of ammunition from his 7.92 Type 53 machine-gun clink-clink-clinking to the rhythm of his hips. These tiny olive figures progress with such stellar slowness through the green and khaki vastness of this valley that from a distance one might think they are static.

These men are parched. Their thirst sits inside them like a tumour. Visions pass through their minds. Wives, girlfriends, beer, soft nights. A baby sister's birthday looms and her scarcely bearded brother manages a smile as he thinks of the tortoise he will give her.

Step back. Is it not clear now? Can you not see back to the day when all this began?

CHAPTER THREE

Gina was dreaming of her last few minutes in Mayo, the tears, the promises to stay in touch on the station platform. The Brackens in a mournful cluster, and Mrs O'Hara from the village grocer's who had questioned her closely on several occasions to see whether it was really and truly possible that she had never met her cousin Annie in Chicago. From nowhere, a woman with dyed-red hair approached, held her hands, and in a voice coated with phlegm and tobacco tar, wished her well.

'Bernie,' she guessed. 'My, you are such a disgrace.'

'Don't I know it. Enjoy yourself with that Stefan of yours. And don't forget the condoms. Them's the fellas, if you can get your hands on them, here in holy Ireland.' She winked and was gone. As Gina waved at her departing back, Bernie turned and croaked, 'A phone call, Gina,' but she was using Mrs Ryan's voice. 'And 'tis lashing out.'

Gina jerked her head off the pillow. She was indeed back at Mrs Ryan's. Phone. Stefan. Gina threw on her kimono robe and ran downstairs to the single phone in the hall. 'Good morning, Mr O'Reilly, Con, I mean,' she remarked to the crumpled figure on the stairs below her. He was wearing a black armband and his eyes were on the steps before him. He looked round at her and shied.

'Jesus Mary and Joseph, girl, you're naked! Merciful hour, what are you about?'

'Oh Con, this is a very respectable Japanese garment. The Japanese are exceedingly modest, you know.'

'The Japanese, modest? Geishers and that class of caper, whole blooming families sitting around in the bathtub, men and women in the nude, not a stitch between them, and that's modest? Not in Wicklow it isn't. Is it me and Madge having a bath together? Modest? And her with her urges and no sense of privacy at all at all? God between us and all harm.'

Gina bit her tongue. Mrs Ryan, waving the phone, cried, 'Gina,' and she slipped by him as Con continued in a single unbroken stream: 'And speaking of harm, sure the gentleman we visited the last time is dead. I'm just off to the funeral. It'll be like Mozart's if Mozart had been buried in Wicklow. Just me and the gravedigger.'

Gina caught fragments of what he was saying. Her heart was bursting with more pressing things.

'His cousin is Church of Ireland – Episcopalian, in your language – minister at Cloncawell, not far from me,' murmured Con sadly to the carpet. 'He's burying poor Harry McCambridge there. The last of the line. So here, I'll be off my dear, or it'll just be the gravedigger and the clergyman, and then Wolfgang where are ye?'

Gina's ear was to the phone as Con's explanation vanished for all time.

*

Bosnia, 1992
The soldiers have paused in wary clusters – see their disbelieving, scolding sergeants driving them apart: such targets in groups! – and they spread out, exhausted, drinking from their water bottles. At length an officer rises, reclips his webbing, and indicates to his sergeant that it is time to move. The men rise like old men from their slumbers, their limbs stiff as they form into a loose line abreast and once again begin their advance, stumbling over the rough ground, their rifles at port.

Sunlight steeples downward, as heat rises in inverted waterfalls, consuming entire platoons. To the left, skirmishers encounter a stream, made visible from afar by the weeping trees which flourish along its course. See the drooping branches dance in the shimmering air.

In an odd, jagged line the skirmishers spread along the stream. Some then cross, bent double as they run, their rifles now menacingly cocked and ready as they splash across the water. Behind them men have deployed in cover, their eyes peering down sights at possible locations for enemies. Five rounds automatic at the first sign of trouble.

The first soldiers safely across, others follow. There are no shots, no defenders of this handsome wide stream, with its rocky, arid beaches on either side. In the spring it would be beachless, an icy foaming torrent rushing to the Miljacka miles away, but on this summer's day it is a lazy brook which draws soldiers to its bubbling generosity. Two of the men drop on their knees to drink, but others remain watchful, scanning distant trees, and beyond them the smouldering skeletons of burnt-out houses.

The fair-haired machine-gunner rests his bipod on the rubble of a ruined storehouse and scrutinizes the land before him down his forward barleycorn sight. Through the air comes the distant sound of gunfire. Silence amid the babble of water and the birdsong, men exchanging looks, water dripping from their half-raised, scooped hands.

Two officers confer as the machine-gunner stays unmoving, his barrel traversing. Through the haze, far-off houses burn, the smoke rising in the heat. The officers wave their men forward, and together they move, alert, feeling that eyes and gunbarrels might be on them. Walking over scorched scrub through walls of heat, fear churning in their bowels, each soldier wondering, Who will be hit first? If me, through the head, please God, neat and clean, or the arm, so that I can walk home.

Home or head or arm: the soldier's trinity.

*

Ireland, 1972

The morning's rain had lifted and a warm soft wind had risen from the south. As they drove down the winding lanes of central Wicklow, thirty miles from Dublin, Gina told Stefan about herself, about the odd spelling of her surname, and her middle name, Du Pre, as in Jacqueline.

'You know her Elgar Cello Concerto?'

'With Barbirolli? Why of course I do.'

'Here, I've got it somewhere in here.' He slowed the car while he rummaged through a box of cassettes on the floor beside her feet, and then rammed one into the player. They listened in silence.

'A kind of un-English name for an English musician, don't you think?' Gina said when the music ended.

'Names,' he laughed. 'Du Pre is French, Elgar is Swedish. Listen to my name: Djurdjev. Very Irish.'

'I know. You told me. So how come?'

'As well as being a tennis player my mother is a linguist. Like her father, my grandad, God bless him, who was an Irish scholar – professor at University College Dublin. My mother was studying at Cambridge when war broke out, and because she was vehemently anti-Nazi she got involved with British Intelligence. That's how she was parachuted into Yugoslavia, where she met my father, who was with the partisans.'

Gina looked at Stefan's high cheekbones, his small and permanent smile on those full lips. With an effort she controlled the urge to lean over and kiss him. He turned to her and said, 'After the war, I was born. My father died of war injuries, long before I knew him, and some years later my mother married again. Someone she met at the tennis club.'

'Tennis,' she laughed. 'After what she'd been through. Are you good at tennis?'

He smiled. 'Not bad. Rather good by Irish standards. Keeps me fit.'

Keeps you fit, she thought, as she wondered about his body. They slowed to allow a man to urge three cows off the track in front of them, and a large black car emerged from a lane. Gina remembered something of Con's words – what was it he was saying about poor Harry McCambridge, dead in old Dean Swift's hospital? – and was about to wonder aloud when Stefan started to speak.

'See that signpost there? Well the Agha in Aghavannagh means field.' He said the word in Irish, *Acha*.

'Agha,' she repeated.

'You have a good ear,' he said.

'You should put your tongue in it some time,' she said, shocked at her brazenness. She froze in embarrassment. The car stopped. He leaned over and began to do her bidding, and she was immediately aroused. She turned and put her lips on his, as the black car slowly vanished from sight.

'And up there,' he said, withdrawing his lips from hers and pointing down the road, 'is the ancient mound of the storytellers. Tomnascela.'

He drove a few more miles and parked the car. They walked beneath a pale wintry sun in a pure blue sky, to a stream. Even in the Irish midwinter insects buzzed through the brilliant yellow flowers of the gorse, and birds sang from their perches on the high black branches of whitethorn bushes. She lay down, feeling him looking at her, and said Yes with those long lingering eyes. Yes again, with a soft, consenting blink.

He leaned forward and kissed her. She put her arms around his neck and kissed him in return, feeling a great ease emanating from the small of her back settle right through her.

'Are you on the pill?'

Nineteen, silly with lust, she did not hesitate. 'Yes,' she lied.

*

Later, they found a hotel and ordered afternoon tea of the ancient Irish variety: a huge silver teapot, and with it a silver salver of sandwiches – ham, cheese and chicken – with scones, tarts and cakes in sinful abundance served by a sinfully flirtatious receptionist–waitress, Esmerelda.

'What are you?' he asked seriously, munching.

'Not much. I'm the quiet girl in class. Boys don't notice me. You wouldn't have, only I opened the door to you. And you?'

'I studied politics at Trinity and did a thesis on Yugoslavia. And then the North began. Because of my studies about intercommunal structures in Yugoslavia, I got a job with the Community Relations Commission in Northern Ireland. That's it.'

'Yugoslavia sure sounds like a fascinating country.'

'It's an amazing country, just about every nationality in Europe.'

'Except the Irish, right?'

'Except, thank God, the Irish. But millions of Muslims. Though they're not a nationality. More a people.'

Gina thought for a while before asking, 'What does that mean?'

Stefan replied, 'I don't know.' His roguish smile caused her heart to lurch. 'But it does sound good, doesn't it? Anyway, the Muslims at least have freedom of worship there.'

'What's your own opinion of the Muslims?' she asked solemnly, trying to keep her turbulence in order.

'That's hard to say.'

'Why?'

'Because I haven't met many of them.'

'Aren't they kind of important?'

'They are important, of course, but you can't just say to someone over there, hey, are you a Muslim? You have to be very delicate.

'You! Delicate!'

'Indeed, and I had to read a lot. Sugar, Treadgold.'

'Is there much in English about the Muslims in Yugoslavia?'

'Apart from those two, virtually nothing.'

'So what did you do? Depend on stuff in Serbo-Croat?'

Gina sensed an elusiveness in his manner. He now busied himself buttering a fresh scone. She pressed him.

'So why don't you write about the place? Wouldn't that make sense, to write in English, for a larger audience? And who knows, it could be real useful in places like Northern Ireland, Canada maybe.'

'You're right. It's a great idea. Yes, I like it. There's one tiny, tiny problem. I don't speak Serbo-Croat.'

'You don't speak . . . Well how did you manage when you went there?'

'Georgina sweet,' he said slowly, 'I just don't know. I'll let you know when I find out. You see, I've never been there.'

There was a silence during which the fire blazed with hearty and irreverent cheer. Stefan laughed. 'It's terrible, isn't it? I just got sucked into the whole business because of my name. People think that in my family we all babbled to one another in Serbo-Croat, but of course we didn't. My mother was – suppose still is – fluent in the language. But then she was fluent in encoding things too, and that doesn't mean she spoke to us in Morse, dot dot dash dash dot. I speak English, reasonable Irish and goodish French. But at UCD being Yugoslav was chic. Girls preferred me if I was Slavic rather than Celtic.'

'I can see you'd need something. You guys. You said you hadn't met *many* Muslims.'

'Did I? Did I really say "many"? A Slavic failing, the intrusive "m". I meant any.'

'Oh witty, *très* witty.'

'And I bluffed and plagiarized my way through the thesis. Shocking, isn't it?'

The maid entered. She took a log from the timber basket and threw it on the fire. The embers sparked beneath the impact, then blinked, stunned. 'I'll get some more,' she said, taking the empty basket. She looked up and her eyes smiled at Gina as she departed. A message, a common desire for the man present, passed unspoken, but sensed. Gina looked back at Stefan.

'So now you know the truth.' He laughed. 'Have some tea.'

'That's not the whole truth. Your Serbo-Croat might just be very poor.'

'Oh, worse than poor. It's non-existent, other than to bid you good-day, *Dobodan*.'

'Have you told me a word of truth? I mean, do you even play tennis?'

'Oh yes, that I do. Tennis, yes.'

He smiled and shook his head, looking for a while into the diminishing, flickering flames.

'I don't know what to believe about you.'

'Believe the truth.'

'What truth?'

'Well, I don't speak Serbo-Croat, but I will. I haven't been to Yugoslavia but I will go. I did a thesis which was a con. I work for the Community Relations Commission. That's a con too. But I'm not.'

They sat silently in the dark. Too early for dinner, the corridors empty, the receptionist keeping her noiseless vigil like a nurse at a deathbed, this was the desolate hour of a country hotel's life. Simultaneously, they both shuddered.

'Kiss me,' she said.

'God, I am just so bloody obedient,' he said as he raised her to her feet.

'After you, when you're done with him,' said Esmerelda, out of nowhere.

'I'll be a while,' said Gina, feeling suddenly brave.

'I can wait.'

'You're sure going to have to.'

CHAPTER FOUR

That night they met some of his friends in a Dublin pub. Peter Burke, a young doctor, spoke enthusiastically about his work, about the long siege-like battles against disease in which he specialized, but Gina's mind was elsewhere, and when Stefan whispered, 'Let's go,' she bade his friends good night and they left.

They went to Stefan's home, a large Victorian pile on Pembroke Road. His mother was away. The guest room was old-fashioned: heavy drapes, gilded mirror, a large bed with weighty woollen blankets, and a bathroom with a huge tub and a handset. When she saw it, Gina heard herself say, 'Can I bathe you?' She trembled at her shamelessness, but he smiled, and said, 'I'd settle for a bath.' He kissed her on the cheeks, whispering with mock pomposity, 'In Ireland one bathes in the sea and baths in the bath.' She laughed as she kissed him back.

He moved his mouth and took her ear gently in his teeth, his tongue flicking in and out. He bent and turned on the water. She stood still as he kissed her again and then removed her clothes. When she was naked, she undressed him.

They were nude before the mirror, him behind her. He pressed himself against her, his half-erect penis against her buttocks, and placed a strong brown hand on the white of her breast. Her fingers touched his thigh: the muscle was rock hard. She looked at her breasts, at her flat belly, at her triangle of pubic hair. She raised her right hand and placed it on her left breast, and gently caressed a nipple. The penis on her buttocks went bone hard. She reached behind her and gently squeezed his testicles. His eyes glazed, his knees buckling, a soft choking sound from his throat rising above the roar of the water.

The bath was nearly full. 'Get in,' he whispered.

She obeyed, the water warm on her shins, and he stepped in beside her. She knelt, and he scooped water over her head, her body stirring within. He cascaded more water over her, then massaged shampoo into her hair. His hands were so firm yet gentle; and her scalp tingled with a pleasure that passed to her breasts and to her groin. An orgasm gathered within her and almost to stem it, a last attempt at restraint, she held herself.

He lathered her hair slowly, with muscular delicacy, the pressure growing in her groin. He paused, removed some suds from her ear, and then kissed it. Such an excitement filled her lower belly that to relieve the intolerable pressure she grabbed his hand and placed it on herself. She climaxed almost instantly.

I can do anything in front of this man, without shame, she exulted, and leaning forward she licked his hard penis. She heard him choke. 'Stand,' he whispered, and when she had done so, he lathered her neck and face, her shoulders and her back, and then, her hands raised skyhigh, her armpits. In delicate detail he soaped her vulva, and that secret place between her buttocks; and then he washed her down with the hand-shower, opening her private lips to complete the cleansing.

They transferred duties. His head lowered, she rubbed shampoo into his fair, tumbling locks, and then rinsed them. She washed his armpits, the hair salty, slightly rank, and she soaped his chest. She took his penis and cleaned that, massaging the glans with suds and water, as he uttered low, deep gasps. Her fingers gently washed his scrotum, weighing them softly in her hand, before soaping between his buttocks.

She lathered his front again; his belly, hard from exercise, its umbilical button as neat as on a Greek statue. His erection was full, pulsing to the rhythm of his heart, and she was deeply tempted to masturbate him there and then, to have him ejaculate over her face, her breasts, in this bath. She shuddered with pleasure at the thought but, deciding against it, she continued to soap him, rubbing lather on his skin then scooping water over his lean hard body.

They towelled each other dry and lay down on the bed. He kissed her again and entered her in a single smooth movement so that she fitted around him as neat as a shell over an egg, and an orgasm erupted from her. Her body was full of him, and she was filled with joy.

She opened her eyes. It was morning, and he was sitting beside her, smiling. Gina found herself asking silently, Let me wake up beside this man every day of my life, God, not just this Sunday morning in Dublin, but all the Sunday mornings you send me, Lord, all the Sunday mornings you send me.

He leaned forward and kissed her. Again they made love. She said nothing about the wishes burning within her.

*

In the concourse of Dublin airport he asked, 'What if you're pregnant?'

'But I'm not, I can't be.'

'But what if you are?'

'How could I be pregnant, stupid?' She put her arms around his waist and pulled him towards her.

'I'm getting an erection,' he whispered in her ear.

'Me too,' she replied. 'Well, you know what I mean.'

He kissed her again, his lips fully against hers, her hand against him.

'Christ, you keep doing that I'm going to come,' he whispered.

'Good,' she replied. He touched her, but amid the sexual clamour she could hear another command from that ancient and abiding instinct which calls for order, food, an assured and common future. Ask me to stay, she urged. Go on.

She said into his ear: 'It's not just sex?' (loathing her wheedling tone).

'Dear Jesus, it's not just sex,' he whispered.

Tears were running down his beautiful Slavic cheeks. She reached up and trapped one, putting the wet fingertip to her mouth. 'What are we to do?' he continued lamely.

'I don't know, I don't know, oh I do not know,' (knowing that she knew).

'You will tell me, won't you? If you're pregnant, you will tell me?'

A woman nearby turned.

'I'm not, I'm not.' Go on, she thought. Fucking well ask me to stay.

She kissed him again, her tongue slipping into his mouth. She could sense the woman staring at them and, ignoring her, Gina rubbed his hardness, and urged silently, *Ask me*. His hand went between her legs and she whimpered. Dear God, was she going to come right here? *Ask me*.

'I want to fuck you so badly,' he said into her ear. 'Oh so badly.'

'You can, Stefan, you can, whenever you want,' she said. *Ask me*. 'My body is yours, everything is.' *Ask me*.

'Oh Georgina, what would you say if—'

'Gina?' said another voice. 'Gina, is that you?'

Gina turned and looked at the woman bobbing beside her. 'Mrs Ryan,' she said airlessly, hastily withdrawing her hand.

'I'm sorry for interrupting you,' said her landlady, glaring at Stefan. 'I might remind your companion this is an airport, not a boudoir.' She handed something to Gina. 'Your passport.' She appraised her briefly. 'In your hurry to rush hither and thither, you left it behind. Sure you weren't like *this* when you arrived.'

Gina was nonplussed, filling the silence with a vacant 'Oh.'

'Mrs Ryan,' she whispered, 'thank you so much.' She took the passport, as another part of her mind whispered to her of the influence which that mere document, her sex and her irredeemably stupid heart were having on her life. Listen, her parts murmured to her, had she not lingered here, would she not already have been rejected at check-in for not having a passport and would she not now be safely on her way towards whatever future this conveyor belt was trying to take her away from?

A voice announced the final call for her flight to the US, and, her heart lifting, Gina decided: I will take control over my life. 'I'll stay, fuck it. I'll stay.'

But she had spoken too softly so that in her moment of triumph, Stefan asked, 'What?' even as Mrs Ryan trotted towards the check-in desk, jubilantly pointing her gloved hand back at Gina and crying, 'Miss, miss, we have a passenger here for New York.' That obedient part of Gina's brain, the part of human nature which accepts laws, attends to governments, obeys events, submits to the conscriptor's edicts, ordered her to go.

The loudspeaker voice spoke again. Stefan was looking straight at her, his face distraught, baffled. 'Miss, miss,' cried Mrs Ryan, catching the young check-in woman's attention. Gina uttered a deep sob. Stefan reached out and grasped her to him, his lips kissing her ear through his tears. 'My love,' he said, 'my love.'

He looked, for one perfect moment, as if he too was about to allow his free and inner self to take precedence over the larger commanding events of life.

'Hurry,' urged Mrs Ryan, 'hurry.' 'Hurry, hurry,' repeated the check-in attendant; Hurry, hurry, cried the entire airport, silently. Stefan surrendered to that bigger compelling world. In a single moment, he heaved her solitary suitcase over to the check-in scales. 'Cutting it fine, aren't you?' said the young woman to Gina. 'Passport? Thank you. Board immediately, gate B29. Now, if you please, Miss Cambell. Immediately.' The belt lurched again.

Gina shoved her treacherous passport into her embroidered shoulder bag, swallowed, and braced herself. She turned and kissed Mrs Ryan, the uncomprehending agent of this departure, thanked her, promised to stay in touch, and said goodbye. She turned back to Stefan.

'Goodbye, Stefan, my lovely, lovely Slav.'

Her own voice created the echo, *Shtefan, my lovely, lovely Shlav*, for he said nothing, but wiped the tears on his cheeks with his hand, which he then wiped over her tears and then her lips.

She kissed his hand, reached into her shoulder bag and took out her camera. She pointed it at him, clicked it and he called, 'Georgina, be of good cheer.'

*

Bosnia, 1992

Cuckoos call as the heat rises in shimmering waves, concealing the flanking infantry. The boy, wearing a shako, dances in their lead, the machine-gunner sauntering behind him.

On a hillside ahead, the outlines of a village materialize. Walls, small paddocks, outhouses, smoke. The forward skirmishers start jinking towards the village, halting behind the cover of stone walls and scanning ahead through rifle sights at the houses, at the splashmarks of projectile-impacts and the rubble beneath them.

Nothing.

The patrol swiftly deploys, darting past open doors and broken windows, as clouds of flies erupt from their banquets.

Here, look, see how earlier visitors came and fired through this still-locked door, hitting the woman beyond it. Observe the pool of blood on the floor, the bullet hole in the wall, bits of door and torso splattered against the inside wall.

But this peasant Serb survived the shooting through the front door of her home. Look. Her bloody footprints – what ugly, splayed peasant toes, do you see? – mark her flight away from her attackers, a fat and barefoot quarry, splashing bloodily to the stairs. Up, up, in panic, she waddles up, step by step, past her sister's postcard from Banja Luka pinned to the wall, past the portrait of President Milošević sent to her by her millionaire nephew, Ivan, who sells Yugo cars in Belgrade, past the photograph of her two soldier sons, now on active service, on to the landing, into the bedroom with the veranda and the outside steps leading to safety.

She slams the bedroom door shut, bolts it. Look, so much blood fountaining out of her fat white peasant flesh, gushing through her futile, grasping fingers – oh dear God, how will she stop it?

A noise. She turns. Behind her, two teenage boys are on her veranda. Look at them. Barely out of infancy. One winks at her, a winsome, engaging gesture, and then raises his rifle and shoots her. She staggers backwards, her hand smearing blood down the walls, the final signature of her fingernails. He shoots her again, and she flops onto the floor. Her sewing basket falls over beside her, and with it the embroidery she had been working on last night, a copy of the postcard from Banja Luka.

Now her body lies with those of other women, their blood blackening in the sun. One young girl is quite naked, spread-eagled. Across this humble village the air is sweet with the scents of decay, of the sickly, intimate smells of human entrails and their contents. Flies joyously chant their busy anthems. The soldiers walk past the bodies, their fingers tense within their trigger guards. The enemy is gone.

Burn the houses, the officer says. So those Turkish pigs can't use them.

The bastards, says one.

Maybe, says the machine-gunner, his eyes are scanning the horizon. Is this any worse than what we have done?

Not as bad as we're going to do, says the boy.

Tough little fellow, jests a soldier. They all exchange manly smiles. The boy grins proudly.

Fill your bottles, says the officer. Then we'll move on.

There is the clink of webbing buckles, rifles, the gurgle of water. Then they head off into the heat, none noticing the memorial stone commemorating victory at this spot in an earlier war, in which Stefan's father received the wounds from which, years later in Ireland, he was to succumb. Instead they are aware of the dust rising behind them, and of the smoke pursuing them from the burning buildings, its fragrance abominable, meaty. Above them the cuckoos chant.

Stand here, at the head of the valley again, and you can see, quite plainly, a line of trees beside that icy, chuckling stream where earlier the men lay in veneration, just as Stefan's parents had once upon a distant day gratefully prostrated themselves at that same spot.

What are they, those trees?

Banks of green willow.

CHAPTER FIVE

Louisiana, 1973

In some ways she was glad to be back home. The weather, the local Howard Johnson, the dee-jays on the radio sunnily identifying the traffic snarl-ups of Baton Rouge, the happy, leisurely rhythms of the language of her own people. Louisiana seemed hardly part of the same planet as the cold and violent city of Belfast which she had never visited but to which her thoughts and heart constantly returned.

The occasional report from there spoke of restaurants blown apart by handbag bombs left by girls; drooping figures tied to lamp-posts, their knees shattered; blocks of houses burning as fleeing residents tottered through the smoke beneath the weight of rescued beds and bric-a-brac, households without houses.

But Gina was back to a comforting world of warmth, of a general and prosperous ease. Her home state lived by the rules of a swampland meridian, where alligators prowled the creeks and hummingbirds hovered and supped, where rain was warm and sunshine often; yet part of her yearned for rain that was cold and bleak and skies that were cloudy and grey.

She threw up some mornings, emerging at breakfast with an entirely contrived bonhomie. Her mother, Beth, had entered one of her hostile cycles. She gazed at Gina daily over the breakfast table, an eyebrow raised, suspicion clearly aroused but still unspoken as she drew from the top of her coffee cup. Karen, her sister, overweight and stuck fast in mid-teen idiocy, either prattled or sulked, unaware of the wordless dynamic between the two other women in the Cambell household.

One morning, with Karen gone to school after gorging herself on four bowls of cereal, her mother looked at Gina steadily, a quizzical smile on her face. 'Whore,' she said. 'Just couldn't wait, could you? I know what kind of girl you are.' She rose, put her coffee cup in the dishwasher, then left the kitchen, shaking her head, laughing softly as she reiterated the word: whore.

No word came from Ireland as day by day she felt this thing commandeer her from within, tugging at the base of her spine, at her heart, at her brain. She lay in bed at night, touching her abdomen, wondering at the mystery of her body, once so ordinary, and now engaged in this private, miraculous industry of creation.

It amazed her. It was separate from her, yet part of her; and when parting occurred, she knew, separation would not. Though young, she was discovering how indissoluble the bonds of motherhood can be. She did not like it; yet she cherished it.

All her attempts to telephone Stefan had come to nothing. The Community Relations Commission reported that he had not been seen in weeks, there was no answer from his flat in Belfast, and she did not know his mother's married name. He was gone and she was alone – aside, that is, from her mother, simmering with barely controlled aggression, and Karen, positively boiling with hormones and ceaselessly gorged animal fats.

'You look down, Gina,' said Doris Sykes, her new French professor. '*Quelle est cette île triste et noire?*' '*Non, ça va, il n'y a qu'une île petite,*' Gina said.

This semester French had been undersubscribed, and because of the poor reputation of Doris's predecessor, Professor Picot, Gina's particular language module had been applied for by her alone.

Doris, a thin, handsome woman in her fifties, was full of energy and she possessed the most penetrating, unwavering gaze Gina had ever known. Her eyes now settled on Gina unblinkingly, and Gina glanced away. 'Look at me, girl. One of the joys of being a teacher is coming across a student who is better than I am. You take my meaning? I do so hate giving compliments. So, listen to my constructions. They are flawless and elegant and are the pride of my life. Imitate and

learn from them and you will benefit. My accent is deficient.
You, now, could speak perfect French if you put your mind
to it. We're going to have to do a lot of work in the lab. In the
meantime, Apollinaire. Have you yet . . ? No? A shame.
Apollinaire. Oh the waste, the abominable waste.'

*

Bosnia, 1992
The machine-gunner stares through the binoculars at the
distant village. The men here are tough, he says. If they were
here, we wouldn't be. They must be in Kisiljak. The Turks
need all their men there.

Chances are the only man left is the baker, says the officer.
You can't get a baker to leave his bakery. Rifle grenades on
the bakery will do, as a start.

He moves back from the brow and whistles half a dozen
men together.

Čabrinović, Tomašević, move down to the left there. On
my signal. Rifle grenades into the bakery there. The bakery,
you hear, not the town hall, the national opera or the fucking
airport; and Tomašević, try not to hit Belgrade, just for once,
but just the little bakery there, you understand.

Obradović, Jovanović, Karadžić – rifle grenades from the
far side.

You, he says to the machine-gunner, you . . .

I know, says the machine-gunner, rising carefully. Stooping
beneath the skyline, he lopes round to the far side of the
village, the boy running after him. Two soldiers follow, bent,
scurrying, following the machine-gunner who, in addition to
the 13 kilos of Type 53 machine-gun, is draped with maybe
30 kilos of ammunition. The boy turns and growls with
pleasure.

Fucking lunatic, says one soldier to the other. I just fucking
hate this shit.

Not as much as me, my friend. I became a father of twins
last week.

What are they?

Serbs, like myself.

The machine-gunner turns and rasps, Listen, father of

Serbs, do what I tell you and you will go home to your Serb children. I'm going to mount the gun just up there – I want you, he says to the other soldier, to feed the ammunition, you boy, to lay the next belt, and you, father of Serbs, to stay nice and safe up there, minding our flank. Check your rifle.

I have checked it.

Good, let's get going.

The father of Serbs hurries to a promontory above them, and the machine-gunner rests his bipod beside a boulder. He opens the feed cover to check the first cartridge is snug against the feed-guide. He closes it and pulls the cocking handle all the way back with his left hand, then pushes it forward until he hears the click. He checks the safety. Good. It is ready to fire. He runs his fingers over the snake-like links of 7.92 ammunition, saying keep it coming, neat and clean, no kinks no misfires.

There is a crack-boom from the far side of the village, and a cloud of smoke rises from the bakery. A door opens and two boys of about fourteen emerge. They have FAZ rifles which dwarf their puny limbs. The machine-gunner presses his trigger, and his weapon consumes the belt of ammunition as if sucking in gobbets of food. There is a din of gunfire, of clattering, discarded cartridges, of the sharp metallic clack of the buffer-spring and bolt slamming backwards and forwards, and the acrid stench of gun-oil and cordite.

The boys are transformed into dead objects instantaneously and their mothers who wailingly follow them, all headscarf and flapping hands, are dispatched as neatly. Wisps of vapour rise from their settling bodies.

There is the whoop of jubilation from the father of Serbs. The boy hisses with joy as he, too, observes the baker burst from the bakery with his Schmeisser afire, about to dance the last dance of his life.

CHAPTER SIX

'Why here?' Gina asked Doris over lunch at the latter's home, Cypress Mound, a wonderful plantation house, antebellum and glacier-white. 'You're too good for here, you know that.'

Doris allowed herself a small smile. 'Well I sure do deserve more students like you, Gina,' she replied. 'I'm lazy, I guess. I love my French and my home. I inherited money. I'm firmly of the opinion everyone should. I could have gone to one of the big schools, but they're so gosh-darned competitive and I'm not. I content myself by writing. And I just adore coming across students like you, the truffles in the *foie gras*.'

After they had eaten a powerful gumbo followed by flan with almond sauce, and then a strong Colombian coffee, Doris offered Gina a liqueur. 'Grand Marnier, perhaps? My daily treat, my dear – why don't you join me?'

Gina laughed and said yes. Doris looked at her over the half-poured glass of liqueur and remarked casually, 'Gina, my dear, you appear to be putting on a few pounds. They suit you, mind, but I do hope you're not gorging on french fries and those hamburger things from McDougald's, are you?'

'McDonald's,' said Gina, smiling, and to her astonishment, the truth marched out: 'I'm pregnant. I got pregnant in Ireland. I met this guy and, well, you know.'

'Will you marry this fine fellow of yours, the one who is so very careless with his seed?'

'No, I'm not going to marry him, I don't even know where he is.'

'What a sex the male sex is, leaving its tissue wherever it expends it. I don't know, really I don't. Are you going to have an abortion? Though not legal, these things can be arranged. Myself, I have a few contacts. Would you . . .?'

Gina shook her head in silence. She was breeding a

mystery, a new power. It redefined her from below, filling her and renewing her, and she could not terminate its command.

'When are you due?'

'August.'

'August? Why that is good news,' cried Doris, suddenly heartened. 'It won't interfere with your studies. We mustn't let a mere trifle like childbirth change your life. Have your child. We will ensure your studies continue regardless. Have another centimetre or two of this intoxicating little citrus concoction.'

'Not now, thanks, I've got lab work.'

'Okay, I'll see you tomorrow. It's a pleasure having you here, one we will repeat, I hope.'

Back in the language lab, Gina put on a tape of Rabelais. She had been studying Strasser's theory on the evidence favouring various pronunciations, especially the fate of the now elided 'i' in *Fay ce que vouldras*. She played it once – was the 'i' there? She reeled the tape back and played it again.

'Are you okay?' said a voice.

'Sure, I'm just trying to catch this sound here.'

'Take care, the spool tends to overwind, then it throws the whole tape right off the capstan.'

She turned to smile at the man who was speaking. He was early twenties, tall, very handsome, solidly built with a soft, kindly face.

'Hi,' he said, 'I'm Warren Bourne. I'm a graduate student. I do part-time work here making a few bucks.'

'Gina Cambell,' she said, waving her spare hand.

He watched as the capstan whirred, taking her way past the bit she wanted. 'They can be real SOBs can't they?' he said. 'We should be using cassettes instead of these goddamned spools. Here, I'm used to it, let me.'

He leaned forward. Without warning, her stomach heaved and she vomited her gumbo, flan and Colombian coffee, heavily laced with Grand Marnier, all over him.

'Gee,' he said.

*

'These things happen,' he said over coke later in the canteen, while she thought, He actually says *gee*.

'I'm sorry, it came just right out of the blue.'

'That's where it didn't come from,' he said, smiling at her.

He said very little else. He was studying comparative linguistics. He spoke of Chomsky, whom Gina knew primarily for his opposition to the war.

'Do you speak Serbo-Croat?' she asked with casual suddenness.

'A bit. Why?'

'I was wondering – is it written in Arabic as well as Roman and Cyrillic?'

'Why would it be written in Arabic?' he asked.

'Because there are a lot of Muslims in Bosnia, and the liturgical language of Muslims is Arabic, and I sort of figured that maybe some people, scholars or even mullahs or whatever they're called, might have chosen to use the orthography of their church. I was just wondering.'

He was silent for a while. 'You don't meet many people like you around here, you know. Most of the students are kind of dead. Orthography, liturgy, you know? Do I sound arrogant? Yeah, I sound arrogant.'

'You don't.'

'Thanks. To answer your question, I don't know.'

'Another coke?' she asked and he replied, 'No, this one's on me,'

'Like my lunch.' They exchanged smiles.

It was three months since she had left Ireland. Her nausea – well, until that afternoon – had been abating. The only letters she received from Ireland came with the familiar hand of a Bracken on the envelope. Nothing from Stefan.

She wrote him another letter.

Dear Stefan,
I write to you but I get no reply – are you getting my letters? If you don't want to write, say so, briefly. I know you've left your work, but I'm sending this letter there to be forwarded. My other letters were sent to your home. I've got no reply from there so I guess you must have moved and nobody's forwarding your stuff.

I can't believe, can't believe, you wouldn't reply to me.

Myself, I've been very busy here, trying to catch up with my classes. I'm way behind in my French, not behind my class but behind my expectations and the expectations of my teacher, a charming old lady called Doris Sykes who has taken a great shine to me. She gives me private tuition and she is very demanding, rightly so.

I think about you a lot, and think about the time we had in Wicklow and in your family home in Dublin. That was wonderful. Thank you for the best fuck I've ever had. I'll never forget it, never, and never forget you and the hours and days we spent together.

Take care, wherever you are. I think of you often and I miss you, but I suppose ocean liners have their routes to follow. In the night I gaze backwards and see our two wakes mingling and sparkling in the moonlight. I will never forget you.

All my love,
Georgina

*

Morning followed morning, and no reply. Could he have been killed in the violence of Northern Ireland? Yet if he hadn't, could a man resist replying to a woman who had told him he was the best fuck of her life?

But surely he must have made arrangements for his mail to be forwarded? He was young and carefree, had certainly not chosen to get her pregnant, and so now he was gone.

She had made a choice. Now she must live with it. Her belly was swelling, but pregnancy gave her face a bloom. Her breasts were bigger and fuller and for the first time in her life, she thought she looked good.

Once the first side-effects had worn off, pregnancy made her feel sexy. She had discovered how to masturbate at twelve, and this she did more often than ever. But now, she sometimes cried afterwards, thinking of Stefan – Stefan in Wicklow, Stefan in Dublin, Stefan bathing her, Stefan making love – before she drifted off to sleep, her heart like lead within her.

Stefan had been living in a war-zone where people were

murdered almost daily. He could not be expected to remember one little student over one weekend. Maybe that was an average weekend for him. The next weekend he was being a charming Slav with another dim American. And the next. Fuck it. It was over.

Warren was a good antidote. He was handsome, steady, and quite solitary. He was more academically intelligent than Stefan, not as much fun, but he was utterly reliable, which Gina found rather attractive. His closest friends were guys back in Philadelphia he played basketball with, and, here in Clapham, his tutor, another Chomsky specialist called David Collins.

One evening Warren drove her over to the Collins's clapboard house in Goodison. She was a little taken aback by the fact that they were black; Warren went up in her estimation for not even thinking it was worth mentioning. And she had instantly got on with Roben, the daughter of an Atlanta dentist – very striking, very self-confident, with the poise born of wealth and an expensive education.

Roben and Gina talked while the two men discussed something to do with faculty politics, Roben dismissing them with a great big yawning gesture. Roben had scarcely disposed of the conversational preliminaries before she smiled at Gina and, with a knowing look, asked how she and Warren were getting on.

'Some would say that Warren is quite a hunk,' Roben teased. Gina made a wry little 'maybe' smile, and let the enquiry drift away.

'You like Doris Sykes?' asked Roben. 'She sure is an odd one, real strange, but kind of nice. And that's some family she comes from. I look at that house, I see darkies in the fields and her granpappy calling for a piece of black ass – bring me yaw sistah, boy, ya heah? Hey, we might even be cousins.'

Roben laughed and Gina laughed with her before saying, 'Yeah, I like Doris just fine.'

'Doris? Well if she has you calling her that then she likes you just fine too. A mighty intimidating woman when she wants. Grown men wilt at her gaze. She's one of the few people round here with a brain between her ears. And that sure is some place of hers, but I think she barely even knows it. Born to riches and you don't know you have them till they're gone, yes sir.'

'Maybe. But she's got a real good heart, and a brain so sharp it's like a needle.'

'A needle without a prick,' said Roben, her eyes flashing mischievously. 'She's one for the girls, I reckon.'

'Is she? Really? I never . . . She never . . .'

'It's a hunch. 'At's all. She never said nor did nothing, and as for her students, uh-huh, never, not Doris. But I kind of sense it, you know?'

'Well now. I should have guessed.'

'"I should have guessed." You? Why should *you* have guessed?'

'I don't know. I like to think I'm good at understanding people.'

'You understand Warren?'

'No, not yet.'

'He's sweet and good and very bright.' She smiled at Gina, silently urging her onwards.

Warren drove her home. As she moved to get out of the car, she turned back. He leaned forward and kissed her softly on the side of the cheek. It was a kiss both promising and irreproachable. She was still thinking fondly about him when she fell asleep.

The next day they met for coffee at eleven.

'I've got to tell you something,' Gina said, impulsively.

'What?'

'I'm pregnant. I had an affair in Ireland before Christmas.'

'Oh.'

'Yeah.'

He stayed silent for what seemed an eternity. Then he looked her in the eye, a thoroughly forced smile on his face. He cleared his throat.

'I kind of guessed something,' he said softly. 'Since you got back, you have really blossomed.'

Gina half registered the 'since you got back', as Warren continued talking. 'I minored in Classics. After that nothing can surprise me. And you're having the baby. You needn't.

That takes guts. Ask me whether I'd prefer if you weren't pregnant, I'd say yes indeed, I'd prefer that you weren't pregnant.'

Yes indeedy. He says yes indeedy, Gina observed to herself. Who else our age says yes indeedy these days? Gee and yes indeedy. My.

Warren forged on. 'But if you hadn't been pregnant you wouldn't have thrown up all over me, right? Then maybe we wouldn't be here, so who am I to complain? It's not often somebody falls in love with somebody who pukes over them.'

Oh. They were both silent for a while, Gina's mind too stunned to reply at first. 'That's a little hasty, isn't it?' she finally managed to say.

His voice was grave. 'You might think so, but it's not hasty for me. I watched you all last year. I spoke to you on half a dozen occasions. You were sweet on every one of them, and you forgot me immediately afterwards. You were and you are the loveliest girl I have ever seen in my life.'

'And when I threw up all over you, then it was true love, right?'

'Something like that, yes. Will you marry me?'

'Will you . . . Hey, let me think about that. You want to take me on a walk first and maybe try to make a big play for me, something like that? Make a pass, that kind of thing? I come from a very traditional family. That's the order we do these things in.'

'It's just I've been waiting a long time.'

'Why don't you start by kissing me again?'

That night they made love. He was concerned about the pregnancy, but she told him not to worry. To her astonishment he was an astoundingly good lover. His body was lean and muscular, full of considerate urgency. Perched within her, he could halt mid-stroke and by some extra-ordinary pressure from his hips, his penis, bring her off without moving.

He did this repeatedly, conveying sexual pleasure in utter silence. When he climaxed, he did so noiselessly. Then he kissed her, and she kissed him, and she expected sleep would follow. But instead, as they kissed, he became erect and in a single move entered her; again she began the delirious rhythm of orgasm, until exhaustion finally claimed her.

She woke in the middle of the night, blinking in confusion. She was in his apartment. He too was awake, lying naked and gazing at her. He said, 'I have dreamed of this for eighteen months, and now it has come true, and I can hardly believe it.'

Her whole body moved with lust at the sight of him, and it was her body, not her brain, which spoke as she opened her legs and his hardness entered her.

'Keep talking like that, my friend, and I might even marry you,' she gasped, the words rolling out without premeditation, and the doors slamming shut behind them, as consequences do.

CHAPTER SEVEN

Sitting at the wrought-iron table on her porch. Doris was incandescent with rage. 'I know the boy, he's good and nice and fine, and it sure isn't my business to judge your life, but goddam it, I'm going to. Gina, do not get married to this man. Do not. I'm not saying things will be easy if you don't get married, they won't, they surely won't, but you can do it, I know you can.'

'You don't understand.'

'You're damned right I don't. Now listen here. Once you get married you'll find new forces at work on your life, the forces of his career, of marriage itself. They're so gosh-darned insidious. You can say you're going to stay free, but for folks like you, with so little money, there's still going to be one primary bread-winner and one primary home-maker.'

'Maybe you're right. But Warren is good and he loves me and I need a home for me and my baby away from my mad, mad mother, and he'll give me that.'

'This is stupid,' Doris spat. 'Saints alive, your mother can't be so mad you're going to marry someone who is wholly unsuited for you.'

'Mad enough for me to leave.'

'Leave then, but there sure is no call for you to marry somebody you should never marry in a million years.'

'Look, he's not like other men, he likes my mind because I'm not afraid of using it.'

'And your body, which you're certainly not afraid of using.'

'Fuck you, Doris, you goddam fucking bitch,' Gina hissed.

Doris stood, trembling, before replying. 'I am so sorry, so very sorry, that was downright inexcusable of me. I only wonder you didn't hit me. You would have been within your rights. Entirely. Hit me still if you want. I deserve it. But before you do, believe me, I was only thinking about what's best for you. My dearest Gina, because I worry about your condition and what you're doing, I'm saying things I don't even mean or think. Look, come and live with me here, in this house, I have so much room. You and the baby can live your own lives, you'll be free to leave whenever you want to go your own way. Gina, my dear – will you think about it?'

Her tone, her look, soothed Gina's rage. She paused to compose herself. 'That sure is real kind of you, Doris, but I couldn't, I truly couldn't.'

Doris rose and said urgently, 'You're my student. Have you the least idea . . . no of course you don't. My life, my vocation, is the odd student of merit who comes my way. My self-esteem demands that I do the best for my students. My very best. Gina, listen to me. I know, I know, what will happen to you. You will do your degree and vanish into a world of diapers and domestic chores and part-time college life. I know it, I know it.'

'We'll see,' said Gina.

'I know it,' said Doris in a low voice, sitting down again, 'I just know it.'

They sat in silence watching the sun plummeting until the rising chime of the mosquitoes told them it was time to go in.

'There's another thing, Gina,' said Doris as she got up from her seat. 'There's you, the inner you, the woman in you. I am what I am and because of what I am, and because I live where I live, an entire part of me remains unfulfilled. May I be honest with you? Please?'

Gina felt her eyes, of their own accord, flash assent.

'Look, I know what it is to live without the pleasure of physical love, and I hate it, hate it,' said Doris. 'I hate waking up in the morning and not feeling arms around me. I daresay you think a woman of my age . . . Well, that's not the case. The years go by, but the urge never vanishes. I am told that even in old folks' homes . . . No matter. So yes, Gina, I hate not feeling the joy of loving sex with somebody else. That is the price I pay for living here, and it's too darned late for me to do anything about it now. I am, thank God, lesbian. I have companionship and love in France. Listen. This I know. I am more than the austere academic people take me for. I love sex. I am not ashamed of my solitary endeavours. They keep me sane. Is Warren sexual? I somehow don't think so.'

Gina laughed. 'No, there you're wrong. Warren is a very sexual person indeed. He's just not very assertive, that's all.'

'Not very assertive? Is that how you describe the most diffident man I have ever met? Not very assertive. My, what a way you have with words. What about the father of the child?'

'History, Doris, he's history. He doesn't even know I'm pregnant.'

'Gina, Gina. History? There's no such thing. It's always present, always. We take our past with us wherever we go. And other people's pasts too.'

*

Her mother was different. Marriage she understood and approved of. 'Well, I think that's quite wonderful, Gina, a woman in your condition getting a husband, and really easy too.'

'Mom . . .'

'Quite wonderful. You're so clever. Who will ever know the truth? Everyone'll think Warren is the father, just like you mean them to think, and that the pair of you were a mite hasty. Well, people are these days, aren't they? I'm sure it's better than when I was a young woman and we all went ignorant and fumbling towards our wedding night. Such horrors.'

'Mom, please.'

'Oh very well, very well. Though I'm sure my father was not as gross in his indulgences as your father was. A different kind of man, as I think you know.'

'Please, Mom, not your father again, not again, please.'

'Good, we are agreed, no need to argue. Now, what about a little drink to celebrate? A mint julep, perhaps. Honey, would you do the honours? Poppa's recipe, not the one you tried last time. Well now. This is fine, just fine.'

Gina scowled at the wall, then rose to concoct the julep according to the method her grandfather had bequeathed to posterity.

*

Bosnia, 1992

The village is silent. Only the flames speak as they lick through the little houses, crackling hungrily. The battle had not been costly. The father of Serbs, whose unchecked gun had jammed, was their only death, killed by the dancing baker. Now, his eyes glinting like a bird of prey, the machine-gunner is stripping and cleaning his weapon, the boy watching beside him.

Nearby Milošević is busy with a young Muslim girl, and Jovanović is propping the body of a dead one against a wall. He has cut off her head and, holding it by its long fair hair, he tries to balance it on the top of the wall. Fuck this, he says as the head falls off again.

Observe, see the smile on that girl's face. Was she not once a happy young woman before the bullets so shattered her body that it was of no use to her killers? Maybe that is why she smiles.

Oh fuck this, says Jovanović as the head rolls to the ground again, its tresses half concealing the face. Jovanović takes a bite out of his apple. Stubborn fucking bitch. Only I am more stubborn. He takes out his bayonet.

The boy looks away from Jovanović's struggles with the dead girl, and says proudly, This is a Serbian gun. He strokes the Type 53. Serbian guns are best. Serbian everything is best. What is that?

The buttstock. Beneath the stock, see here, is the catch. I push it and twist the butt a quarter turn, either way, it doesn't matter. It is a masterpiece.

Now stay there, orders Jovanović to the disobedient body.

And it is a Serbian masterpiece, says the boy.

It is Serbian. But it is a copy of a German machine-gun, the MG 42.

We are using a German machine-gun? My grandfather was

a Četnik and he fought the Germans, yet we are using a
German machine-gun?

He would use anything to kill an enemy of Serbia, wouldn't
he?

Yes.

Well then. And anyway, the MG 42 was a copy of a Polish
machine-gun, and the Polish machine-gun was developed
from the American Browning Automatic Rifle, and that was
a development from the Lewis gun from 1917.

There is a bellow. The boy glances over. Jovanović is
kicking the body in despair. Behave yourself. You, BEHAVE
YOURSELF NOW.

Nineteen seventeen. But that is centuries ago.

Yes. Hold this. And so you see this gun is not just this gun
or that gun, it is based on what we know and learn over
generations. That's civilization.

Please, says Jovanović. Please. For once, just once, would
you please be a little co-operative? Please?

The Muslim girl's body stands poised for one second and
then slumps sideways. The head still grins idiotically on its
perch on the wall, the hair hanging over those whimsical eyes.

Here, pass me the housing there, says the machine-gunner.
The housing, I said, the housing.

Stay there, Jovanović commands, but the head rolls off its
perch anyway.

You say you have never killed anyone, says the machine-
gunner to the boy. So, make your first kill a close kill.
Nothing like it. A body loses thirteen grams at the moment of
death, and it goes right by you.

Perfect, cries Jovanović, perfect. He has balanced the head
on the top of the wall, hovering three feet above the corpse,
which rests against the base of the wall like a slumbering
headless cartoon Mexican.

A work of art, he continues, a fucking work of art. He
wipes the blade on his trouser thigh and takes a bite of his
apple, asking through the juice and the saliva, Has anyone got
a camera?

The grey-haired officer arrives and says, Time to move. No
survivors, okay?

Please, pleads Jovanović. Has no one got a camera?

The machine-gunner silently draws his bayonet and goes to the girl Miloš has been busy with. There is the sound of a breaking ribcage, an animal shriek rising into the enclosing forest and up to the mountainside above, where wolves lift their heads and blink in the caverns of shade. In the sunbaked meadowland, the cuckoos still chant. On the ground, Jovanović's girl still grins, a smile that celebrates her departure from history.

CHAPTER EIGHT

Nineteen years earlier, in August 1973, within a few days of the birth of the girl with the smiling face, Gina's son was born. She called him Tom, Tom of the storytellers. Doris's forecasts about the advantages of an August birth proved wrong. The campus had no crèche, and Gina and Warren could not afford a full-time babysitter. Gina's mother, Beth, moreover, was taking a disastrous interest in the baby and his future.

'Such an easy birth,' she observed as she stitched a garment with a sinister resemblance to babywear. 'How I suffered. Yet you seem to drop them as easy as slaves littering in a cottonfield.'

'Mother,' said Gina, looking at a discomfited Warren, who in silence watched his twirling thumbs, while Karen, fat, distracted and temporarily content, mimed to music in her earphones.

'Thomas here must be baptized,' Beth continued. 'Episcopalian, naturally. We are not the negroes of my childhood, Gina, strumming on our banjos.'

Gina replied in a steady, controlled voice, 'Mother, please, it is Tom, and I am absolutely not going to baptize him. Why are you talking like that? *Nigras, strummin.* It's ridiculous. We're not that kind of folk and you know it.' Karen, rocking her head to and fro, said nothing. Warren sat and gazed at his feet.

Beth looked up from her sewing and smiled loftily. 'My poor dead father, had he but lived to hear those words.' She shook her head sadly. 'I might also remind you that I am young enough to give young Thomas another aunt or a nice little uncle. Or maybe one of each. You are not the only one around here who can play fast and loose with their morals.'

'Now hold on there a second,' Warren murmured to the floor.

'We got to go,' said Gina.

'Poor Thomas has just arrived. How could you? Well might young Thomas look so longingly at his quietly adoring grandmother, busy here sewing him a Tennessee bonnet.'

'A Tennessee . . .?'

'Bonnet, dear, a Tennessee bonnet, for his delicate skull – he has my head, I see, and I have my father's – sewn by his neglected grandmother's loving hands. Go if you have to, dear, I'll just keep myself busy here sewing clothes for your semi-illegitimate offspring. Still, real good of you to drop by. Ignore us poor middle-aged ones, do.'

'Tom has an appointment at the clinic, you know that.'

'And we're going to be late,' said Warren mildly. 'Unless . . .'

Beth looked at Gina sympathetically. 'These little irritations of yours – I understand them, truly I do. Nature did not intend that families be divided like this. I have so much to give – so much experience. Think about it, Gina – move back here. Does this here bonnet not show I can give so much to you and young Thomas? The three of you should live here. It would spare you the torment that was my lot. Oh I had to struggle, so hard, so very very hard, to attain whatever modest academic achievement I managed . . .'

Gina stared at her mother, knowing some lethal culmination was to hand.

'. . . and virtually an orphan I worked at my master's alone, unaided.'

Incredulity overwhelmed Gina's determination not to be provoked. 'Master's? What master's?'

'No matter. It was not to be. I am determined that my daughter should not suffer the hindrances which destroyed my own academic ambitions.'

'Mother!'

'Does it not please you, Gina, to be welcomed in the home you so nearly brought shame on? Now you can achieve what family tragedy and my sense of duty prevented me from achieving.'

Gina was about to speak but her mother had already risen.

'Maternal duties, *yet* again. Karen, come help me here. The peach cobbler calls. I do trust Warren enjoys fatherhood, even the limited variety which fate has permitted him.'

Distracted, Karen did not respond as her mother departed; Gina envied her vast inviolability. She looked over at Warren, who was sitting in a silence all of his own. 'Honey,' she said. He smiled a small smile in acknowledgement, and shrugged his shoulders.

Later, in the car, he asked why her mother was so insistent they move in with her. 'Control,' said Gina simply. 'Can't you see she just loves control?'

He thought for a while. 'I think she's mad.'

'Well for lansakes, ain't you the regular li'l ol' Sherlock Holmes,' she declared, smiling.

*

Doris had not seen Tom because she had had a persistent head-cold. Only when it had passed did she invite Gina up to Cypress Mound where, as always, their conversation moved backwards and forwards in English and French without either really noticing. 'Oh you charmer,' said Doris, lifting Tom. 'He has the charm, he has it, yes he has, oh yes 'e 'asums.'

Gina was still registering the astonishing scene of The Terror of Clapham University talking baby talk as Doris kissed him. 'Oh my boy, my beautiful, beautiful boy,' she murmured. Did she have tears in her eyes? No, it wasn't possible. But did she?

'I would have done anything for a child, even married – can you believe that? But of course though men are a mad race – all that preposterous testosterone, endocrinal plutonium – no man was ever misguided enough to suggest marriage. I was always too frank in my disdain. All that dissembling while they fumble with your underwear. No, no, too terrible.'

'Doris, come on, no man ever fumbled with your underwear outside a laundry. Come on.'

'Nor inside either, I trust. A most terrible thought. But one can still *imagine* the necessary prelude to, oh dear me, *copulation*. What a shudder-making idea. Admittedly, for the time being, the deed is necessary for the continuation of the human race, until, that is, science perfects more wholesome techniques of reproduction. But I confess, you who do this are so *heroic*. You endure such ordeals at the hands of the enemy, and uncomplainingly, solely that the genes of our sex be transmitted from the past into the future. I am dumb with gratitude. I am mere womanly flesh, and my womanly flesh fairly curdles at the thought.'

'Doris, it's not too late, you should try it some time. For pleasure, of course.'

'Pleasure,' murmured Doris. 'Ugh. Oh I think not, my iddle widdle ums, my iddle widdle ums.'

'You have the enemy in your hands there I believe.'

'Ah, now. We must live in hope. There are exceptions, remember, there are exceptions. Rimbaud, Verlaine, my beloved Alain-Fournier. Possibly Tom will be an exception – brave and proud and sensitive and true, an Apollo or an Apollinaire.'

Doris ruminatively stroked the baby in her lap with a strong, gentle hand. 'It is not merely a question of enmity but preference. To favour women suggests a superior intellect.'

'Most men would agree.'

Doris laughed. 'You hear Momma, young Tom? Isn't she so clever-wever, so vewwy, vewwy, clever-wever?'

She looked over at Gina again and now her eyes were sparkling. 'Tom. Such an unadventurous name for such a sterling little fellow. I shall call him Augustin, my wild, wild Augustin, who will trudge bare-legged along river banks scouring the rushes for moorhens' and wild ducks' eggs. He will raid woodlands for snared pheasants and will set off fireworks out of season. My wild, wild urchin.'

Gina smiled. '*Le Grand Meaulnes*, Augustin Meaulnes. I just adored him when I was a teenager. Didn't even you fall in love with him, Doris, when you first read him?'

'In a certain zoological sense, yes, rather in the way that one can admire the amiable character of a dog or the courage of a particular horse. But I did not say "I want to meet the incarnation of this fictional character." Never. Gwendolen Harleth, yes. I think I would have slain for her. Oh how I

adored her, and how I detested Daniel Deronda. A perfect
fool, a drivelling idiot, a man.'

'Invented by a woman who admired him.'

'These little imperfections litter the history of our sex. But
Gina, I am no bigot. Men too have their moments. We cannot
put what they have made into womanspeak, alas. I have
always said that we cannot understand any work of art in
translation, any culture in translation. The simple adjective in
Le Grand Meaulnes defies translation. It takes its meaning, its
countless meanings, from the sentence in which it stands. It is
the perfect example of contextual coloration. Alone, the word
is dead. Set properly, it glitters like a diamond surrounded by
amethysts.'

'Tom finds this very interesting.'

'I'm sure he does, and I am so glad you have taught him
French so young. It is the language of the archangels. English,
on the other hand, is incapable of mastering such a luminous
understanding of the twin processes of memory and of
forgetting, of *"Les souvenirs sont cors de chasse, Dont meurt
le bruit parmi le vent"*. In English it is simply embarrassing.
Memories are hunting horns whose sound dies on the wind.
Bah! Gibberish! It is of course – because of the resonances of
each word and because of the linear rhythms – utterly
untranslatable. In English one gets no sense of that dreadful
sense of mortality as memory dies amid the wind. *Bruit* not
sound, *parmi* is nothing in English – amid, within, among. A
priceless, perfect preposition.'

Tom made a noise and Doris smiled down at the gurgling
pink object on her lap. 'When you get to my age, my boy, you
understand the importance of memory, you understand how
imperfectly we record and recollect, yet fail to understand
those imperfections. Apollinaire knew that, though he was
dead at thirty-eight.'

'Flu,' said Gina absently. 'The very thing you've been trying
to protect me and Tom from.'

'Flu merely finished him off. A young man like him would
never have died otherwise. Apollinaire. What a calamity, with
so much more to give. He was, you know, a classic European,
not French at all. Half Polish, half Italian, and like all civilized

people he loved France. He did not die alone. With him died Europe. What a waste. My two adored men. Alain-Fournier also, of course, and four years apart.'

Doris stroked Tom's scalp gently. 'Tom, Tom, stay at home and write great words.'

Kissing him, she passed him to Gina who put him to her breast, where he began to gorge himself. Doris watched with envy while Gina suckled the boy.

'Oh to have done that but once in my life,' breathed Doris. 'Just once.'

For a moment there was silence as Gina's mind reached into Doris's.

'Then do it now, Doris,' she whispered suddenly. 'Here. Feed him.'

'Oh I could not.'

'You could, you could. You can give him no food but you can give him comfort. Comfort him, Doris, comfort him.'

Gina saw in Doris's eyes an almost ecstatic expectation.

'A moment,' said Doris, unbuttoning her blouse. She reached behind her and undid her brassiere then, lifting a cup, she exposed a breast. Its nipple was pink and puckered. Trembling, Doris took Tom in her arms. He blinked.

Doris put the boy to her breast, he took the nipple and sucked, and Doris cried, 'Oh, Oh, Oh,' and then was silent. Gina watched and felt emotions stirring strangely within her – maternal, sexual, possessive, proud, joyful – none of these things yet all of them.

Doris's eyes were glinting like an eagle's as they gazed at the little man at her breast, and she began a gentle murmur which gradually became a song, in a thin and improbably crystal-pure voice, from which Gina heard snatches of words – *'Raging fires, raging fires. God the Mother guard my child, guard my child. Hear my cry. Hear my cry'.*

The song faded in the air and there was the sound of a contented baby sucking.

Gina, remembering Henri Alban, Alain-Fournier, murmured, ' "*C'est d'abord comme une voix tremblante qui, de très loin, ose à peine chanter sa joie.* "' (At first it is like some quavering voice, overwhelmed with joy.) Doris flashed a look of understanding at her and continued, '"*Cet air que je ne connais pas, c'est aussi une prière, une supplication au bonheur de ne pas être trop cruel, un salut et comme un agenouillement devant le bonheur.*"' (This melody, it is unknown to me, yet it sounds as much like a prayer, an entreaty to fate not to be too cruel, a salute and a genuflexion before happiness.)

They were silent for a time before Gina asked, 'So what is it, this prayer to happiness?'

'A Hebridean lullaby, I believe, which I have altered slightly. The original and unliberated Scottish version, bowed down by all that fearful Celtic doom, maintains the ludicrous heresy that God the Mother was and is a man.' Doris chuckled in derision. 'What a notion. Why, that's just like saying God was and is a hedgehog. No. This is what's called a smooring song, a women's work song turned to the purposes of slumber. Labours and lullabies, the duties of women.'

'But not of hedgehogs?'

'Hmm. Hedgehogs at least are mammals, and, today, I finally understood something of mammalhood.' She paused and wiped a joyful tear from her eye. 'Sweet Jesus, have you the least idea what you have just done for me? Thank you. Gina, be my friend. Move in, the three of you. I have sinful amounts of space. Move in, do.'

Gina shook her head. 'I can't.'

CHAPTER NINE

Warren had bought the crawfish from a man over at Terrebonne, and they seemed such a perfect dish for a Sunday lunch.

'Clear the afternoon,' Gina warned their guests in Warren's cramped old apartment which she had moved into. Beth had Tom for the day and was probably at this moment grooming him to be Jefferson Davis. Gina directed her visitors to their places, putting Dave the Chomsky enthusiast beside Doris.

'A delight and a joy,' said Dave, drawing back Doris's chair for her and smiling tightly at the back of her head.

Warren looked stressed. He had not wanted this little party. Doris made him nervous, and their other guest, Sebastian Brownchurch, an aged Englishman and visiting professor, was scarcely less intimidating; but he had been chosen because Doris liked and admired his brain, and his appetites, which seemed of the neutered homosexual variety.

Soon Doris and Dave were flirting with wild improbability in medieval French. Professor Brownchurch – he urged them all to call him Sebastian, but the name did not rise easily to their lips, so gaunt and Gielgudian he appeared – soon settled into an effortless conversation with Roben about the poetry of Provence.

At around seven o'clock, with everybody quite drunk, Doris excused herself to go to the bathroom, the treacherous acoustic qualities of which Gina had been but dimly aware of. Moments later, there was the thud of a gastric explosion, followed by the sound of a torrent pouring into the toilet-bowl. Gina instantly raised her voice and Dave began to shout, 'Here, let me clear up these dishes for you,' and started clattering saucepans, ladles and plates with frantic gusto.

But all this did not quite conceal the succession of

concussions from within the bathroom. Gina bawled despairingly, 'Music anybody?'

'Tape deck blew this morning,' whispered Warren in a voice thinned by a pessimism which life had repeatedly vindicated. A long slow fart followed from the bathroom, and Professor Brownchurch and Roben and Gina began to bellow pleasantries at one another while Dave animatedly collided pot with pan until finally there was the welcome sound of flushing.

Doris returned looking grim. Warren mused, shaking his head at the table, while everyone else babbled. Doris interrupted the jabbering to declare with mordant relish, 'An interesting reptile, the misnamed crawfish. It is, of course, not a fish at all, the word coming from the Old French *crevice*, and that in turn coming from the Old High German, *krebiz*, meaning crab. I can well believe it. That was just like giving birth to a litter of crabs, fully grown, and with angry claws. I suspect the pleasure will not be mine alone.'

They all laughed at her frankness and had begun to leave, when Professor Brownchurch interrupted the polite industry of departure to make a subsidiary exit towards the toilet.

Gina had to stop herself breaking into song to drown out the noises which boomed from inside the bathroom, as Roben wept with laughter and Dave became ominously thoughtful. When Professor Brownchurch emerged, blinking, Dave pushed past him. Soon a noise like a tureen of potatoes being emptied into bathwater rang over the dining table. By this time tears were streaming down all their faces.

'Seat's nice and warm,' said Dave, emerging. Roben murmured 'Good,' and slipped into the toilet, recoiling briefly at the door. The sound of an elephant breaking wind gusted through the dining room, followed by the roar of gravel cascading into a swimming pool. Doris let out a long hysterical snort of joy before the smile on her face suddenly died.

'My, is it fragrant in there,' said Roben with a respectful tone as she emerged.

Dave rose, mumbling an excuse-me-please, and Roben said, 'Hold up there, buster, you're out of turn. Anybody else to go in first?' Doris looked beseechingly at the door, smiled weakly and like a little bird fluttered back into the bathroom.

Dave said, 'Believe me, you might soon wish that I'd gone in there.' Then he was silent as he examined the tablecloth for small faults. A long unbirdlike sound of gas bubbling through a warm marsh exited the toilet and patrolled the dining room, followed by some minor detonations.

Doris emerged and Dave pushed past her, pausing only momentarily in shock before slamming the door behind him, an eructation following only a moment later.

'Close,' mused Roben. The sound of an Icelandic geyser echoed through the silent room. Gina stuffed her napkin in her mouth and felt tears trickling down her cheeks.

'Time to go, honey,' said Roben after Dave reappeared, 'before fresh calamities befall us. We got time to make it back home before it strikes again, partner?'

Dave muttered indistinctly, his face grey, his eyes rolling. They hurried out, Gina and Warren accompanying them to their car while Professor Brownchurch slid into the bathroom.

'Toodle-oo, soopah pahty, simply loved the food, and adawed the diah-weah,' called Roben. 'Let's split, Dave, I feel something boiling down below.'

When Gina and Warren returned inside, Doris was back in the toilet. Professor Brownchurch, meanwhile, looking pale and baffled, was no longer a force to be reckoned with.

'I think I will take some air,' he said, and vanished.

'My turn,' said Gina in a thin voice, and fled into the bathroom.

'Well, that was a successful evening, all things considered,' said Doris brightly as Gina emerged from the bathroom.

'We don't have any gasoline handy, do we Warren?' said Gina 'That bathroom's not what it once was. The poor thing.'

She giggled and helped herself to more wine. 'I think I'll have some of that,' said Doris.

'If you'll excuse me,' said Warren, hastily vanishing towards the seat of ease, while Gina and Doris roared 'The Battle Hymn of the Republic' and 'Dixie' until they were in uncontrollable hysterics.

When Professor Brownchurch reappeared, blinking as if emerging from a century-long sleep, he asked for and noted down the name of the supplier of the crawfish, observing dryly, 'I must remember this. V-A-S-I-T-C-H. It could come in useful one day.'

*

'I detest that bathroom and I hate this apartment,' Gina declared after a couple of days' contemplation. 'Warren, hon, we simply got to move.'

Warren said, 'I agree about the bathroom. The other night . . . oh my. Sure, but where?'

'Doris's. Doris would have us, I know it. She's lonely, she would love to have Tom around.'

'Doris's? Great. What'll you tell your mother?'

'That we'd love to but won't move in with her while all her manfriends are trying to make an uncle or an aunt for little Tom, that's what I'll tell her.'

'I don't think she'll like that,' said Warren. She looked to see if he was joking. He wasn't.

She told her mother that poor Doris was getting old, had had a bad fall, and she and Warren were temporarily moving in until she was through convalescence.

'I do approve. Father would have done too, probably does, in that Valhalla where his noble soul resides. Our class has always looked after the less fortunate. Such duties come with rank. And the Sykes were once fine people, though sadly reduced in recent times.'

'Mother,' muttered Gina. 'You should see a doctor.'

'An obstetrician might be more appropriate for a young woman like me.'

*

Within a month, the three of them had moved into Cypress Mound, a majestic heap designed, Doris told them, by the great Henry Howard. Its main structure was columned and galleried, but in its rear was a sort of afterthought, a plain extension with an A-roof and a tiny east-facing porch. This was what Gina and Warren were to occupy. It was perfect.

Sure enough, soon after they had set up home there, Beth phoned Doris to enquire how she was. Doris reported the call to Gina while Gina was unpacking a cardboard box of books. 'You once told me to fuck off, or something on those lines, if I remember correctly,' said Doris.

'I did,' said Gina, examining a book's spine, 'and would do again, given the same provocation.'

'My, you are such a charming young woman sometimes. Your mother has many of your qualities.'

'Enough,' murmured Gina. 'On with your tale.'

'Well, I nearly uttered those same words to your mother. As an imprecation, they do not readily come to my lips. She asked me how I was after my fall, and I said, fine, fine – see, you have me lying! – and she replied that maybe I thought I was fine, but women of my age often got confused.

'"My age?" I whispered. "Yes, your age, my dear," she replied, my, oh so jaunty, adding, "It's hard for you to admit your frailty to a young, fertile woman like me, Doris. I understand, and I forgive you." And then she hung up on me. I couldn't speak for an hour afterwards, I was so mad. I will make an orphan of you if she suggests a few herbal remedies for me. In the meantime, thank you very much indeed for the cover story which started all this.'

'You're welcome. Please don't mention it again.'

'Believe me, I won't. And why does she go on about her father so?'

'He joined the Army when she was little, the war, and never came back. I guess he ran off with some woman. It's never really talked about. I think she felt rejected. She's obsessive about him.'

'Really? I hadn't noticed. And this Tennessee bonnet thing,' said Doris, musingly. 'What is it?'

'You mean . . . ? I assumed you knew and I didn't have the nerve to ask you. It'll be interesting to see when it finally arrives.'

It never did. One day Beth simply stopped her sewing and no further mention was made of it. Tom embarked upon his journey into childhood from infancy with his skull unprotected from the sun's rays, and Beth gradually accepted that Gina and Warren and Tom lived at Cypress Mound. It was so.

Part Two

CHAPTER TEN

1975, Ireland

When Tom was nearly two, Gina took him to Ireland to stay with the Brackens. The pulse of motherhood was revived in Maureen's breast with a passion when she saw him. She kissed him, and he astonished her by reaching out and kissing her in return.

'Did you see that, Noelly? By heaven, you were never so affectionate.'

'My fierce intelligence, Ma, still prevents any public displays of affection. But you know I'm fond of you, even in your dotage.'

Gina laughed. 'Well it's good to see that you haven't changed.'

He had. He was about five inches taller, and a ludicrous combination of down and stubble burst in odd clumps about his skin. But adolescence had not dimmed his boyishness, even though he was reading Dostoevsky as he eavesdropped on their conversation.

Paula was now studying electronics in Limerick. The twins were no longer just the twins. From being inseparable they were now quite separable, Cormac becoming a robust Gaelic footballer and Liam playing the fiddle with serious and energetic application.

Maureen said, 'It's amazing. You produce this thing, totally dependent on you, and slowly it acquires characteristics which make it an entirely separate person. Where does it all come from? There's no music in my family, nor in Matt's, yet out of nowhere we produce this budding musician.'

'I'd ask questions if I were Dad,' sniffed Noelly. 'The postman whistled a lot. Maybe Ma gave him something to whistle about.'

Maureen looked heavenwards. 'May God forgive you.'

'Tetchy today, are we? My fault, I didn't give you your Complan yet.'

Maureen scowled amiably at Noelly. 'Come on, Gina, I think this little fellow needs changing.'

'Already?' cried Noelly. 'But sure you only changed me an hour ago.'

'Is it against the law to murder a teenage male?' asked Maureen.

'Absolutely not,' replied Gina.

In the bathroom, Gina sensed the question approach, manoeuvring like a large beast in a cattlefold. 'You must have known Warren a while,' said Maureen as she cleaned Tom, adding at a tangent, 'Boys are so much slower than girls.'

'So my mother keeps telling me. Proudly, I might add. Yes. We got kind of impetuous when I got back. Tom wasn't planned, but I don't regret it one bit.'

'Regret this little fellow? Oh stop smiling at me like that or I'll never let you back to America, you little flirt.'

Tom was standing in his new red trousers. 'Fell off the bath, hit the floor, banged my head,' he recited.

'That happened to him six months ago. The biggest event in his life. Boasts about it to everybody, Tom, don't you, hey?'

'Here,' said Tom, pointing to his forehead.

'Here, I'll kiss it better,' offered Maureen.

Tom obediently offered his forehead, then scrambled down from the linen box and toddled off out of the bathroom.

'He'll go for Noelly,' said Gina. 'He loves men.'

He did go for Noelly, running to him and pushing his book aside.

'Up,' he said to Noelly, 'up.'

Noelly lifted him up and put his mouth against the child's neck to blow into it, making a long, wet, flatulent noise. Tom roared with delight.

'You know who you look like, young fellow me lad?' said Noelly jocularly, looking steadily into Tom's eyes. 'Stefan thingummy.'

A hand from the past seized Gina's heart. Her ears thundered, and she just managed to detect and suppress a sob of incredulity before she turned and walked to the far corner of the kitchen, Noelly's voice following her. 'Ma, what was the name of the fellow staying here that you had the crush on? Oh begod it was shocking, Gina, she couldn't keep her hands off him.'

'What was that?' asked Maureen, distracted, her hands in a towel.

'Ma, what was your man's name, the fellow you fancied? Da nearly put you on the pill on account of him.'

'Enough of that talk now, Noelly, and in front of the child as well. The pill indeed.'

'Of course, no need for the pill at your age. Da had a rough time with the ould business a couple of summers ago and Ma was doing bed and breakfast for a while,' Noelly explained to Gina. 'This Stefan fellow stayed for a week of Ma's breakfasts, and God love him, the eejit even paid for them too. But what was his second name, Ma?'

'Talk of the devil,' said Maureen, still absently towelling her hands. 'Didn't he only phone the other day. Now what's that his name is? He said he might be in the area, could he look us up. I said of course, a pleasure to see him.'

'If only we could remember your name, Luigi,' said Noelly.

Maureen ignored him. 'Paula will be pleased.'

'Pleased? Paula? Ma, Paula will be all make-up and perfume and party frocks and God bless my soul, Stefan, what a surprise to see you, and here's me in my rags, I hardly know where to look, I'm so ashamed you'll have to take them off for me, my bedroom's the third on the left, I'll join you in a minute.'

'Noelly, God forgive you, she's far too young for Stefan.'

'Ah, yes, but does she know that? She comes over all puce and plump, and you can hear her hormones clank into action whenever she sees him. It's true love, Ma, true love.'

'That'll be nice, seeing Stefan again,' said Maureen ruminatively. 'You'll like Stefan, Gina.'

Gina, struck by a mental blizzard, managed to say, 'Stefan, that's Irish for Stephen, isn't it?'

'Yes, if it was Stefain, but it's not, it's Stefan, and Stefan's a Bulgarian,' said Noelly. 'Nice as Bulgarians go, but a

Bulgarian nonetheless. One locks one's doors.'

'No, he's not Bulgarian,' said Maureen, carrying a fresh towel for the bathroom. 'You young ignoramus. And what's that about locking doors? God forgive you. God forgive you indeed.'

'I'm sure you lock your doors against somebody beginning with a B. Can it be Belgians? Bolivians? Boers? It must be Boers. Sorry, Bulgaria. You too, Belgium.'

'Noelly, shut up. Stefan is Irish but his family is or was from somewhere in central Europe. His second name, I'm happy to say, is impossible.'

'But we cherish your memory, thingummy,' proclaimed Noelly, 'whoever you are.'

Gina, her mind spinning in panic, declared suddenly, 'I've really got to go and see Josey in Dublin.' She looked to see if Maureen and Noelly had detected anything in her voice. Nothing. Maureen was folding up the towel and Noelly was on the floor playing with Tom. 'It'll be nice seeing Josey,' she said lamely, unheard.

*

Maureen was slicing bread, as Gina and the three boys buttered and spread jam on it, the boys promptly consuming it in unchewed, crocodilian gulps.

'You're gaining on me, lads,' said Maureen. 'Slow it down. So, Paula, your young man is coming after all.'

'Ma,' said Paula, squirming.

'Yup,' said Noelly, licking jam from his fingers. 'You're welcome to my bedroom, only my bed is single, and three would be a crowd.'

'Ma, make him stop.'

'Throw the teapot at him,' advised Maureen. 'Don't come whingeing to me.'

'Just you wait, Noelly Bracken, just you wait,' said Paula.

'Come on now, Noelly, enough's enough.'

'Sure, amn't I only toughening her up for life? Our Paulie'll soon be able to take on Mohammed Ali, fifteen rounds in the ring.' He paused. 'And another twenty in the showers.'

'Gina,' said Maureen, 'you see that bread knife there?'

'This one here?'

'That's the one. Stick it in him.'

'Certainly. Any particular place?'

'The throat.'

Noelly uttered a great adolescent, animal yelp and, spluttering with laughter and showering the table with half-chewed breadcrumbs, rose and backed towards the wall. 'Gina,' he cried, 'what's a poor boy to do?'

'Stay silent, I reckon,' said Gina, smiling at Noelly. 'For a minute if you can bear it.'

'A whole minute?'

Gina nodded. Noelly put on a show of dumb agony and a long period of silence followed.

'At last,' said Paula, 'Paradise.'

'Bliss,' interjected Liam.

'Bliss,' agreed Cormac. 'So when's your man coming?'

'He's going to ring and tell us. Noelly'll have to move in with the twins.'

'Why? Can't he tuck in with Gina?'

'Noelly,' barked his mother. 'That's enough of that!'

'But Ma! Me minute's up! Fair's fair.'

'Jesus Mary and Joseph, I'm not talking about the shagging minute. What'll I do about you, child, what'll I do?'

'A bit late for contraceptives. They're fierce about them fellas in this household, oh fierce,' he explained to Gina.

'Well, look,' she said, 'I've got to see friends in Dublin, and I'm sure you'd like to meet your friend, Ludwig or whatever – you know, the one with the name – without outsiders cluttering up the house.'

'Outsiders, girl?' Maureen tutted dismissively. 'What outsiders?'

When Gina went to bed, her brain was humming with Stefan. Will he find me attractive still? she asked herself as she undressed. Naked, she looked at her reflection in the mirror, and she touched herself, imagining him standing behind her, as once he had, feeling her arousal start. She went to bed thinking of Stefan, as she always did when she worked herself to orgasm. As she lay drifting towards sleep, she could smell an odd, sweet odour; Maureen must have been polishing in the room. She awoke when Tom began to mutter about his head, then slept again.

*

She was dressing Tom when the phone rang and, distantly, somebody answered it. She froze, Tom's little shirt halfway over his head. She felt her heart stop as she listened to the murmuring.

Tom grumbled, 'Mom, it hurts,' and Gina pulled the shirt the rest of the way over his head. 'Ow,' said Tom. 'You hurt my ear.' She kissed his ear. 'Sorry, hon,' she whispered. 'Shhh.'

'Shhh,' agreed Tom. The pair of them listened. The phone was put down. Had he telephoned? 'Okay,' said Gina, 'let's get you dressed, buster.'

In the kitchen, Maureen was preparing eggs.

'If your friend is coming, I suppose I'd better tell Josey when I'll be visiting her,' said Gina, her voicing ringing with falseness.

'Who's for breakfast? I can't be in here all day breaking eggs on the off-chance,' cried Maureen.

'I'll need to tell her.'

'Is anybody coming to breakfast at all at all, or am I alone in this house?'

'I can't just turn up.'

'Cormac! Liam! Noelly! Paula! In the name of the divine Jesus, will you get a move on.'

'What do you think?' asked Gina.

'Paula! What's happened to you, girl?'

'Drowned, I think,' suggested Liam, sauntering in. 'She's been in the bathroom since February.'

'Ma, what does Paula bloody do in there all day?' chimed in a ruffled Cormac, following his twin. Tom shouted a welcome to them, and Liam picked him up, murmuring, 'Ah ye big lump ye, sure you're only a big lump, what are ye?'

'A big lump,' cried Tom. 'A big lump.'

The phone rang and was ignored. Liam said, 'Go on, what are you?' 'A big lump.' The phone still rang. Answer it, urged Gina silently. Answer the goddamned phone.

Maureen said, 'None of you stir, that's all right, Ma will do everything around here. Saints preserve us, what a family.'

Cormac went out, and Gina strained her ears to hear what was being said. 'Well would you look at Lady Muck,' cried Maureen as Paula shuffled in.

Gina stopped herself telling Maureen to shut up as she tried to hear the conversation.

'Ma, every time I get into the bathroom I've got these disgusting brothers trying to get in after me. I never get a moment's peace, it's enough to drive a saint mad.'

'A constipated saint,' said Noelly as he slunk in, looking wrecked.

'Good afternoon, young sir, I trust you have had enough sleep. The twelve hours did you, I take it?' said Maureen, shovelling out scrambled eggs.

'Somewhat less than your young master is used to, elderly female retainer, but your good intentions are noted. Take a day off at the end of the year.'

'Did you get any sleep at all at all? You look a ruin.'

'Make that half a day. How's my Tom this fine morning?'

Tom sat on Noelly's lap and announced, 'Mom hurt my ear.'

'The brute,' said Noelly. 'The brute. Did you try hitting her back?'

'Noelly!' barked Maureen.

'Here,' he continued, unconcerned, 'have some toast, young fellow-me-lad. There you are.'

'Mom hurt my ear,' said Tom.

'Sadist,' hissed Noelly. 'Here now, eat that.'

'Mom hurt my ear.'

'Needle's stuck here. Help. Will torture shut you up?'

Cormac returned and said, 'Ma, is there any more toast?' Gina fidgeted furiously. Maureen replied sharply, 'What in the name of God is that if it's not a toaster? Is there any toast indeed! Did you ever hear the like of it, Gina?'

'So what do you think, should I ring Josey?'

'Josey? Josey who?'

'Josey O'Flaherty.'

'Joe C. O'Flaherty,' announced Noelly in an American

accent, 'film prodooser and stoodent of life. Know him well, Horatio.'

'She, it's a she. A friend in Dublin, and I thought I'd stay with her when your friend, thingummy, is coming here, you know, so I'm not in the way.'

'In the way indeed. More eggs, anybody? Eggs, Gina? Oh you haven't eaten your first lot, and look at Tom, the creature, half-starved are you? Is Mammy neglecting you?'

'Mom hurt my ear,' he said, rubbing his ear.

'Fell off the bath, hit the floor, bumped my head,' intoned Noelly. Tom crowed with delight and repeated the mantra. Everybody laughed except Gina, who felt irritation mounting. The telephone rang again and again was ignored.

'Now look, I'm not getting that, so who's going to?' said Maureen from the head of the table. 'Gina, you look as if you want to.'

'No, no,' Gina heard herself almost shriek, 'no, not at all.'

'Let it ring, so,' said Maureen. When it stopped she departed and returned. 'That's it, the phone's off the hook, now can we have our breakfast in peace, please?'

Through a voice as taut as cheesewire, Gina said, 'So, Maureen, what do you think, should I phone Josey and say I'm coming and should I tell her when?'

'Gina, do what you like. Everyone else does around here.'

Noelly began to clear the plates away. 'Gina,' he said with a sudden earnestness, 'you've hardly eaten a thing.'

'I'm not hungry,' she replied.

'Are you well?' asked Noelly. 'You haven't been overdoing it or anything?'

'No, no, I'll just put Tom on his pot for a few minutes, see if anything happens.'

'We do the same with Paula,' observed Noelly, walking to the sink. 'The results are often quite interesting.'

'Noelly, you're foul. Just you wait until people make jokes like that about you.'

'Ah Paula, I was only messing. Sure aren't we all only human?' he said in oddly solemn tone. Gina looked at him. His eyes appeared to speak to her before he turned hurriedly away.

CHAPTER ELEVEN

As Matt drove her to the station, with Maureen calling farewells from the doorway, Gina tentatively asked, 'When's your friend arriving?'

'Stefan? He's not. He rang this morning. He's got to go to Dublin.'

'Dublin?' said Gina, swivelling in astonishment. 'But no one called here.'

'He tried. Paula and her bloody friends, natter natter natter, so he rang me in the office. Something's come up.'

'How's he going to get to Dublin?' asked Gina in a shrill but wary voice.

'Didn't ask. Train'd be great, sure I'll introduce the pair of you, company for the journey.'

'What?' said Gina, appalled. She groped for words. None came.

At the station, Matt scurried the length of the deplorably brief train of carriages, staring through mud-caked windows, while Gina, Tom in hand, scrutinized her shoes, murmuring, 'Oh God, why have you done this?'

'Not here. Pity. Now, get you on in here,' Matt said, opening a door in the rearmost carriage, which smelt like an old people's home. The single passenger there was a teenage girl: an equally young train guard was talking to her.

A whistle blew and Matt said, 'See you soon.' He lowered the window, stepped outside, and shut the door behind him. The guard walked to the rear window and signalled, and the stationmaster on the platform waved a flag at the driver.

Gina, her heart uplifted at her liberation, leaned out to kiss Matt. 'Grand,' said Matt, smacking his lips in delight, and then turned at the sound of a car horn, as a taxi skidded to a halt in the car park. A figure leapt out of the car. The stationmaster blew a whistle, and the train gave a testing tug on the carriage. It lurched forward an inch. Matt strode over and spoke urgently to the stationmaster, who pointed at his watch. The train began to move. Gina sat, paralysed.

The newcomer jogged down the platform with healthy ease. Was it Stefan? She did not dare look closely. The guard in the carriage walked past Gina and sat beside the teenage girl. The train moved away from Matt, as slowly as if it were being winched up a steep slope. The Stefan-figure – was it him? – spoke briefly to Matt and then moved towards the train, loping confidently.

Gina looked at the furthest door. The guard had left his schleifen key in the lock. Gina rose, walked swiftly to the rear door, twisted the key once to lock it and, unseen, returned to her seat, where she sat with lowered face.

She could see the far door handle jolt as it was twisted, but the door did not open. The train gathered momentum. The handle twisted again. Nothing. The train quickened. Her heart thudded, her stomach heaved: this was her doing.

The man then abandoned the lower door and began to run towards the next one up: Gina's door. She turned her face away as he drew alongside. He was so close each could have heard the other's whisper through the still-open window.

Her fingers tingled as she gazed at the space between her feet, thinking of those Slavic cheekbones, those strong athlete's shoulders, a mere foot away. He would make it after all. That was it. She was about to meet him again. She glimpsed his hand on the window frame. The handle on her side of the door began to turn. Gina felt a great surge of joy, her lips mouthing a welcome.

'Please,' he said, and the face vanished backwards, the carriage handle ceasing to turn, the train leaving him behind. Through the diminishing angle of window she could see the figure, cursing heavenwards and standing marooned on the edge of the platform, where it began to shelve downwards.

*

Bosnia, 1992
They are bivouacked near Sjeniste, and are in good cheer,

Milošević especially. Three women, ha ha ha, daughter, mother, grandmother, and the grandmother was not all that old, under fifty, he laughs, a cherubic smile across his barely bearded face.

Their lorry has an improvised four-barrel ZPU 14.5 mm anti-aircraft mounting on its back, with ammunition panniers on the outside, and a Muslim captive within. Night slides suddenly up the mountain like a dark lake filling from below. The driver takes several bottles of wine from his cab, apologizing for their condition – all this blood, do forgive me – but here, a quick wipe, look, as good as new, there now.

They eat pork grilled over charcoal by one of Arkan's men who had once worked in the Munich Hyatt, and it is perfect, juicy and crunchy on the outside and white and chewy inside. The boy drinks wine from the billycan he shares with the machine-gunner, and a slick of grease rests across its surface.

This is good, says the boy. I'll remember this day always. Such a memory, to last for ever and ever. This is what life is all about, isn't it, making good memories, to tell your children?

What will you tell your children?

Simply of how you and I fought for freedom.

Good. Excellent. You can't beat the plain truth.

*

Had it been Please, or *Pleashe*?

Gina was haunted by a dream, by a silence, the strange and haunting silence of the seabed, ending in 'Please'. She could have spoken to him. She could have opened her door. She did not. Sin upon sin.

She knew some sins remain with you for ever, their consequences plaguing lifetimes begun long after the sin itself is forgotten.

The truth remained absurd. She had spent a few days with him almost three years ago. Can one weekend create such enduring emotions? Can such brief moments so change a life?

And if that was the case, why had she not welcomed the chance to see him again? Why had she gone to such extraordinary lengths to avoid him? And more decisions had awaited her. She didn't go to Josey's in Dublin – Stefan might turn up there. So she took a taxi to Mrs Ryan's.

Her host was delighted to see her. 'But did you hear?' she cried, exultant with bad news. 'Poor Mr O'Reilly's gone. Killed by a truck, and would you believe it, outlived by his mother. Sure she came to see me the other day. Drove herself in and out, and all over the road, like a heifer killing mice. She was raging, raging, over her pension. Some whippersnapper in the British embassy objecting to something or other, not that that excused her crashing into poor Mr O Dálaigh's new Ford, and him fierce, oh fierce now, on the matter of law and order.'

Gina opened her mouth to interrupt the flow, but Mrs Ryan continued regardless.

'All for a pension. I said to her, I said, "For the love of God Mrs O'Reilly, why didn't you write?" Her eyes, she said. Couldn't see well enough to write. Did you ever hear the like? Her husband was drowned, you know. Some mailship or other, she said. The *Leinster*, I think she said. You ever hear of it? Nor I either. And there was poor Mr O Dálaigh's Cortina, bonnets and bumpers all over the place, quite the little scrapyard.'

Tom suddenly seized Gina's attention, enabling her to say, 'You haven't met Tom. Tom, say hello.'

'Tom here would love a meal, I'm sure.'

The salty, salival smell of frying soon filled the house as Mrs Ryan cooked a huge heap of sausages and pudding, tomatoes, rashers of crispy bacon, potato bread and eggs and bustled in with them.

'You don't mind if I just join you for a couple of minutes now, do you?' said Mrs Ryan. 'Here, young fellow, let me cut the pudding for you. There we are. Here. And the sausage. Not Haffners, I'm sorry to say. They don't make them like they used to – sure isn't that the way with everything? Now. What's been happening in your life, so?'

'Well, I'm married, as you can see. This is my son, my husband had to stay working but I was dying to see Ireland again and my friends the Brackens in Mayo.'

'And what happened to the young gentleman you were with at the airport?'

Gina busied her mouth with a pretence of eating before replying, 'We lost touch.'

'A nice young gentleman, as it turned out,' Mrs Ryan mused. 'I'd caught the bus out, and he gave me a lift back to Dublin, told me he thought you would probably come back to live here. Well I certainly hoped so after the carry-on at the airport. But what would I know what young people get up to these days?' she said, mouthing the words directly at Gina, apparently so that Tom wouldn't catch them.

Gina gave her a wan smile and said nothing. That night she woke, sweat on her forehead and tears on her cheeks, after a long dream in which Stefan had fallen under the wheels of a railway carriage, whispering, 'Please, *pleashe*,' as he died. Now Stefan's son lay beside her. She thought of the pretty young girl in the train. Not long before, Gina had been like that, with all her life and its vast promises resting before her. One weekend had changed everything.

Gina and Tom spent three sad and desolate days in Dublin. She would have preferred to return to Mayo but, trapped in her iron mesh of deceit, could not. The weather was poor and Gina felt lonely, especially after Tom had fallen asleep, and she sat in their room, listening to the traffic hissing on the wet road in the dark night outside.

On the last day she bought a large map of Wicklow from Eason's on O'Connell Street, hired a car and drove south, retracing the route of years before. Men raised welcoming hands at her approach. In one tiny village stood a solitary cow amid its dung, almost as if it had been biding there these three years.

'The place of the storyteller,' she whispered to Tom as they sat on an old tree bole. She wrapped him up against the slight drizzle which came in from the west. 'And maybe the spot where you were conceived.' She shuddered and pulled Tom closer to her.

She returned to Mayo. Matt never mentioned the man on the platform and nor did she. Her ignorance remained intact and some days later Maureen and Matt drove her to Shannon

Airport with Noelly, the only child free for the journey, and they made her swear not to come to Ireland without Warren. She returned the invitation. 'Our friend Doris has spare rooms galore. She'd love to have you. She adores big noisy families.'

'Excuse me,' said Noelly. 'This description, "big noisy families". To whom, pray, is it intended to apply?' He had a grin on his face.

'Bye, Noelly,' she replied, kissing him as Matt and Maureen busied themselves with her bags. 'Bye, my Gina.' He kissed and hugged her and whispered, 'Oh were you my age, such kisses would I give you.' And then he touched her lips with his. A pulse passed between them. She inhaled, and she smelt aftershave, Noelly's first.

'Noelly,' she said. The smell was familiar.

*

'Tell me the truth,' said Warren as he drove from the airport. He looked meaningfully at her, sniffed, changed gear and asked: 'Are you okay?'

'Just tired.'

Back home, Gina was asleep the second her head hit the pillow; and was awake only a couple of hours later. Her body was living the rhythms of Irish time. The surging Doppler-din of crickets told her she was home.

Her emotions baffled her. She thought about the look on Stefan's face as the train drew away. But she had not been looking directly at him, and must have invented the image of despair which troubled her. So she wondered: how much of what we do and think is impelled by our own fantasies? Can we tell them from the truth? And what is truth?

She fell asleep. She heard Warren rising, moved to get up also, but plummeted to the warm, comforting depths of profound slumber. When she woke Tom was curled up round her, and for the moment her heart was restored to peace.

But sitting on the porch that October, the sun descending in fiery abandon to the west and with Doris and Warren both teaching, she said to herself, I can never live with this. I can never live with the errors I have made. I cannot live with my misery.

But then that other voice said that she must. For Tom, for common sense, for the reason that all people must put their lives together after adversity. And this was not a calamity: look at old Mrs O'Reilly raising her children through the years – mad Madge, Con, and Rory. Yet there she was, still alive, the best part of a hundred years of age, minding mad Madge even now.

She thought: we shape and form our lives from the base clay given to us. Order is merely a fiction, a creativity over chaos, and her duty was to impose a purpose on that chaos which was of her own making. Take her marriage, for a start: now largely sexless, and loveless too.

She knew that lives are assembled from the imperfections of half-recalled truths, mangled in the remembering. Her duty was to Tom. She must forget Stefan.

She thought then of Noelly and smiled. What a boy. But in that mischievous teenager was the kernel of a passionate and intelligent man. Some woman was going to be very lucky indeed.

CHAPTER TWELVE

Louisiana, 1980

Tom came into the breakfast room where Gina was sitting scribbling notes for her thesis on Apollinaire. She had so much writing to do, so much to read, that sometimes it made her sleepless with worry. 'Mom, can we go now?' he asked. 'Can we? Can we go now, Mom, please, please?'

'McDonald's isn't open at this time, hon, it isn't even eight.'

She looked and saw Stefan smiling back at her. She bent and kissed Tom suddenly. 'Mom,' he said disgustedly, wiping his cheek, 'I'm all wet.'

There was a knock on the connecting door.

'Hi,' said Gina, instantly pulling herself together. 'Come on in, Warren's off plotting a coup or a putsch.'

'Men,' sniffed Doris.

'Coffee?' asked Gina, half expecting a sideways enquiry about her thesis.

'Sure.'

Gina poured and Doris lifted the cup to her lips. 'Ooo, be still my beating heart, you sure do make it strong.'

'Caffeine-courage. I promised Tom I'd take him to McDonald's, goddam it.'

'Do you know I have never been to a McDonald's. Is that extraordinary?'

'You want to join us? First in a lifetime? We're meeting Beth at Atlas, she's been getting her watch repaired. Hey – two birds with one stone – I'll go in the Impala, you can drive the VW in. Beth's borrowing it while the Saab's brakes are being done. Beth sure would love to see you again. You gentry folk can lament the good old days, talk about Jim Bowie.'

'Bowie was just trash,' said Doris. 'What can you say about

a man who invents a knife the size of a spade, other than that he has to be a man?'

'Exactly!' cried Gina. 'Mom loves talk like that.'

Gina's relationship with her mother had improved vastly. Age had calmed the rages which had troubled Beth for much of her life, and now Gina looked forward to their meetings.

'Come on,' she urged. 'I just know Tom would love to give you a guided tour of a McDonald's menu.'

'Isn't it odd how we seek the approval of children?' wondered Doris aloud. 'There he is, a man-child, the enemy in embryo, and I desperately want his good opinion. Why, I even let him have a shower with me that time he snuck in, trying to get a look-see. The only man ever to see me nude. "Lovely big jubblies," he said, the rascal. Is there anything left in that nice little pot of yours?'

'He's his father's son all right,' said Gina, smiling, pouring more coffee. 'I just wonder how many women his father is liking right now.'

Doris looked at her intently.

'Sorry, that was stupid,' said Gina, irritated with herself. 'But you know he's there in my brain, hiding, saying nothing, and then, wham, and he suddenly emerges, and I can't help it, he's standing there, with that goddamned smile of his, taking over things. It's not fair, I know it. Warren is a good man, he's loyal and hard-working and he looks after Tom as if he were his own, and I don't consciously hanker after Stefan, but I can't stop him catching me off-guard and I feel so pathetic, Jesus, so *female*.'

'That's not a bad way to feel. "*On ne nait pas femme: on le devient.*"'

'I don't think de Beauvoir has the least idea what it is to be a woman.'

'No self-pity please. You've been dealt the hand, play it.'

Gina laughed bitterly. 'Sometimes you want more than the hand.'

Doris was silent for a while. 'I don't know what it is to have a young sister or daughter, although I do – alas – know what it means to have a nephew. I guess the way I think about you is a cross between the three.'

'Thanks. I've met your nephew.'

Doris laughed. 'Sister, daughter, niece, I meant.' She paused. 'Look, just don't offer me secrets which might embarrass you later.'

'There's nothing I could tell you which would embarrass me. Warren and I just aren't getting on any more. Sexually, or any other way. Simple as that. And there's things in my head.'

'Stefan things,' said Doris.

'In part, yes. What I'm talking to you about is not just sex, right? Well I don't think so. Sometimes it's hard to say.'

'Read that goddam bastard Freud and it's always hard to say.'

'Maybe. Oh I guess what I'm trying to say is something happened with Tom's father, something inside me that never happened before and sure hasn't since, and sometimes when I think about it all gone for ever, I could cry.'

Doris reached over and placed her hand on her friend's arm. 'Gina, honey, come on, your life's not so bad. We've all got to get over our pasts. I got over mine, Papa drinking Tennessee whiskey every night, smoking cigars, Mama sitting silently alone.'

Gina sensed something new emerging. Doris looked at her, almost for permission, and she flashed a signal of assent.

'I used to feel real angry about it, but not now. I guess they were people whose inadequacy is not punished, as it would have been if they were poor. I used to play here with my doll Arabella. Strange. Three people, all alone like three spacemen marooned in orbit in their suits, the radios not working, circling impotently round one another so that a passing Martian might think, my, but they're having a good time.

'It wasn't bad, mind, it wasn't a hell for me, though I think it was for my mother. Then I was sent away to the academy, and that's where I grew up. I learnt odd, disgusting rumours of sex from other girls. But I used to get those sensations, you know. We all get them, but they surprise you when they arrive, they're so unrelated to anything you're used to. I would lie in bed thinking about Ruth Niven, a girl in the class above me, with long blonde hair. God, did I adore her. And those stirrings, they frightened me so, in that strange place which, like most girls, I knew I shouldn't touch.

'But I placated them in the only way possible, then I felt a terrible shame for doing so. Nothing came of my crush, of course. I never even kissed Ruth Niven. She's a grandmother over Opelousas way now, on her third husband, I hear, and no doubt good for another brace. Not seen her in thirty years. Fine looking, I'm told.

'But I'm rambling. There's a point to all this. Is there any coffee left in that delightful little pot of yours? Thank you. Truth is, I knew nothing about me, absolutely nothing, by the time I went to Radcliffe. There I met Audrey Weinstein, Jewish, of course. You know, I had never even seen a Jew. So lovely. Every time I saw her, I felt this turmoil inside me, terrible and wonderful at the same time.

'She came round to my room one time, I was nineteen. She was a real fine French scholar, her mother was French. We were discussing Villon, I remember, and she was sitting beside me on the bed, and she turned and looked at me, and her eyes caught mine, and oh, I fell, how I fell. She leaned forward and kissed me, and if I live a thousand years, I will never experience again that kiss on my lips, that joy in my heart. I kissed her back, and she stopped and asked me if I knew what was happening, and I replied, sure, though I didn't, not the least idea, and she replied, good, and I thought, God, guide me through this, let me get it right, whatever it is, but Audrey, God bless her, steered me right. I knew then that my fate was to love women, but first of all, to love and to serve Audrey Weinstein, day and night, to the end of my life.

'I'll be brief because, believe me, this is not easy, so no questions, okay? I have not told you this before. I do not know why I am telling you now. Too much coffee, probably.

'We were together for about five years. Audrey was in Paris when it fell to the Germans. I, God forgive me, was here. As an American she could have left freely up until the end of 1941. She didn't. Instead she got involved in the Resistance. She vanished without trace some time around 1942. Audrey's *reseau*, without exception, went to the firing squad or the gas chamber. As far as I know, not a single survivor. Not one.'

A long silence filled the sunlit morning room. Doris's face was iron-grey.

'You are the second person I have told this story to. Françoise is the other. I have had other lovers, but Audrey Weinstein is the love of my life. I dream of her still. I said it hurt just now, but that's not entirely true. You can love the dead, you know. Is it too terrible to admit that I think of Audrey sexually even now? Does that repulse you? I hope not. The truth is, that is the moment I feel closest to her. It is a seance of a kind. I get other seances too, such as when I smell her hair beside me in the early morning when I am half awake and day is breaking through the drapes, and then I am immediately transported back to Radcliffe some two score years ago, the happiest and greatest moments in my life.'

Again there was silence. Gina felt tears beneath her eyelids and looked up at Doris. Her face was steel-hard, but her eyes shone with happiness.

'God, I loved Audrey Weinstein. I adored her. I adore her. I always will. When I die, wherever she is, I will be also. I know this more certainly than I know anything. Even if at death we vanish and are no more than scattered molecules to be dispersed by wind and rain then that is fine. It is a fate in common. And a fate in common is all I've ever wanted for me and for Audrey.

'There now. I have told you something that I have not told even Françoise, though she knows that my first love was Audrey. So. You understand. You are not alone. That is all.'

Gina rose from the table, walked over to her friend, bent down and kissed her. 'Doris,' she said, and kissed her cheek again. Doris turned and looked at her, their faces only inches apart. Her eyes were now full of tears. 'You must understand something,' she said. 'When I think of Audrey, I feel only happiness. Her memory gives me joy. Maybe you can do the same with Stefan.'

Gina smiled.

'Well,' sniffed Doris, 'this is a fine way to start our morning's shopping and our visit to cholesterol city.'

CHAPTER THIRTEEN

Beth was standing outside the main west entrance to the Atlas store. Her recently repaired watch shone on her wrist, she had on an elegant straw hat against the sun, and was wearing the old, patterned blue shoes Gina had bought for her forty-fourth birthday.

'Mom,' said Gina, kissing her.

'Honey,' said her mother. 'Hi, Doris.'

'How are you, Beth? Love the hat.'

Beth looked at her sharply, alert for satire. Doris was gazing at the hat in genuine admiration. Beth's face relaxed. 'I'm glad you like it, I got it last year in Galveston.'

'Suits you.'

'Thank you. I would wait to hear a compliment like that from my own family for a full century, and in vain.'

'Granma, are you older or younger than Doris?' Tom chimed in.

A long silence filled the street, broken only by Beth asking glacially, 'What is the penalty in this state for the murder of a grandson? I will happily pay it.'

'Just settle for having to eat McDonald's, mom. That's enough,' said Gina.

'You know my parents never allowed me to go to the soda fountain when I was his age,' said Doris as they strolled to the parking lot. 'There was Gavrilo's over on Mormal and Arras, and lord I longed to go there and eat one of their sundaes, like I saw other kids devouring. Not the Sykes, though. Not for the likes of us. All that coffee's made me so light-headed.'

They walked into the lot where their two cars were parked. Ahead of them, a figure beside a yellow pick-up truck was fumbling in his pockets.

'There's Mr Vasitch,' said Tom solemnly.

'Yeah, I see him,' replied Gina, rummaging through her purse. 'Did I give you my keys, mother? No, silly me, here they are.'

The yellow pick-up ahead coughed and came to life. Gina looked up, and saw it reversing out of its space, clouds of blue-black smoke belching from its exhaust.

'Gina, if it's okay with you, hon, why doesn't Doris come with me?' Beth said. 'You don't look too good, Doris, if you don't mind my saying so.'

Gina again looked up the parking lot. The yellow pick-up stalled at her gaze.

'I don't mind one bit,' said Doris. 'I don't feel too great.'

'Fine,' said Gina. 'We'll meet you outside. But Mom – don't forget, if I'm not there go round the block, the cops here like illegal parking the way Golden Meadow cops love cars going forty.' She looked up the lot again. The yellow pick-up was now moving slowly towards them.

She gave her mother the keys. 'You know, the gears are different than the kind you're used to?'

'No problem,' declared her mother.

'Okay, I'll see you outside Holweg's in about five minutes.'

'I'll back out now while I still can,' said Beth. 'Manual is what I prefer. I'll cruise around the block if you aren't out, okay?' Doris got into the passenger's side and put on her seat belt.

Standing behind her mother's car, Gina looked up and saw the yellow pick-up slowly advancing, weaving, touching the fender of a parked car before veering right.

She glanced down at Tom. His eyes were on the approaching truck.

'Mommy,' he said. 'Look at this guy here.'

There was an empty parking space across the parking lot in front of Beth's car, with the perimeter wall beyond it.

The pick-up collided lightly with the fender of another parked car, and then picked up speed.

'Tom, quick,' said Gina, pushing him into the protected space, with a car on either side. In front of them, her mother was about to reverse away from them. Down the central lane, the pick-up rumbled towards them with sinister deliberation, bouncing off cars as it found its one true lane and accelerated.

'Look, Mommy, it's Mr Vasitch,' laughed Tom. 'Drunk again!'

'Jesus!' cried Gina, pushing Tom back further towards the wall, even as the pick-up collided with the nose of the car beside them, bounced back into the lane then went towards the exit and vanished.

Tom cried with delight at their near miss. 'Mommy, I thought Mr Vasitch was going to hit us,' he said. He turned his knee-buckling smile on her, and took her hand. They had faced danger together and had come through it.

Then she heard the high revs of the VW engine.

Beth, hand on the steering wheel, was gazing over her shoulder, away from them, but the VW bounded forwards, with Doris wide-eyed in the passenger seat. Gina looked down at Tom, who was gazing up at her with Stefan's smile. In a single leap, the howling car flew past Gina, the smile on Tom's face vanishing in that moment as he was swept from her.

The VW hit the wall with a bang like a ship's boiler in a foundry, smashing the brickwork into rubble. Gina was paralysed for a second, as if she were alone in the universe; then she began to move with awful slowness towards the wreckage, the twisted metal and the ruins of a broken wall. There was the sound of liquids gushing, of tired steel wilting. Somewhere in that debris was her son.

As she hefted bits of concrete and razor-sharp lengths of metal away from where Tom must be, Gina heard noises, distantly: her own voice calling, '*Tom! Tom!*' and Doris's voice, calling her as she frantically rummaged through broken bricks as if they were pillows in a summer sale.

'Not me, Tom,' Gina heard herself scream. 'Not me, Tom.' Her hands burrowed deeper through the brutal brick edges, and blood, her son's arterial blood, she was sure, came spurt-spurt-spurting over her as the car hissed beside her, defeated.

Then Doris's voice was screaming, 'Gina, Gina, stop, stop,' and there was a sudden silence in the lot.

Doris was looking at Gina and saying something, but she

couldn't hear what, and a stranger – where the fuck was everybody? – was pulling at her arm, and she pushed the stranger away, and Doris kept on shouting, and there was a voice beside her, and Gina turned, intending to kill the person interrupting this . . .

It was Tom. She reached out to him and she saw he was bleeding. Gina cried, 'Tom,' and held him, trying to staunch the blood wherever it was coming from, but she could not, and the more she tried to stop the bleeding, the more he bled, until he was covered in a shining lake of blood.

Through the din of her own terror, of her own screaming, she heard Doris calling to her to stop, and she stopped and saw that the blood over Tom was coming from her hands, and he stood before her, white and terrified. Her fingernails were hanging by thin ropes.

And seeing her shattered fingers holding Tom alive, Gina felt a great smile of relief on her face, and looked at Doris in joy. But Doris did not return that look.

A woman's shoe protruded from the far end of the rubble. It was blue and patterned. Gently Gina reached forward and removed a brick. A wrist extended from beneath it, with a familiar wristwatch on it, and some part of Gina said, 'Just like Mom's.'

*

Bosnia, 1992
It is night, and the boy is awoken by a long thin scream. The boy waits for the scream to stop but it does not.

Finally it dies, diminishing through the keys until a perfect silence follows.

In that silence the boy's heartbeat slows, until at length he hears a voice whisper in his ear. Boy, your time has come.

Dressed, he follows the machine-gunner to a huddle beneath a blanket, illuminated by a truck headlight.

What is it? he whispers.

Mehmet, says the machine-gunner in an even voice. What remains of him.

What remains of him? Is he alive?

An interesting question. We know this. His eyes are gone

so he cannot see. His ears have been punctured so he cannot hear. His prick is gone so he can no longer produce little Mehmets. His tongue is gone – look, there it is, see how long it is – so he cannot speak. His trachea is cut so he cannot even wail. Yet he still lives. Does he feel anything? He does not. Milošević shoved a dipstick up his spinal column. It wasn't easy, but Milošević is a determined man. Deaf, dumb, blind, unmanned, paralysed. He lives, certainly, but is he alive?

The machine-gunner presents a small gun in the palm of his hand.

Answer the question, the machine-gunner says. Feel no guilt, for you are favouring him. He will know nothing of it, will rejoice as his soul passes to that sullen hall the Muslims call paradise. That is a Remington Derringer. American, two .41-inch rounds, as they say, what we call 10 mm, hard to get, so we must be careful not to waste them. Just above the ear. Aim for the ear on the other side through the head, and then sense the thirteen grams passing by you.

The boy takes the gun and points it. The Derringer barrel touches the Muslim's ear.

From the Muslim comes the sound of a hiss, a pocket of air bubbling up through catarrh.

The boy steps back and cries, What is that?

Our question has been answered. He is alive and he lives.

Shaking but determined, the boy raises the Remington and points it just above the Muslim's bloodied ear. There are teethmarks on the lobe. He squeezes the trigger slowly.

The Muslim's head snaps up and down. Something passes by the boy – an aroma, a sensation, thirteen grams – and there is the sound of gas escaping, a mildly odorous wheezing noise, then silence. Death, done by his hand. Life ended, the purest of powers.

CHAPTER FOURTEEN

Louisiana, 1980

Sleepless, Gina rose early to do some ironing. The hiss of steam and the sweet acridity of the starch filled her early morning senses and she was taken back to one forgotten childhood afternoon, her mother working on shirts beside her. Twenty years on, Gina stood still, alarmed by the intrusive intimacy of those smells and of her mother's closeness.

She thought of her negligence, of all the times she had mocked her mother with Karen, of all the unseen deeds of kindness which had enriched her childhood. Only now, just released from hospital, did she feel the yawning sense of loss, of business uncompleted, of unjust and random severance. And yet there had come a new union. Karen, now finally emerged from the worst of adolescent self-indulgence, had shown herself to be a loyal and affectionate friend whom she could turn to, and depend upon.

Clumsily, she unplugged the iron with her bandaged hands and wandered to the elegant balustrades beside the porch. Beyond the house, interspersed through the cypress, stood hardwood hammocks of bay and mahogany, and a stately blue heron, probably out hunting catfish in the swamp beyond the oak grove, flapped gracefully by.

Grief held her, stealing something she had not even been aware was present. We have one chance to get things right. Do we always choose the wrong path? Is that what original sin is all about?

This will not happen to Tom, she said. Tom will not be taken unawares by bereavement: I will let him feel no guilt when I go. I will return to the soil, will be remembered, and then be forgotten and will be no more than the cry of the frog or the flight of a Louisiana heron, recycled proteins and amino-acids for use by some other living thing.

*

'Did kids get spots in your day, Doris?' Karen asked, examining herself in the mirror two hours later in her mother's house. 'You don't read about them in Jane Austen or the Brontës, any more than you do fucking or, what is it? Tribadism. Rubbing off.'

'Sweet child. Thank you for the translation. Ah yes, the Brontës, Jane Austen,' murmured Doris, idly polishing Beth's silver teapot. 'I'm real touched you think they were peers of mine.'

'Doris, tell me,' said Karen, posing and studying her still-large frame before the mirror. 'You think I'm burly? That Jennifer Haig was saying I am. She right?'

'Jennifer Haig is an oaf. Your figure, my dear, is comely, not burly. Men, I'm sure, find your amplitude of bosom more than attractive.'

'I don't know about that, but they sure do like my tits. Not my zits though. Lord above. Ah Jesus, will you just look at that.'

'Please, I beseech you, child, please, not in front of the mirror. Your mother had nice things, you know. That mirror is genuine ormolu, and this teapot is a Mouton. Alexander Mouton, governor of Louisiana, you've heard of him? Of course you haven't. Yes, I guess we had spots in our day. Nutrition had not reached the sophisticated level of fraudulence to which science has now raised it. We ate what we liked. And I recall two spots. One when I was fourteen, the other shortly after my sixteenth birthday.'

'Shit, I got the goddam Black Death rampaging all over my face, and she tells me about two zits around the time of Black Death One. Oh fuck, have you ever seen spots like these? Lord above.'

The front door opened and a genial, large man entered. 'All right, ladies,' he announced. 'We got everything under control here.'

'Everything under . . . Jesus, who are you?' whispered
Karen.

'Chuck, Chuck Mitton, and me and my good buddies are
here to move all this here furniture out, once you good ladies
have gone.'

'Mr Mitton,' said Gina, 'please. These are our last
moments in our old home.'

'Miss, we got a real tight schedule, and we got to get out of
here by noon.'

'And this is not noon,' said Doris, with a chilling asperity.
'Go, if you please. Are you Mittons thus reduced, to hunting
orphans out of their homes? It must be true what they say
about your tribe. The best of you perished at Shiloh.'

'Okay, so where do we start?' said Karen, in a low, awed
voice, after the routed Chuck had fled. Their mother's house
had been rented, not owned, as they had always thought, and
the time to vacate their old home had come. Now the two
sisters sat, unmoving, gazing at certainty and known things,
from which they would now depart for ever.

Gina rose. 'So let's do it. Whatever's in Mom's room goes
to charity, apart from the stuff in her jewellery case. You
want her silver-handled hairbrush? You sure? Okay, I'll keep
that. I love it. Always have.'

All morning, they wandered through the house, fingering
drapes, touching furnishings, choking back tears as memories
besieged them with every item. Finally, only one piece of
furniture was of real interest – a Victorian-type roll-top
bureau. 'You want this?' asked Karen.

'Yes and no. You?'

'I don't know,' said Karen. 'Can we have a time-out? I got
to go to the bathroom.' She left and Gina asked, 'What do
you think, Doris?'

'Well, Victorian, mahogany, fine carved legs, elegant
drawers, woodwork's good, nice inlay. It was your grandfather's. Beth's daddy.'

'What? How did you know that?' asked Gina, amazed. 'I
don't recall her ever saying that.'

'There you go. Bought it for a couple of bucks on his last
furlough before he shipped out. Nobody wanted Victorian

stuff back then. Your grandmother hated it. Beth said it was just about the most precious thing she had from him.'

'And she never said a word to us,' said Gina.

'Some things we can't tell our nearest and dearest, and they never know what they really should.'

Warren emerged from the basement. 'More junk down there than you can imagine. Look, this magazine from 1956, *Mechanix Illustrated*, about a thousand miles of piping – was your mother a copper thief? I don't know, nothing worth fighting about, that's for sure.'

Karen reappeared, declaring, 'Wow, serious. My last shit in the old home, oops, hi there, Warren.'

Warren managed a little smile and said that he would check out back.

'Quite the little lady,' said Doris, looking at Karen.

'So what do we do with the bureau?' asked Gina.

'You keep it,' insisted Karen.

Gina laughed. 'Only I'll never get it through that door.'

'It breaks down,' said Doris. 'Into four parts.'

'Doris, what a brain,' said Karen. 'Ladies and gentlemen, the foremost pussy-diving dyke in the land.'

'If people on campus only knew how you spoke to me, I think they'd die.'

'That's only because you're such a fraud. I can just see you, pretending to be austere and terrifying and a frigid-Brigid old virgin, when in reality you're just a soft and cuddly lessie.'

'Karen,' Gina said, 'believe me, believe me, Doris has teeth. You watch what you say. She comes with a government health warning.'

'That easy, huh? And I thought I was quick.'

'You,' said Doris, hitting Karen softly over the forehead with the *Mechanix Illustrated*.

'It's a mystery to me,' said Karen. 'A mystery. Tried it twice with girls at Loyola. It's okay, sort of, but it sure as hell ain't the real thing.'

The doorbell chimed. Doris smiled, 'Chuck to my rescue.'

'Correct,' declared Karen as she ushered the man in.

'Good afternoon, ladies, and after noon it is. An hour and

five minutes after noon to be precise, and my schedule for the
day lies in ruins, y'hear?'

'Mr Mitton,' said Doris. 'A joy to see you. So you're here
to move things such as that, for example.'

'That . . .' and Chuck paused. 'Well now . . .'

'Mr Mitton, it breaks down into four parts,' said Doris.
'Provided you and your fragile companions have no fear of
carrying weights . . .'

'Us? Weights? Huh. Live and breathe weights.'

Karen muttered, 'Okay then, I guess I'd better check out
Mom's stuff, see what's what. Albums 'n' stuff. Doris, help,
be brave beside me.'

Karen walked to Gina, placed her forehead on her sister's
shoulder, and sighed. 'Murder,' she said, 'pure fucking
murder.'

*

Chuck, as blind to grief as a gravedigger, started to explain
the desk to Gina. 'See, the side here, it comes off like this. Hi,
Al. Gina, this is Al. Al, this here is Gina. See, and this item –
give me a hand here, Al, stop gawking – easy now – comes off
like this. My, so damn neat. Ain't it though? You all ever see
anything as sweet as this? Goddam.'

'It sure is neat,' said Gina. 'I'll just leave you to it.' She
turned and headed for the kitchen. 'Well lookee here,' said Al.
Gina slowed.

'What you got there?' said Chuck.

'Don't rightly know,' said Al. Gina looked back as Chuck
took something from him.

'Letters, for a Georgina Cambell? She family?'

Gina felt an icy smile arrange itself upon her face as she
said, 'Yes, that's family, I'll have those please.'

'Sure.' Chuck passed a small bundle to Gina, then turned
back to the bureau. 'Al, grab that there corner and lift it
towards you. Towards you, Al, towards you, why don't you
just once, in a goddam while . . . that's right . . . slowly does
it now, nice and easy, there you go.'

With her heart hammering, her mind's eye suddenly seeing
again the Vasitch vehicle nearing with its terrible epiphany,
Gina took the bundle, strolled into the kitchen, and put it

onto the table. The letters were all addressed to her. She lifted one and gazed dully at the Irish stamp, beside it a datemark of eight years before. Another had the face of Marshall Tito. She shuffled through the collection. Some Irish, some Yugoslavian, all unopened. She turned the top letter over, knowing full well what she would find.

CHAPTER FIFTEEN

'Hi,' said Doris, looking up over her spectacles as Gina entered her study. 'Be with you in a minute.'

Gina, suddenly ill at ease, put her shoulder bag onto the little two-seater meridienne and gazed through the window towards the distant refineries and the warm grey mist which concealed the plain's northward journey towards the curve of the earth and beyond.

'You seem far away,' Gina heard Doris say as she put down her pen.

She pointed through the window. 'Lake Superior, Canada.'

'Which is where a lot of people from around here originally came from. Maybe it's not so far. We're too inclined to be impressed by distance and time. I apologize for keeping you. I have a lot on my mind.'

'What is it, Doris?' asked Gina, sensing something important and putting off her own announcement. 'Are you okay?'

'Yes and no. I was writing to Françoise. She is unwell.'

'Oh Doris.'

'Hush. There's something else too. I have been trying to summon up the nerve to tell you, and it isn't easy.' She cleared her throat. 'I'm moving to France. There now. I've said it.'

Gina cried with genuine joy, 'Oh but that's marvellous.'

'You think so? Truly? I was so worried you'd feel, I don't know, hurt, maybe. Stupid of me.'

'Pretty stupid, Doris,' said Gina, shaking her head.

'Please do not be so keen to agree with me. It was Beth's death which warned me I was letting things drift. So . . . I'm leaving. I'm going to France, to Françoise, to spend the rest of my life with her.'

'I think that's wonderful, simply wonderful.'

'Oh Gina, I am so pleased, so relieved, I was worried that

you might think I wanted rid of you, and nothing could be further from the truth.'

Gina smiled fondly at Doris. 'Quite the reverse. It's time for us to move on too. We have a bit of capital now, not a huge amount but enough.'

'Gina,' said Doris, a look of affection on her face. 'You don't have to . . .'

'No, I know that.'

'Stay here as long as you like. I cannot sell this house. When I die, it will of course go to my wastrel of a nephew, Newton. My grandmother's maiden name, you see, was Newton. She was the daughter of the crudest man a Sykes ever met or married. The Sykes' strategic marriage. Maybe young Newton's worthless loins will yet produce a daughter to grace this place. In the meantime, Gina, you know you are welcome to stay here as long as you want.'

'That would be real fine, but Warren and I have got to go our own way.'

'A drink would be in order at this juncture,' decided Doris. 'It is early for Cointreau, but what the heck. Too early for you, my dear, I'm sure. A cola perhaps?'

Gina watched her prepare the drinks and saw for the first time an unsteadiness in Doris's hand – age was stealing up on her old friend. She said nothing until they had both sipped from their glasses and then asked, 'And Françoise? You didn't say what her problem was. Is it serious?'

'Oh, yes, it's serious enough. It is a cancer of the lymph glands. I steadfastly decline to acquire knowledge about such things until absolutely necessary. The Sykes have traditionally succumbed in gallant and silent ignorance to all manner of diseases in the past, as I intend to. At all events, I will not repeat the mistakes of my youth. I will be with her as soon as I have tidied up what loose ends there are here.'

'Who's going to look after Françoise till you get over there? Will she be okay?'

'She will. Her children, of course, will mind her until I arrive to seize that sublimely rewarding duty. Me. No other. You know, my heart burns with happiness at the thought.' She smiled, and as she gazed at Gina a look of shrewdness suddenly took over her face. 'But I have a feeling you wanted to tell me something?'

Gina sat silently for a while and then told her about the trove of letters. She drew one from her pocket. 'This is the first.'

Doris lifted the letter and put on her reading glasses. She turned it over, examining it closely. 'I can't read the postal date. What is it?'

'March, eight years ago. There are more.'

'Like this, all unopened?'

'Yes.'

'And your mother intercepted and hid them, is that correct, and you have now discovered them?'

Gina nodded.

'Burn them. Live with the world which is, not the fictional one you missed.'

'Oh come on, Doris!'

'Gina. You're a married woman. You've got a home, a husband who loves you, a child who thinks Warren is his father.'

'I won't, can't, burn them. Here. You take them. Mind them. Keep them. One day maybe . . .'

'One day never,' said Doris. 'But I will take them and I will mind them as you ask because you ask. They will be in my safekeeping.' She looked intently at Gina.

'There's something else, isn't there?' Her eyes probed the inside of Gina's mind. 'What is it?'

Gina swallowed and nodded. 'You're right. I went off the pill in hospital.'

'You're pregnant.'

Gina nodded, a tear running down her cheek, and leaning forward Doris kissed its moist track. 'My dearest child,' she said, her fingers running over Gina's hair and brow. And as Gina began to weep more fully, Doris whispered, 'Hush now. And be of good cheer.'

*

'You sure are lucky,' said Erwin Spruce, realtor. 'What I got here is the keys to the Terraine place over on Old Cody Road.

Named after Colonel Cody, killed at New Orleans, one of the handful what was, and must have been a tolerable old fool and all to have managed that. You know Old Cody Road? Just outside the town, heading towards Route 308. Right next to the Johnson spread. You know the Johnsons? Course you do. Oldest family in the parish.'

The Terraines had gone, said Erwin, he to his immortal reward, she to her sister in Birmingham. Gina found the house, after getting instructions from a group of kids playing yard basketball, in one of a row of rather extravagant-looking 1930s houses built, Erwin had told her, by a unregenerately confederate developer who had modelled them on Rosemount, Jefferson Davis's old home.

Admittedly the Terraine place was seriously run-down after three decades of trench warfare within, but it was magnificent – two storeys above basement, double-fronted, with a fine porch running the width of the front and a wide, eight-step approach to the central front door leading to a broad hallway, with rooms either side. From the rear doors an expanse of lawn, dotted with shrubs, ran down to an old lane and a creek, beyond which lay the drained and elegant parkland of the Johnson estate.

Gina wrote to Stefan.

I nearly lifted the telephone to call Warren over, to buy the house immediately. I was beside myself with agitation and excitement.

Three days later we bought it. Bang. And we met our new neighbour, Eleanor Johnson. Very grand, very rich, very bawdy, riding her horse Potoriek. She stopped and made friends with us. She's sweet and sexy. You'd like her. She calls Warren Hutch. Guess why.

Stefan, I feel we belong here and I can't begin to tell you what it means. Things like roots. That's what you have, you see, a sense of who and what you are. I have not. Getting a house gives me a sense of self, of purpose.

*

One month later, Gina stood in a room off the hall in Cody,

a homeless vase in her hand, looking hard at a youthful removal man whose eyes appeared to have lost the art of focusing. He stood poised, indecisive, a chair balanced in his hand, the fingers of the other hand tapping rhythm on his hip bone.

'Excuse me, not there,' growled an unusually stressed Warren. 'There, not there, NOT THERE.'

'Do what the folks ask you, Wayne,' said a voice. 'Hi there, Mrs Bourne, I just dropped in, see how my men're doin'.'

Gina smiled wearily at Chuck Mitton. 'This is one fine specimen you got here.'

'Him? My sister's boy. You heard the man, Wayne, put the chair down.'

Wayne half did, and Chuck sighed admiringly.

'That's a real fine day's work you done there, son, your mom'll be mighty proud of you. Hell, your uncle's damn near bursting,' a 'huh, nephews' look written large across his rueful face. Gina looked at the chaos mounting in the hall, two men bearing the large bureau in to join the mounting crates of books already there.

'Oh my,' she whispered.

'Miss Sykes ain't around, is she?' asked Chuck. 'No? Ain't that a relief. Wayne, you hearing me? That Miss Sykes, don't you even think about crossing her. She looks at you and you like to die. You hear me?'

'I hear you fine.'

'Good, 'cause . . . Aw shit. Looky here. Shit.'

An ingratiating leer settled on Chuck's face as Doris's voice came from the hallway, 'Ah, Mr Mitton. What a delight. My heart always rejoices at the sight of the Mittons.'

'I'm real glad about that, Miss Sykes.'

Doris entered, her eyes on Wayne, still poised with the chair touching the ground.

'What a charming boy,' she said, walking to Gina, touching her hands and smiling. 'So here it is. Your new home. And it is so, so elegant.'

She gestured around the room and again caught sight of Wayne, still frozen. 'Mr Mitton, why is this young gentleman's mouth hanging open? Has he a respiratory problem?'

'Respirat— No, I don't believe so, Miss Sykes.'

'That will do for the moment, Mr Mitton, I thank you.' Chuck Mitton blinked, barked an incoherent order to young Wayne, and the pair of them turned and left.

Doris sank into the one armchair present and said, 'I speak only from theory, because we Sykes are more like lichen than human beings, the way we cling. But the best advice I can give you is just to sit here looking haggard, just like that, Warren, and let the men smash whatever they want to – they will anyway, regardless of your wishes – and when they've gone you can allocate the next ten years to cleaning up the mess. My dear Mr Mitton, back already?'

'Yeah, we got a visitor.'

A nose peeked into the room followed by two bottles of vintage champagne, dripping condensation – Eleanor Johnson. A moment of general recognition followed. Eleanor and Doris shook hands with the cordiality of ancient suspicion, the latest moves in a dance through the ages.

'A long time, Eleanor. A long, long time. You have put on some weight. Avoirdupoids suits you.'

'Yes I have, I'm glad you like it. Douglas approves.'

'This would be a very sorry world if we women were to spend our time chasing the good opinion of men.'

'To that one, Doris, you can plead not guilty.'

'You noticed. How very acute.'

An aloof smile flitted across Eleanor's features as she turned to include Gina and Warren, on their packing cases, in her conversation.

'You all feel up to a glass or two of a humble Laurent Perrier '76?'

Gina and Warren assented, passively, as those in the thrall of moving home accept authority of almost any kind. 'Doris?'

'Myself, I think not, my dear,' she declared. 'You have company enough. Poor Wayne there is already dizzy with love.'

Poor Wayne was lingering by the door, pretending to do something with an occasional table.

'I must go. I will leave you in the capable hands of a Johnson,' said Doris to Gina. The two stood in the centre of the room, their hands in one another's, their eyes focused. 'So,' Doris said heavily.

'Doris,' said Gina.

They were silent, and then they embraced. There were tears.

'Come now. This is not goodbye,' sniffed Doris. 'We are not schoolgirls.' She turned and said, 'Warren,' offering him a cheek. No further word was spoken. She left.

CHAPTER SIXTEEN

'I can,' said Eleanor Johnson, 'be impossibly boring talking about my second favourite topic.' She and Gina were sitting beside the Johnson pool. 'The Johnsons always were an unsavoury lot. Good at finding the quickest, worst way to make plenty of money. Such as that creature Isaac Newton. Such a man.'

'Isaac Newton? Is this your connection to Doris?'

'She has admitted that disgrace to you? Then you are a true friend of hers. She deplores the connection. Me, I revel in it. Newton invented the Lewis gun. The Lewis gun makes this and Cypress Mound what they are. Such fortunes – and we kept those fortunes by intermarriage. There is so much unfounded, pagan superstition about incest. We have prospered wonderfully from it. Sex with your cousin isn't so very bad, you know.'

'It sure would be with me. I don't have any cousins.'

'That wouldn't make it bad, just a little bit solitary. But often the best, in my experience. Anyway, you have your Hutch. I do so adore your husband. So very clever. All those words, in so many languages. And just fancy being named after a rabbit-home.'

'You're in luck,' said Gina. 'I left a note for him, and here he is now.' Warren was rounding the bend of the drive.

'My, and he walked all the way, my hero,' breathed Eleanor, as Warren approached up the drive. Douglas emerged from the house with their daughters, Lindsay and Philippa, waving a fat hand of hello.

'And look, Hutch even had the foresight to wear his Bermudas,' Eleanor declared amiably. 'You couldn't turn down the volume of those oh-so-tasteful shorts just the eensiest-weeniest bit, darling Hutch, now could you?' she called. 'And look, your grandfather's tennis shoes too. How delightful. Was the poor dear from Oklahoma?'

'I've had them since MIT,' said Warren uncomfortably.

'We too have our family heirlooms. Priceless legacies, I agree. Douglas, sweetie, what are you doing with our children and that precious Tom?'

Stefan, she looked at him with such fondness. You should have seen it. She too is entranced by that secret him, the Bosnian thing which nobody knows about but which still makes him him.

'I thought I'd take them to look at the white-tailed deer and the loggerhead turtles over at the Marshalls. Can Tom come too? You want to join us, Warren, you and Tom, leave the wives here, give them a clear run at us both while we're gone?'

'For shame,' said Eleanor, winking at Gina. 'As if we would.'

'Can we, Mom? Please, Dad, can I, please, can I?' pleaded Tom.

Oh Stefan, were you to hear his voice, Bosnian and Irish but pure Louisiana, a bayou boy. When they were gone, Eleanor suggested we had a swim. I said I didn't have a costume. Come on, she said, who needs a costume? It's just the two of us. We went to the house beside the pool where we undressed and showered. I turned to walk towards the pool when I caught sight of myself and Eleanor in the mirror, both of us naked. My, I felt such a pulse, a twinge, amps tingling you know where, with the warm air on the bare skin of her body.

I must have let a look come to my eye, because Eleanor looked up, saw my expression, smiled and said, 'Yeah, I know, I sometimes feel like that too. Nice. But very, very dangerous.'

For a moment we stared in the mirror, kind of interested. A memory came back. Eleanor said to me, appreciative but real casual, 'Nice tits,' then, touching her breast, posing, lightly running her hands over herself, said, 'Eat your heart out, boys.'

You know, for a second I wondered whether we were going to kiss. We just looked each other in the eye. I smiled – I think – and said, 'You only go in for family.'

Eleanor made a face and walked off. My, she has such a body, such smooth tanned skin. I am glad you did not see her, Stefan, for if you did, you would never look at me again.

Eleanor turned and dove into the pool. I stood watching her, wondering about the moment which had just passed, and just then another memory arrived of how once we lay beside a cold stream in December, ten thousand years ago.

Oh Stefan, beside that pool I thought of you and grieved for you and thought of the opportunities which are gone, irretrievable. And then I lowered myself gently into the water. A hot Louisiana sun burned in the western sky. I would have preferred the water to be cold, with mud between my toes and a weak December sun shining from the Irish skies, and I know that will never be.

*

Bosnia, 1992.
Beneath a dark Bosnian sky, the boy is looking through night glasses at the lightless streets of Sarajevo. I see nothing, he says.

Here, you, the machine-gunner says to the radio operator. Look.

What? says the radio operator, the stink of slivovitz on his breath. There is nothing there.

Look, the figures beneath the promontory there. One, two, three, no four. Fuck. We're being infiltrated. This is a raid.

Fuck off, says the radio operator, unaware of the tiny red light which suddenly appears on his forehead. He laughs. This place is impregnable.

Then he is dead, the silenced bullet emptying his skull, his body promptly making brief, final hissing noises. The boy and the machine-gunner had peeled left and right the moment they had seen the lethal droplet on his brow. Another silenced round slams into a tree next to the boy's head. He turns and drops, the next bullet arriving ten centimetres lower, purring over his scalp. He gazes into the dark. He sees something, a movement of darkness on darkness, like muscles moving beneath a panther's black fur. He fires his FAZ directly into the centre of the darkness. There is a grunt, a sigh, the noise of limbs collapsing. A weapon slips down a hill followed by uncoordinated limbs, a body tumbling. The victim's name is Izzet Ibrahimović. He is the same age as his killer and has not eaten meat or seen mains electric light in a year. He ate an egg the previous month. When this war began he was a school-boy and weighed sixty kilograms. At the time of his death, he is still a schoolboy, is three centimetres taller and weighs five kilograms less.

Around the boy gunfire erupts from the finally awaking garrison, automatic fire spraying through the brush and the scrub, wild cries in the dark.

It has taken these attackers three days to get to this point in irreversible futility; three days inching up the sides of a mountain, as stationary as stick-insects during the day, and snatching at sleep while wedged in between rocks or roped to shrubs. Dozing in the sun, waking exhausted, tormented by daydreamt nightmares of discovery, foul of mouth, and breeches full of shit.

Then night-climbs, coordinated meticulously by rope signals and tiny torches whose batteries alone cost twenty Deutschmarks each: the annual salary of the doctor in Sarajevo Hospital who an hour ago abandoned the attempt to save the mother of the young soldier who was the first to die in this assault. She had been shot by a sniper that very afternoon as she laid flowers on her husband's grave, her son never discovering that for a few brief hours he was an orphan.

These attackers have trained for a month for this. None of them has drunk in a day, or touched food since they began, yet still they follow the doomed plan to turn the flank and spread panic the length of the Serbian line. Their silent approach now foiled, they are floundering up the steep, densely shrubbed slope, their war cries emerging as thin and airless whinnies.

A flare is fired. The attackers freeze for the merest second on the hillside. Joyfully, the boy gets a clean headshot into his first clear target, who flies backwards, a marionette flailing in the phosphoreal glow of a soldier's midnight sun.

Another flare is fired and the boy sees some enemy crouching beside a bunker. He empties a magazine into them. There are screams, shots, the pandemonium of men losing their sense of purpose under fire. Instinctively he knows the moment is his.

He changes magazine and empties the fresh one into the grey huddle of collapsing, demoralized figures. Oh courage is his and he has mastery; wisdom is his and he has mystery. One youngster whimpers on the ground, Mother. The boy's heart rejoices at the word. Weep, Muslim whore, he says as he kills her son.

A further flare lofts into the sky, and he sees a half dozen of the remaining survivors of the ill-fated assault. One of them has an M16 in his hands, which he drops in surrender. The boy shoots him neatly through the forehead, and then methodically shoots the survivors. Finally, one wounded Muslim remains alive, lying on the ground, gazing unwaveringly at him in the flarelight. The boy moves nearer, to look closely into the dark, unyielding eyes of the doomed. The eyes close at his gaze. Their owner knows that in moments he will die. The boy draws his bayonet. Mother, he says, as the blade kisses the thin chest of the young Bosnian.

The boy presses down with the blade between the ribs, like a crowbar through a doorjamb, and into the thumping muscle of aorta and ventricle. The Bosnian speaks wordless rage through clenched teeth, hissing defiance as his body begins its journey to the chemistry of humus, clay and decay.

Thirteen grams escape. It is over. The boy remains kneeling beside the settling corpse, lays his hand on the lifeless still-warm forehead, and the only emotion he feels is envy.

Part Three

CHAPTER SEVENTEEN

Ireland, 1987

The three of them arrived at Shannon Airport at dawn. Warren had joined Gina and Tom at Atlanta from a conference in Los Angeles, and was even more exhausted than they were. He had added to his woes by drinking heavily on the flight. Gina said nothing, largely because she had spent the journey weighing her emotions at the implications of returning to the land of Tom's father.

Now, foul-breathed amidst the foul-breathed, with Warren reeking of various spirits and in an odd and assertive humour Gina had never seen him in before, they waited at the carousel for their bags. Tom, thin, sinister and aged, stood apart from them, casting his pink-rimmed eyes around the hall, apparently looking for somebody to throttle.

In silence, Warren heaved a bag off the carousel. 'How many bags do we have?' Gina asked. She smiled at the man beside her and said, 'Sorry, looks like we're stealing yours,' and he said, 'That's okay.'

Thatsh okay. Did he say, *Thatsh* okay? By the time she was able to look again at where the man had been standing, he was gone. Gina, stunned, said nothing. There was a din in her ears. 'Did that man get his bag?' she asked of no one.

Tom, a suitcase in his hand, drifted away, looking back at Warren with a subdued loathing. Had his real father just gone through customs? Was that possible? Gina's heart paused mid-beat as she approached the customs clearing area, but there was no sign of anyone resembling Stefan. Uniformed officers watched the incoming passengers.

The three of them were waved through, and at the far side of the concourse stood the Brackens, talking to a man with his back to her. Was that him? Could that be Stefan?

'No one's here yet,' declared Gina in a decisive voice. 'What we need is some coffee, clear our heads.'

Warren followed as Gina forged her way towards the coffee-dock. She ordered two coffees and a coke, Warren standing impatiently beside her with poor Tom still simmering with teenage disdain for the entire world.

At the cash desk, Gina reached into her purse, and only then realized she had no Irish money. 'I'm sorry,' she said to the teenage cashier. 'I only have dollars.'

'Oh sure that's all right, we get them fellas the odd time,' the girl replied cheerfully. 'That'll be two dollars, please.'

'Two dollars!' murmured Warren, shaking his head.

'Hush, Warren,' said Gina, handing over a five-dollar bill, and as she was given her change she looked back across the concourse. Matt and Maureen, now unaccompanied, were scanning the arrivals gate. Gina uttered a cry of disingenuous joy, 'Look! There's Maureen and Matt.'

Tom was studying his shoes. 'Warren, Warren,' declared Gina. 'Look! Maureen! Matt!'

'Great.' He was swaying with fatigue. Gina grabbed him and steered him towards the welcoming Brackens. There was a general hubbub of greeting.

After Gina had disengaged herself from their warm and communal embrace, she called her son over. 'Tom, of course, you remember.' Tom shifted uncomfortably from one foot to the next. 'And this is Warren.'

'Hi,' said Warren. 'Tell me, how much should two coffees and a coke cost in this country?'

*

'With all your luggage, we've brought the two cars,' said Matt as they threaded their way through the airport car park. 'Here we are. Now, Maureen can have the Mercedes and I'll drive th'ould banger here,' he added, gesturing grandly at the ancient model beside him.

'You want to keep Matt company, Tom?' asked Maureen.

'Sure.'

'Some car,' said Gina. 'Never seen anything like it. What is it?'

'A Volkswagen,' said Matt. 'An old Volkswagen.'

'Hey. This was a good car. It's old, sure, twenty years old, but it got here, didn't it?' said Tom suddenly. 'Not as good as the Beetle, but then what was?'

He peered into the side window. 'This is a 1964 twin-carburettor, 54-horsepower 1500S. Rear-wheel drive of course. But it's got a good cruise speed, seventy easy.'

Matt looked in wonder at him. 'Well you won't catch me driving this yoke at seventy,' he declared. 'But you got it spot on, spot on so you did. How did you get it right, just like that?'

'The 1500 body-style is easy. See the heat control? Levers. Turn-knobs came in 1964. The body stripe makes it a twin-carb. In 1965 they added plated fittings around the indicator. This car doesn't have those. Therefore a '64.'

There was a stunned silence in the car park. 'Okay, genius,' said Gina, 'you can bore Matt to death with two hundred miles of autobabble.'

She instantly regretted her words. Tom, so easy to hurt, looked abashed. Matt walked forward and put his arm around him, saying, 'By God, I'd love to travel with Tom, so I would.'

A small nervous smile appeared on Tom's face.

'Right,' said Gina. 'So Warren and I will travel with Maureen.'

The two women gallantly conversed as they drove north, an odd, yawning exchange, while Warren snored in the back. When they arrived at the Brackens' home, Gina checked her watch and saw in disbelief that it was only noon.

'Honey, I'm pooped, wiped out,' said Warren. 'My brain's in California, and I wish I were too, I've got to go to bed. I'm seeing things here.'

'You can't go to bed the moment you arrive, Warren, come on.'

'Unless I go to bed, I'm going to be a zombie for the entire trip.'

Matt showed Warren his room, and he did not emerge at all that evening. The twins, grown, bounding and extrovert, arrived with friends, musical instruments and much laughter, and there was music until Gina, almost broken by fatigue, fled to bed leaving Tom behind. She woke at seven, and Warren was standing beside her, fully dressed. He had a cup of coffee in his hand, which he gave her.

'I'm sorry, I shouldn't have gone to bed like that. I just had to.'

'You shouldn't and you didn't have to.'

'You weren't in California.'

'Don't make excuses.'

'Don't start, now just don't start. I'm going for a walk. I'll see you later.'

She felt pains beneath her kidneys. Only two a.m. back home. She dozed, her rest interrupted by devils sticking red hot barbs into her. When she awoke, the vast energy of the Bracken household, despite its late night, was already unleashing its powers. She showered and dressed and then walked into the kitchen–breakfast room. It was festooned with flowers. Maureen and Matt were picking them up, feeling them, lifting them from the vases and the glasses and the cups and the teapot they had been placed in.

'How in the name of God did he . . . ?' Matt intoned wondrously.

'What is it?' asked Gina.

'This,' said Matt, passing her a note.

Dear Matt and Maureen,

Please forgive my bad manners in going to bed when I arrived. I'm kind of shy anyway, and I was so tired I couldn't even think, never mind make conversation. I promise you I will be more communicative in future.

However, I am an American. I am not without resource. I can get flowers, even at this hour. This is my last boast. I will be in touch later in the day.

Please show this letter to Gina. I am sorry.

Sincerely,

Warren.

Maureen looked at Gina and waited until she had finished the letter.

'This wasn't necessary, you know,' said Maureen.

'It was.'

'It wasn't. If he was good enough for you to marry, he was good enough for us.'

'Maureen, you know, you just know, how stupid that is.'

'That's delightful talk, calling me stupid in my own kitchen, and it not yet breakfast,' laughed Maureen. Her eyes narrowed as she looked at her friend more closely. 'Are you all right, Gina?'

'Tired,' she replied, her back aching again.

*

'Warren is basically so *shy*. He's real good in the academic world, he's highly respected, even Chomsky says nice things about him in his papers. He was the keynote speaker at a conference in California before he came here. On the podium he's confident, smooth, immensely clever. Speaks a dozen languages, and can communicate personally in none of them.'

'As I say, love, you chose him, and you don't get a higher compliment than that.'

'Can you believe it, he used to be worse. But just getting a home of his own made such a difference to him. He was quite devastated when I lost the baby. Devastated.'

Gina paused and was about to say, 'He did so want children of his own, you know.' She stopped herself in time, amazed at how simply the truth could escape through the carefully wrapped tissues of falsehood.

They were sitting on the south-facing wooden bench in the gardens which Maureen had created from the derelict bog of a decade and a half before. It was a rare and perfect Easter, spring bursting out everywhere, daffodils and tulips in full bloom beneath vast blue skies.

Cormac and Liam instantly befriended Tom and all three had gone off to a Gaelic football match. Matt was taking Warren to see the Céide fields, the Stone Age agricultural settlement which had recently been uncovered and reconstructed.

'I didn't realize jet lag could be this bad,' said Gina. 'I mean, a whole week. And the back-aches.'

'How are you feeling now?'

'Dizzy. Is that a swallow? Already?'

'A doomed swallow, I'd say, at this time of year,' said Maureen, consulting her watch. 'Look at the time. They'll be here any minute now, God willing. Families are mad things, you know, mad entirely. You want them to leave you and you don't, when they go you want to know everything about them. The Irish mammy, sure it's a beast inside us all, as you'll discover.'

Gina smiled. 'It'll be a while yet,' she replied.

'No it won't. It'll be like that,' Maureen clicked her fingers. 'One day Noelly was a little boy with a squeaky voice, the next he was an army officer in the Lebanon, fluent in Arabic and wise in the ways of whatever it is soldiers are wise in. Girls and guns, probably. Listen, it'll be the same with Tom and his little mother one day.'

'Little mother.'

'Women are pests, fools or saints to their children. He'll go one day, and then whenever the phone rings your heart'll surge, hoping it's him, like mine does for Noelly or Paula. Now stay here,' said Maureen. 'I've got a few things need seeing to.'

Maureen rose and went into the house, and Gina sat back, feeling dizzy. Sleep in its mercy dreamlessly enveloped her. She was awoken by a voice whispering in her ear, 'We've just got time for a quickie.'

She opened her eyes. Noelly's face, adult, strong but strikingly that of the youngster she had last seen well over a decade before, was about a foot away. Paula was just over his shoulder and scowling at him, with Maureen standing beside them both. 'Where did I get this monster?' she asked the sky.

'Gina, pay no attention to this beast,' said Paula, pushing him aside and hugging her friend where she lay. Gina returned the embrace, crying, 'Oh how are you, Paula, Paula, how are you!'

Noelly said ruefully, 'Lost interest in me, have you? I'm too old for you now, is that it?'

'You'll never be too old for me, Noelly, you know that,' cried Gina, tears welling in her eyes. 'Come here, you you you . . .'

'Mmmmm,' groaned Noelly as he embraced and kissed her. 'Leave me in peace everyone, I need to be alone with the woman I love.'

'A randy old monster, that's what I have for a son,' Maureen complained happily.

'Da spittin' image o' me ma,' intoned Noelly.

'Out of my way, you,' declared Gina. 'Come here, Paulie, dearest.' Her friend was gazing back at her in silent affection. Brother and sister joined in holding Gina. A sob rose in her throat.

'Gina, we can have a threesome,' mused Noelly. 'It's been ages since Paula and I . . . Ow ow ow,' and he ran away, pursued by Paula who was hitting him vigorously about the head. Noelly was nearly thirty, Paula just over, and they were behaving like teenagers.

'I could do with some food and peace,' observed Maureen. 'Are you hungry?'

Gina nodded, wiping a tear from her cheek.

'Come on the pair of you, lunchtime,' called Maureen.

Noelly came sauntering towards them, straightening his clothes. 'No wonder I have no luck with women, my darling sister has me exhausted satisfying her voracious needs.'

Paula hit him in the kidneys, and he let out a theatrical cry before putting his arm around Gina and turning to Maureen. 'Christ, Mam, I'm bloody starving. I could eat a horse, which is what we normally get here,' he added confidentially to Gina. 'Ah! What is that smell? Let me at it!' He uttered a cat-like snarl and hungrily rolled his eyes. 'Lamb chops, my favourite,' said Noelly.

Lamb chops and the Brackens: a memory chimed in Gina's brain, and a strange nostalgia filled her heart.

'Gina, if you've gone all vegetarian and don't want your chop, I'll eat it.' And the memory pulsed inside her mind, light in the fog; and then the fog closed in as again she felt a pain in her back. She thought, lumbago. At my age.

CHAPTER EIGHTEEN

'Rain like that, it's hard to believe that you could ever yearn for it,' said Noelly, looking through the pub window at the wet mist outside, wiping its grey muzzle on the pane. 'But we all did. Dreamt of home, rain. Wet shoulders and the smell of clay and horses with water dripping down over their hooves. Fellows who knew nothing about the countryside, Dublin fellows, great soldiers, solid men, the kind you want beside you when things get difficult, would talk endlessly about the green fields of Meath and sing of the Curragh of Kildare. Identity is a grand thing altogether for giving you notions about what you're not.'

Warren had gone back to the States as planned and the lads were playing football. Paula had returned to Dublin and Maureen was helping Matt in his office.

'The things that happen,' said Noelly. 'You never can tell. Tom going to Latin Mass with Liam. That's amazing. What was he raised as?'

'Nothing. But Maureen was saying you went through a phase . . .'

'I did. For a while. There was a priest here used the old rite. And I loved the Latin. Still do. I did it at school. Six years of it. It's a lovely language. But as for religion, I don't know what I believe in now.'

Gina looked at the profile of the man she had known as a boy, then covered in spots and full of strange, knockabout intelligence, now a linguist and a soldier. Maureen had whispered confidentially, half with pride and half with dread, that he was a commandant – major – with the Irish special forces, the Rangers. Maureen told her he never spoke of his work.

'Fancy a drive?' he said suddenly.

'Yes,' she said, and waving him away went to pay for the drinks.

'It's little enough you understand about Irish taboos, leaping up and paying for a fellow's pint like that,' he jested as they left. He was looking down at her, his blue eyes full of humour.

'Noelly, darling, what would I understand of taboos?' she asked. Their eyes met. Gina, hooking an arm around Noelly's neck, kissed him fully on the lips. As their lips touched she thought, Oh you madwoman, you mad insane idiot, he'll find this disgusting.

He did not. His tongue went into her mouth and she pressed her hips against his. She sank her tongue deep into his mouth. He stayed stock still and hard against her. Thank God, she thought, I can still do it. She heard his breath. It echoed hers.

'Not here,' he said. 'Knowing my luck my sergeant's going to come through here any second.'

She laughed, giddy, and they ran through the clean air into some disued stables. He bent and kissed her again and said, 'Gina, Gina, I've wanted to do that for half my life or more.'

'Men, the things they say,' she whispered, the madness growing as that private part of her, moist and insistent, took command of her will. 'Oh this is idiocy, impossible.' She pressed herself against him as his tongue entered her ear, her toes curling in delight. His hand went down, found her and flickered lightly upon her softness. Oh where did he learn to do that so well?

'You want to do it all, Gina?'

'Yes, yes,' she said, pressing her mouth to his, 'but where?'

'In the rain,' he said.

'Yes, anywhere,' she laughed, running out of the stable into a tropical downpour.

'Here,' he cried, 'over this wall.'

'This wall,' she repeated. She scrambled over the drystone wall, moss and lichen staining her sodden cream skirt and white blouse, her hair in rats' tails. He was on her instantly, the rain lashing over his face as he sank his mouth on her and they shed their clothes. She took him in her hand, and pushing him backwards, she was down on him, salt and the secret mustiness of the male filling her mouth. He groaned and said, 'No, no, you'll make me come.'

'Good,' she whispered, feeling powerful, alive. And when she had finished, she lay back in the grass, smiling joyfully, for a young man was naked beside her in the rain, his clothes randomly scattered in the long green grass. The two of them lay silently in the dripping wetness and she felt no cold.

A hand began to stroke her breast and she covered it with her own, smiling into the great grey sky. Noelly's tongue went into her ear, and then he was on her, his shoulders above her shoulders, his belly on hers, his hardness touching her. 'Is it okay?' he asked.

'Yes, yes, God yes.'

With a long, gentle thrust he was in and she was filled deeper than she had been since that day, so distant it was a dream. This is me, me, unfucked little me, she thought, with this fine young male body fucking me, fucking me, as Noelly's muscularity became more urgent and inside her she felt those large rearrangements which precede an orgasm. She smiled, raised her feet to the sky and was filled completely.

Later they lay together on the warm and sodden earth as the rain softened to a drizzle. She nuzzled her nose into the hair in his armpit.

'Your body hasn't changed a bit, not with the pregnancy or the miscarriage, you look like you always did,' he said.

'How would *you* know?' she taunted.

He laughed. 'Well I do, as it happens. Promise you won't kill me? Promise.'

'Kill you, after what you just did? Bottle you maybe, kill you never.'

'Ha. We'll see. I once hid in your bedroom and watched you undress.'

'You didn't! Noelly!' she cried, sitting up.

'I did, I did, and I loved it.'

'What did you see?'

'Everything. God I was so aroused.'

She didn't remember the night at all, nor the smell of his

aftershave, but nonetheless her voice caught as she asked softly, 'And did you?'

'Not then, with you there. What if you'd caught me?'

'Done it for you, probably,' she whispered.

'So then I spent half the night waiting for you to go to sleep. Just as I thought it was safe, Tom bellowed, "Fell over, bumped my head." I didn't get out till about four, straight into the bathroom, *finally*, and then to bed.'

He licked the skin of her armpit and something inside her moved, softly, and she rejoiced at the rediscovery of all that sexual energy she thought had been dying. She said, 'A long wait.'

'Very long, but worth it.'

Then his mouth was on hers again and he was in her once more and, resting her heels on his kidneys, she uttered the impious prayers, Thank God for sex, thank God for fucking.

In the car she said, 'What are we going to do? Just look at us, look at us. Christ.'

'Go home and shower.'

'What if your parents are there? Or Tom, God forbid.'

'We'll just say we got caught in the rain. It'll be okay. Who in the name of God would think . . .?'

'With an old woman like me.'

'Precisely,' he said triumphantly. 'The clinching argument.' He kissed her. 'Gina,' he added, a catch in his voice.

'Shhhh,' she said, putting a finger on his lips.

*

Bosnia, 1992

The boy and the machine-gunner lie in the sun. Around them the alpine meadows are dense with wild flowers, and ubiquitous cuckoo-song fills the air.

You are good, says the machine-gunner. Is your father a fighter?

My father's father and mother were both heroes. They fought the Nazis. As for my father. A sheep.

They are resting in the garden of the old hotel which had been an Olympics centre less than a decade before. A young woman with dark-red hair approaches them, looking not at the boy but at the machine-gunner. *Dobodan*, she says. They return the greeting.

She asks the machine-gunner, Where have you been fighting?

We have both been fighting, he replies.

He is just a boy, she says.

He is a soldier and I trust him.

Is he a man?

He is.

I am, says the boy, sitting up straight in the sunlight.

There is a Turkish cemetery here, you know, says the young woman, down by the stream there. There are gravestones there, hidden in the grasses. Do you want to see the old gravestones, the last Muslim ones to be permitted in Serbian Bosnia?

I have seen those graves before, says the machine-gunner. As you know.

As I know, Mihail.

The boy laughs. Mihail. We call him Šarac, after his machine-gun. Šarac.

I have been called that since I was a conscript ten years ago. It is a good name.

Wouldn't you like to look at the graves, says the woman, the three of us? Wouldn't that be interesting?

Show them to my friend, says the machine-gunner.

The woman looks at the boy carefully before replying, Yes, all right. Is he ready for those graves?

Oh yes. Oh yes.

The two – the boy, the woman – go down to the long grasses.

Here, says the woman, see this stone.

With her hand she clears away the long stems of grass, bent double. The boy behind her gazes at her buttocks showing through her dress. She is so old, almost thirty. A grandmother nearly. But lust fills his throat as he looks at her body.

Arabic writing, here, in the centre of Pale, she says. Muslim barbarians.

The boy bends forward, and sees hanging breasts through her loose blouse, her nipples. His throat is almost shut tight with lust. He has to stop himself reaching out and fondling her. He hears himself breathing, loudly, long, endlessly, senses his own fierce erection, feels a choking sensation gathering in his throat.

Are you really a soldier? She is smiling. She flicks him with a piece of grass.

Don't do that.

How old are you?

Younger than you, says his thin, faint voice.

Lie here, beside me, she says.

The boy lies back in the long grass. The woman takes off her blouse, her skirt. He looks at her breasts, and he feels hot liquids gathering and simmering at his core.

He reaches for her. Gently, my little man, gently, she whispers.

Later, she says, My boyfriend takes all his new girls here. I do not mind. That is human nature.

Who is your boyfriend? asks the boy.

Mihail. Didn't you know? He doesn't speak of me? No. Of course. Typical. He is only sometimes my boyfriend. He is free. So am I. Is that not what the war is about? Freedom? And then she leans forward and kisses him on the lips, and gently he kisses her in return.

CHAPTER NINETEEN

Louisiana, 1987
The sun was on its downward journey beyond the Johnson place to the distant woodlands of Evesham Parish to the west. Gina lay on the coaster in the shade of the porch, a jug of lemonade beside her, her back hurting again. Doris's latest letter from France lay before her. She had recovered from Françoise's death very well. She was alone but seemed content. She exercised a lot, she reported, when the heat permitted. She swam in the spring and in the autumn, but not much in the summer.

Naked Germans everywhere. I peer through my apartment windows and see them passing and wonder, Was it your father, or yours, or yours, who killed my Audrey?

Do not mistake me. I am not tormented by memory. But it is part of me.

Françoise barely suffered, whereas Audrey, I know, must have done. The animal noises of those in the trucks trundling east, beasts swaying on weakening knees, the old, the young, the weak sliding to the floor. How can I banish these memories of something I do not remember? I gaze through my window and see the sons and daughters, grandsons and grand-daughters, bright pretty things, with clear skin and clean fair locks of hair, of the men and women who despatched my Audrey and her people to their death camps.

These young people, they are so fine, and so nice when I meet them. They are free and take lovers easily. They laugh in the long warm Midi evening as I never did. They laugh because they do not know that on the horizon,

behind them, are the camps. They cannot smell them. All
I can do is remember something I have no memory of,
and see Audrey in my dreams.

But I am happy, my dearest Gina, in as much as
happiness is achievable at my age. My bones know where
they are headed, and my soul is poised to fly beyond
them to wherever and so I am content.

Columns of heat shimmered on the seared, dun lawn. The
hummingbirds had fled. There was no sound of cars or
distant children or animals, no movement of any kind, just
that sun-struck silence.

An insect chirruped forlornly in a tuft of dried grass
beneath the oleander and then thought better of it. A cardinal
fluttered in the stand of wild palm and mimosa where once
she had killed a snake, a moccasin, she thought, using a spade
with deadly deliberation. Her mind drifted backwards;
wilderness, cultivation.

She took up her pen.

Dear Stefan,

It is a long time since I wrote to you. No matter. You
do not apparently notice my neglect. Do you notice I
am growing older? Little lines appearing, while you
remain ageless, young, beautiful, your mouth on my
breast. I was thinking about that just yesterday. You
know why.

Stefan, listen, I had an affair in Ireland with a boy you
once knew. It was wonderful. But young Noelly is not
you. Still, it was good, Stefan, so good.

I know now you will never be gone from me. I rise in
the morning and part of that which rises is you. If I
laugh, part of that laughter is yours. Stefan, listen – I
know this correspondence is unhealthy, morbid,
obsessional. But it is me. It keeps me going, and
sometimes I think some special force is at work.

God, do I sound like some stupid Californian? But
you cannot inhabit me the way you do without there
being something extraordinary about it. It is uncanny, as

*if you no longer need to exist as a separate person. You
are part of me.*

*Romantic rubbish, Doris would say, but that is
because you are a man. Her Audrey is part of her.
Audrey awaits her. One day I will await you or you
me.*

*Oh Stefan, you should see Tom, he is so handsome, so
like you, with such a thin, delicate face. I could never
understand what the Russian pan-Slavicists were so
obsessed with until I met you.*

*Tom was transformed by Ireland. He had been so
difficult, moody, aloof. I had even begun to despair of
him, neither liking his company nor having the will to
improve him. Yet it all turned out so well. Ireland
reached into him, made him very political just like his
dad. Nelson Mandela is on his wall. He talks of human
rights in Guatemala, he reads, is so passionate . . .
Clapham U is so deadly dull. He is like a star. Our star.*

*Was that you in Shannon Airport? Did I miss you
again? And was it not better that I did? What would I
have said to you, jet-lagged, withered, cross? Old, dear
God, old.*

*Warren and I finally made our wills the other day. We
have enlisted in the campus organ-transplant scheme.
Liver, heart and kidney have been marked for delivery to
strangers. We have prepared for death.*

*I have secretly started learning Serbo-Croat. I have
bought tapes, grammars. I will be fluent one day, and we
will converse in the language of your father. I follow the
path laid for me by circumstance and by my own powers
of decision. I must be strong, but mere strength is
meaningless. After all the standing stones of Ozymandias
are strong.*

*I thank God I knew and know you. You are mine for
all eternity.*

Gina paused, feeling an odd kick beneath her ribs in her back,
and irrationally she turned to see if somebody had sneaked up
behind her.

But there was nobody there. The sharp pain subsided, leaving a little memory in the small of her back.

*

'You okay, Mom?' Tom said to her that evening. She was lying down on the sofa.

'No, my back kind of hurts, here,' she gestured.

'Let me. Old age, I guess,' he teased. He sat beside her and began to massage her, inexpertly but gently.

'You and your secrets. A good masseur and an expert on automobiles.'

'I'm not an expert on automobiles.'

'Yes, you are. You stunned poor old Matt with what you knew.'

'I don't know about automobiles. I just know about Volkswagens.'

'Why do you know about Volkswagens? Oh that feels better.'

'Because it was a Volkswagen which nearly killed us and killed your mom, that's why. Its clutch went, that's what happened.'

Gina lay in silence and then said, 'You wouldn't think that, would you, of a German car?'

'Yeah well. They're not all German. VW've got plants all over the world. São Paulo. Pennsylvania. There's a big one in Vogosca. That VW had had a new gearbox. Vogosca clutches have a reputation for slipping.'

'Is that right? You are one smart cookie,' said Gina decisively.

'My mom certainly is. Is my dad, whoever he is?'

Gina let that hang in the air. Neither said anything.

'Thanks for the massage.'

''S okay.' To Gina's intense pleasure, he kissed the back of her head as he rose. She watched his thin body walking away from her. She closed her eyes and she heard his voice again.

'Who is my dad, Mom? Because it sure as hell isn't the father I grew up with. Look, don't get me wrong, I couldn't have a better dad. He's not great at saying things, but he's pretty good at meaning them. He loves me, and I know it. But listen. I'm the wrong blood group. I'm B positive. So are you. Dad is Rh negative. He is not my father. Can't be. So who is?'

So finally I told him about you, Stefan. Obviously he wasn't too happy at hearing about his mother's sex life. What teenage boy is? But you know, the amazing thing, after the first shock, and as we talked, he grew real proud of his background, of the partisans in Yugoslavia, wanting to know what his grandfather might have done. Of course I couldn't tell him much, but I told him what I remembered from what you'd told me, and I dressed it up a bit from what I've read.

My great joy is to tell you that Tom now is real good to me. He made me go to the clinic, get my back checked out. My normal doctor, Ann Gemeti, is on maternity leave. That's a real shame because she's so laid-back and cool, tells you more about herself than you tell her. Guess sleeps around more than she should and doesn't give a damn who knows. You'd like her. Instead, I got this old guy called Tuchmann. He put me on a new kind of aspirin, green-coated to form a wall with the stomach lining, and I feel much better, and you know, I probably wouldn't have gone to see him if Tom hadn't made me.

But I have Tom and I have you, and I have Eleanor and Roben and letters from Doris. My life drifts by. I suppose that is what life is like for most people, drifting by. Sometimes I think I'm mad, writing these letters to nobody, but then sometimes I am so fucking lonely I could die.

I know now the greater part of our lives is solitary, based on events conducted in the vast warehouse of recollection, of prediction, of fantasy. How much of all our relationships are fictions of our own invention, based on characters we only dimly perceive within the uncertain theatre of our imaginations?

You are my invention, Stefan. But you were a fantasy figure before you left my life. I created you and I created the love I feel for you and the two are now indistinguishable. I commune with you, by letter and by other

*ways I have told nobody of, will tell nobody. It is a vital
part of my life, and a complete secret.*

*So here I am, my life pretty much shaped out. I hardly
see Warren. He could be having an affair, and I would
neither know nor care. Eleanor maybe? He is very good
in bed when he chooses to be. As for me, I have you in
my warehouse, now and always, in my dreams, when I
walk and when I swim and when I lie in the sun and
when I read. Always present in every part of my life.*

*My back and stomach are hurting me. I will go to bed
now.*

Thank God I met you. Thank God.

Then she posted that letter with all the others in her mother's
old bureau.

CHAPTER TWENTY

Samo Sloga Srbina Spasava, his mother had told him: togetherness alone protects the Serbs. She sang him the song-cycles of Serbia, and crooned of the childhood love and tribal togetherness that so warmly enfolded him in the ski chalet. The snow fell in thick stifling blankets around them, jets of steam whinnying out of the burning logs as she whispered the legends of the Field of Blackbirds, of those who had fought the infidel Turk and had perished there.

The bastard sons and daughters of the Turk still live here, she told him. So too do the worthless Croat scum, Catholic posers. See them dress, men with hairspray, platform shoes. Sodomites: contemptible. So different from Serbs, who are strong and straight and true. But listen, she abjured: his Serbness for now must remain a secret – until, that is, the coming dawn. The long dark night which had begun for Serbia five hundred years ago would soon be lifting. Where there are no wounds now, there soon will be. Hush child. Let us sleep now.

On another occasion, she told him of the more recent travails of his, her, people. One third of the population of Serbia was killed in the First World War by the Croat and Muslim soldiers of the Hapsburgs. Yet when peace arrived, we Serbs even shared our home with our killers. Then those very people joined with the Nazis, raped our women, stole our children, murdered our men. The Croats were given their own fascist state, and Croat churchmen preached extermination from the pulpit. SS divisions were raised amongst the Croats and the Muslims, Kama and Handschar, their insignia – a scimitar to cut Serb throats.

My parents joined the partisans, not because they were communist but because the partisans had guns. And your father's father, he too fought the Nazis, he too was a warrior for Serbia. A giant of a warrior, for Serbia. It was all for Serbia and the Serb.

After the war, we once again forgave our oppressors, and once again allowed them to share our state with us. Was ever a nation so kind, so wilfully hospitable, so suicidally generous, as were the Serbs? What creatures we invited into our home – the sly and treacherous Catholic, with allies everywhere, or the barbarian Muslim, stupid, illiterate, who belongs in Anatolia.

Without the interfering Turk, the meddlesome Hapsburgs, the Serb family would stretch from Trst in Transylvania to Greece. Our granaries of Vojvodina would feed Europe. Our vineyards in Dalmatia would produce Europe's finest wines. Our slopes would provide the finest skiing, our Adriatic coast would have the best seas and the fattest fish. Our athletes would be legendary, our workplaces would hum with industry. We are the one great nation of Europe which has not achieved greatness. But we will.

And in this Serbia, each evening, our young people will gather at a humble Serbian hearth, the simple forum for the wisdom of the old, and there they can hear their elders as they tell of our heroes, our Serb heroes, who fought for Serb and for Serbia – Marko Kraljević, Miloš Obilic, Vuk Brancović, Prince Lazar and Hrebeljanović.

Mercy has been our undoing. When we have spared the viper, the viper has in due course slain us. Grow to be a Serb hero who will always slay the viper, most especially the viper which seeks mercy. For that is the most dangerous viper of them all.

All this, she told him so secretly that not even his father knew. But that was long ago, before the Black Swan killed her, before he was alone.

*

The pains grew worse, and neither Tom's massages nor the painkillers prescribed by Dr Tuchmann now had any effect. Dr Gemeti was back from her maternity leave, and Gina went to see her.

'I'm really sorry I wasn't around when you first took ill,' she said, leafing through her file. She looked up at Gina and smiled. 'I don't want you worrying now, you hear? These things work out most of the time.'

'How's the baby?'

'Image of her father. If I can remember what he looked like.' Ann laughed. 'A ski instructor during the winter Olympics. Ain't that the maddest thing?'

'You tell all your patients this?'

'No,' said Ann, smiling. 'Just the ones I know who've been in the same boat. You remember where Tom was conceived?'

'I think so. On a hill.'

'So was Sara. Night-time. Guy reciting Shelley to me. All these funny little headstones nearby. Weird.'

'Why Sara?'

'Oh because the father was . . . but hey, you're not here to listen to my sexual reminiscences, *fascinating* though they are. This has been going on far too long. Nine months, ain't it? Shit. Leave this to me. High time to get moving, y'hear?'

*

They are on the hilltops outside Sarajevo. There are trenches and, behind, a large area of freshly dug earth. The gunner colonel beside them says, Best fucking city in the world before the fucking Turks and their ayatollahs took over.

The machine-gunner, Šarac: Good for girls. Muslim, Hungarian, American.

The colonel: American girls? Perverts. Smoke dope and fuck their brothers. And Muslims. Don't keep their arseholes clean, isn't that right? And UN soldiers everywhere telling us we should live in peace with these primitives, allah-this and allah-that.

Šarac: The UN give you much trouble?

The colonel: The UN give us much trouble? Children, mere children. My men have taken people from the UN and shot them before their eyes, and the UN offers to suck our pricks. Worse than American women. Or women generally. Here, see that funny green roof over there? Next to the old post office?

Yes.

My sister lives there. A traitor to Serbia. She is loyal to the ayatollahs, those Turks and heathens. I have tried to drop shots on her as she goes behind, yes behind, the coward, that long wall to the market, with our small-mortar battery there.

Šarac: You're trying to snipe with a mortar? Why don't you just shell the house?

The colonel: Why don't I just shell the house? Because it's *my* house. You know I phoned her last month promising her, finally, I would shell it unless she sent out Deutschmarks in rent. So she sold her husband's gold teeth, the Muslim pig, to pay me the rent. She doesn't know I killed him, and I'm sorry about that. She's a good girl, basically, my sister, I just wish she'd see sense.

You phoned her? says the boy, silent until now.

Yes, we could back then, but now those Muslim animals have cut the lines. That's what this war is all about. Bastards. Look! – his voice incredulous – There she is, the bitch, coming out of *my* house—

The boy says: What is that smell?

Šarac looks at him steadily. You mean you don't know?

—And look! She's wearing my Loden coat. Oh the bitch. Fuck her anyway. The cunt. Number one mortar. Fire one round on bearing X-Ray One!

As usual, mocks the voice from the mortar position. Moments later there is a crack of a round being fired.

Right twenty mils, screeches the colonel, right twenty, no right thirty, sharply now, sharply, and FIRE! There are two more sharp thuds from the small mortar emplacement behind the trenches.

Missed! Missed again, comes the incredulous shriek. Fire for effect!

A salvo of mortar bombs sails through the sky. After the rippling explosions of the bombs, a voice in Canadian English says to nobody: Cool.

Šarac, unperturbed by the mortars, and looking intently at the boy, says: So you don't know? Ah.

He walks the boy to some freshly dug earth, and begins to shift it with his foot. Fat, beetle-like black flies are slowly rummaging through the blood-thickened topsoil with large, earth-moving legs. In the muck, the boy can see an eyebrow. What is this? he asks.

The men you killed here.

His stomach heaves at the stench, vomit bubbles.

Mortars fire again, two sharp cracks. The colonel curses and another voice, in English, says, Bonus.

We missed again, and look at the cunt, she didn't even notice, you incompetent fucking cretins, you couldn't drop an apple in a bucket beside your bed. Mortars, mortars, come on now, one last try.

A young woman in civilian clothes approaches the boy. You speak English, Serbian?

I speak sort of English, yes.

Hi. I'm from Canada, 100 per cent Canadian and 120 per cent Serb. Some jive job, hey. These Bosnian dudes wasted, like, in microtime. I mean like wow, heavy, man. So cool.

What? says the boy.

A kid like you, what would you know. And you hear the latest? They're going to exchange these stiffs for living Serb prisoners. Well who's winning this war! Our guys for these stiffs . . . all *right*. Jeez, the smell.

The boy's eyes lift from the human debris beneath his feet to the city from which those young men had come. What had driven them to this end? What is important to the Muslims, apart from their lives? What did his father say about the Muslims, about what they cherished?

The colonel is still ranting. She was, the bitch, wearing my Loden coat.

Listen, says the boy to Šarac. There are other ways to fight this war. We need to kill, but we need to do more. Kill a hundred children and a year later the Muslims produce another hundred. There are better ways to attack them.

What are you talking about? asks Šarac.

We can destroy their books.

Books? says the colonel, overhearing him. Never had any time for books.

Look, says the boy, can you see the main museum beside the bend in the river, next to the Principiv Most?

My sister bought me my Loden coat at the market there. Is that it, the building with the grey pointed thing?

You are from Sarajevo and you don't know the difference between the mosque and the museum? The pointed thing is a minaret – you know what a minaret is, do you? Look, see there, closer, the thing with all the roofs.

Yes the roofs. You should have said. Of course, the museum, I know it well. Not worth attacking. Books, manuscripts, rubbish.

To them it is their history, their legends. Destroy them and you destroy their lies.

*

Gina had had tests done after her meeting with Ann Gemeti, and there was no doubt what the test were for: cancer.

I have no weight loss, and I have no lumps anywhere. And I feel real fine, overall. But I am so scared, Stefan. So very scared.

Will you ever come back to me? Straight lines that have crossed do not meet again, even in infinity, but you and I are real, not straight lines, and this real person is scared she has cancer. Dear Christ, I am scared.

She barely slept the night before her next appointment with Dr Gemeti. When she did, she dreamt with the lopsided clarity unique to the worst dreams. The dream said with diamond certainty: Gina, this thing will kill you. You will wither like an old apple and die.

Gina awoke, ill with terror, her brain dizzy with exhaustion and yet razor-edged, sharp. She padded around the house awhile, then returned to bed, then rose again and went to the bathroom and sat on the toilet and wondered – will it eat my bowels, so that even my most private deeds become matters of public discussion?

A grey dawn seeped into the distant waters of Pontchartrain, and she felt her heart go cold within her. She saw Tom off to school and Warren to work, and she was alone again. She went to the bathroom to release whatever liquids had gathered within her. All morning her bowels and her bladder retained nothing, thin poisonous juices squirting miserably from her.

She drove to the clinic early. She thought her legs were going to buckle as she walked in to see Ann Gemeti.

'Cut to the chase, Gina,' said the doctor, all flippancy banished. 'Things are not as simple as we hoped. The sonography is through, and it appears that you have a couple of tumours on your ovaries. That's the bad news. Here's the good news. As you know, we did bloods tests, what we call lymphoangiographic evaluation. You came up negative. Absolutely negative. Malignant tumours provoke the appearance of things called antigens. We trace these in the blood by markers. You have no antigens. You have benign tumours. It's not good news, but it's certainly not bad. And we are going to have to operate.'

'When?'

'Now. Sort of.'

*

The colonel takes the boy's advice. Serb gunners fire high explosive and phosphorous shells into Gazi Husrev-beg's library of 25,000 books, setting fire to the world's largest unexamined collection of Persian, Turkish, Arabian documents and 800-year-old virgin census rolls. As the citizens of Sarajevo – Serb and Jew, Croat and Muslim – run to save the contents of their museum, the besieging marksmen and mortar crews have a large and happy harvest. The boy even gets a difficult 300-metre headshot into one of the men bearing the colonel's sister's body.

You are good boys, says the colonel later. Stay here as long as you want.

Our unit is re-forming near Pale. We must go, says Šarac.

You are a dangerous youngster, the colonel says to the boy as they leave. A very dangerous youngster.

Twelve hours after the bombardment, the burning ashes from the library still swirl like flocks of maddened starlings over the city as a UN representative arrives to negotiate the return of the Bosnian bodies. Far from being impressed by the night's work, he seems deeply angry.

Have some slivovitz, says the colonel heartily. Let me tell you an interesting little story. He passes the newcomer his binoculars. Now, do you see that green coat down there?

CHAPTER TWENTY-ONE

Gina awoke to a thin electronic hum.

No, I'll go back to sleep.

The hum hummed.

Sleep; blissful blankness, through which a doctor murmurs, Good news at last. All is well. Benign. All is well.

She is filled with relief. Crisis over.

In her sleep, she moved slightly and within her pelvic vault a little demon smiled and prodded her. Pain, as powerfully evocative as an atom of woodsmoke, passed through her back.

Then peace, a dream. Walking the Wicklow Hills again. A cuckoo sings invisibly. She is striding through a bed of ling, larkspur, wild gentian; and rosemary, crushed beneath her feet, surrenders its aroma to the sunlight. A distant stream topples down peat and stone, a silver vein, twinkling, inconstant as it improvises its giddy way downhill. Willows wave along its banks.

She awoke to a sense of threat, though she spoke to no one. Odd. Had she not been told all was well? She slept again, sleep patrolled by dark terrors. When she awoke, beside her she found another woman doctor, her presence oozing gravity.

'Gina, I have news for you,' she said in a voice which her patient would have understood had she addressed her in Chinese. 'We have opened you up around your ovaries, and you have problems there. The tumours, they were malignant. You have had ovarian cancer, and we don't know how successful we've been in excising it.'

'Hi, Warren,' said Gina, as he moved into focus and took her hand.

'Have you understood what I've told you?' asked the doctor. 'Gina, have you?'

Gina, suddenly terrified, paused for a moment to control her body.

'Do I have cancer still?'

'Yes, probably. But listen. You must know. The prognosis for this kind of condition can often be very good.'

'Often,' remarked Gina in somebody else's voice.

'You've got to look on the bright side, no matter what.'

'You mean you don't know.'

'I don't know anything, *for sure*. I'm a doctor, not God. I can tell you this. We got to the ovaries just about in time. There might still be cancer cells inside you, there might not be. If there are we can attack them with very particular types of drugs that target and kill them and prevent them reproducing. You must see things this way – this is a fight we can win.'

She left. So who was the doctor with the good news? Had she dreamt him into existence? It was possible – did not much of her life result from her imaginings? What, now, was real?

Warren was. He sat alone with her, saying nothing. Gina felt a smile settle on her face like a deathmask as fatigue began to claim her again. 'Well now,' she said, before plummeting, exhausted, into an evil sleep. Beneath her had opened a void. She felt her bed falling through it into the cancer ward we all fear. She saw herself in a bed, saw the woebegone gallantry of those doomed to die appallingly.

She cried inwardly: Can they not perish decently, invisibly?

Her dreamself sneered: They? We. Me.

And her dreamself whispered: Healthy visitors will avert their eyes from me and hurry on, hurling their pale flowers in a trashcan before they flee to the ocean and sunshine, hot dogs and iced coke. Back here apothecaries will fumble with my body; and, punctured and tortured, full of futile potions, I will wither like an old apple and die.

Wither like an old apple and die.

Gina awoke, sick with fear. In the deepest part of her mind a question formed: Tuchmann – is it because of Tuchmann not moving in time that I'm in trouble? If Ann Gemeti had been around, would I have been okay?

Do not ask that question, said Doris, speaking within her.

You cannot undo the done. Deal with what is, not with what might have been.

When she turned to Warren, he was gone.

Gina wondered briefly if she had been dreaming everything, and in an awful epiphany, knew she had not. Suddenly, she was absolutely certain she had a cancer which might kill her.

But it will not, she swore. I will see my boy to manhood. I will.

When she slept she dreamt of a green hill, of a line of men, a stream and trees, and of a place called Igman where Ann Gemeti got herself pregnant.

Stefan, these guys, these oncologists, behave towards me with the same punctilious care that they would show an expensive electron microscope which might not function if handled badly.

I lie here and listen. I cannot write with ease which is why I am telling you this. You must listen. Listen.

What do the doctors see in my bed? Not me. What then? A vehicle bearing on its chassis the freight called cancer, towards which they mimic personal concern. But this is a tale that is repeatedly told, and the look on their faces, though outwardly quite ordinary, is lifeless, inert, as truthful as a rumour.

I lie in my bed and think of what has been and what has not been and what will never be. I mean, Stefan, this might be it. My life, such as it is and was, might soon be over. Nothing achieved. Nothing. A few miserable years of mediocrity, of hopes unfilled, then death.

I am a poor patient. I have reacted badly to the anaesthetic. I should have recovered from the operation long ago. Look at how long I'm taking to recover from you.

Is this silly, talking to you like this? You are gone. The past is the past. Let it lie there. Then I say, no, the past is never the past. Turn a corner and it is there, leering at us, its hand on our throat.

Dr Ammyon, a Canadian oncologist, visited Gina often, talking, probing, feeling. One day he said: 'We're done here. Not much more we can do. Time for you to go off and have you some chemotherapy.'

Gina let the word sink in. *Chemotherapy*. 'Look. I was told that I didn't have cancer, just benign tumours, nothing to worry about, whip them out, everything's fine and dandy. What's going on here?'

'These things happen. We got to the tumours reasonably early. You were lucky that Dr Tuchmann urged surgery as early as he did.'

'Urged surgery as early as he did? What the fuck are you talking about? He told me I was overworking, had nothing to worry about.'

'This kind of talk will get you nowhere.'

'How come I was told, TOLD, that I didn't have cancer? How come? Months were wasted. Months. I got a boy at home, what am I going to do?'

'Look, lymphoangriographic evaluation showed no antigens. We're not to blame because your body didn't realize what was being done to it. Blame it, not us.'

'I'm not talking about the lymphowhatever, I'm talking about NOT being examined properly nearly a year ago when the symptoms started. I'm talking about being TOLD I didn't have cancer and then waking up and being told that I did have cancer, with I don't know how much time before I die.'

'Nobody said anything about death, Mrs Bourne.'

'Nobody ever says a fucking word about death here.'

Dr Ammyon used a different tone. 'Okay. Briefly. Cancer developed in your ovaries. The tumours had obvious ascites, which means, simply, that it was more advanced than we'd have liked, but they don't seem to have spread outside the pelvic rim area – into the liver, say. We got a histological extension – malignant, that is – to the colon, and removed it. We think there are traces of that still present within your pelvic rim, hence the need for chemotherapy. Overall, we're pleased.'

'Pleased? That's perfect. And what if it's in my liver?'

'We don't believe it's in your liver.'

'In my liver is serious?'

'Yeah, I guess.'

'So, am I going to die?'

'We're all going to die, Mrs Bourne.'

'This is a hospital, not a Philosophy faculty. I know that. I mean, what can I expect?'

He looked steadily at her ear. 'You can expect a long life, Mrs Bourne. There's a place in Galveston which specializes in your kinds of illness. We're going to send you there and you'll be right as rain.'

Only clipped him. Be right as rain in a couple of days, whispered an old man from her past.

When Dr Ammyon had gone, tears poured down her cheeks. Stop this, she told her eyes, stop it, crying will do you no good.

Stefan, she thought.

Georgina, be of good cheer, he said.

I will be. She slept.

*

Angela, a vast, sullen and silent woman, arrived with Gina's meal – meatloaf and light fruit salad. Gina toyed with it. Dr Ammyon reappeared with a Dr Eapper, another oncologist, who gave a statistical picture of the cure rates for her kind of cancer, which seemed good. The two men left, without Ammyon looking at her once.

Karen arrived from New Orleans, where she was working in Loyola. They talked about the illness, and Gina suddenly began to tell Karen for the first time in detail of Tom's discovery about his background and about Stefan.

They sat in silence then, which Gina ended by asking, 'You think I'm going to die, Karen?'

Karen shook her head. 'Impossible. Not my big sister, not a chance in hell. Not one.'

'Fine. But I still worry.'

'Worrying won't do you no good.'

'Any good.'

'Oh you, typical big sister, you in your bed correcting my grammar, you ain't never going to die.'

Gina laughed politely and Karen began to cry. A voice inside Gina's head whispered: Georgina, be of good cheer.

CHAPTER TWENTY-TWO

The patients drifted beneath the stressed cantilever and plate-glass roofs at the Boylan Clinic in Galveston, aliens on a strange planet. Some chose anonymity, the slippered shuffled. Others were purposeful, striding defiantly, eyes challenging, civil rights marchers in Alabama. And other harrowed souls opted for abjectness, meekly wandering with their eyes down, trackers following the faint trail of life. Whatever their gait or mien, all bore their blue plastic Boylan files.

Gina had steadfastly declined to allow Warren to accompany her. 'I might be ill, but I'm not unwell,' she argued.

'Ah come on, this is not right.'

'It's right. Believe me, it's right for me, so it's right.'

Gina had been given her file when she arrived at reception. It was her passport to life in the clinic. It admitted her to the immigration area of examination, where three specialists wordlessly read its contents. One, a Dr Ancre, looked young enough to be her son, yet in that flagrant boyhood flaunted an ancient gravity.

That evening Gina was hooked to a drip which fed her intravenous cyclophosphamide. Dr Ancre had warned her of what lay ahead. 'It's the way we do things here. We take the patient to extremes. We hammer the cancer as hard as we can, and the patient gets hammered too, *almost* to beyond their endurance. The patient has will. The cancer doesn't. Understand?'

Understand? Almost, she thought. She lay in her bed, as discomfort spread through her body. Even her eyelids hurt. Some time after midnight, nausea began to churn within her, rumbling and threatening. Sweat ran in torrents for one hour, two hours, and cramps in her stomach focused into a single pain which gradually resembled a red-hot needle through her guts; yet she could not throw up.

Time passed. What did *almost* mean? The contents of her stomach continuously rose and fell to the edge of her throat, like sea against a sea-wall, while insects with sharp teeth busily quarried in the muscles of her arms, her legs. Slowly, the ocean within her began to subside. She whispered a prayer of thanks; and then vomit erupted from the seat of her stomach, a violent spouting of acids and bile and fragments of long-forgotten meals.

The agony faded and died. Gina whimpered in gratitude, and rang for an orderly to clean her. She took a sip of water, but instead of cleansing her mouth, it combined with the detritus coating her gums and tongue, causing her to retch again. Struggling for a breath of uncontaminated air she thought she had reached *almost*.

But she could hear her gut gurgle as it prepared its troops for the next attack.

Now she knew she must hope for nothing, expect nothing, but instead let the tempests of illness find their own rhythm. Her mind was numb. Reason had long since vanished in the meaninglessness of the most sinister word in the English language, *almost*. The only other word in her mind was, when. When will this stop? When does *almost* do the decent thing and let me die in peace?

A certain moment arrived mid-vomit when she realized that she was not vomiting, only dreaming that she was. She had finally fallen asleep. She closed her eyes and slept again. When she woke it was noon and she knew that orderlies had changed and washed her. She did not stir. Her limbs lay as she found them, crumpled and folded oddly, like a victim of a high-rise fall. She felt a certain pleasure in the deep lassitude which bound her to the bed, and was able, when she collected her wits, to thank God that it was over, that she had reached *almost* and triumphed. It was over.

It was not.

*

Back home, Gina's hair began to fall out. At first it hardly mattered. She felt so terrible that her scalp was the least of her worries. She had no doubt: she would have chosen death over the chemo – what she did not understand was how these children treating her knew how finely to judge *almost*.

She went to Atlas, and bought half a dozen Indian-made light cotton headscarves which she could bind tightly around her head, over her ears and pinned at the back, but they did not hide her vampirized face, or the deep circles under her eyes. She frightened people; on seeing her, strangers would instantly lower their faces, as if she bore some plague which eye contact alone could communicate.

When she entered Pricerite with Tom, her head bound to hide her baldness, she noticed two young women – both pretty, both with magnificent hair – exchange looks. She could imagine their conversation when she was gone – God, did you *see* that poor woman, she looked so BAD, my, I felt I was dyin' just lookin' at her.

Gina and Tom wandered down the aisles, Tom dawdling, gawking, a clumsy wildebeest. She pushed the cart past a group of teenage girls and sensed Tom pause to gaze hungrily at them. She stopped to examine some sweet potatoes, and a jet of vomit fountained out of her, all over the vegetable shelves, a lance of agony jack-knifing her in two.

She found herself leaning on a display case of cellophane-wrapped apples, supermarket staff clustered around her, as if shielding other shoppers, and she realized: this is it, as bad as it gets, can't get worse, God, can it, you bastard, can it?

She looked up. Tom, his back to her, was still looking at the group of girls. Gina blinked back the tears and heard somebody talking to her in low, urgent tones. There was a singing in her ears, a terrible taste in her mouth and throat, and her brain recited, you bastard God, you fucking bastard.

Gina felt a chair being placed beneath her and forced against the back of her knees so that she sat down on it, and she began to smell, for the first time in public, the rank fragrance of her own vomit.

'No,' she sobbed in disbelief. 'No.'

'Are you all right, ma'am?' she heard a managerial voice enquire. Gina looked up at the concerned face of a man ten years her junior. Is nobody my age any more? She wanted to say, 'I'm not drunk, it's not what you think.' But she could say nothing, so she merely lowered her face and shook her head.

'I'm fine,' she managed to whisper.

'I don't think so,' said the manager. 'Can we call anybody for you, get them to come and collect you?'

Gina looked up and saw the terrible mess she had made of the vegetable department. 'Oh God,' she whimpered. Beyond the manager, Gina saw Tom at that moment turn. The look of concern that rose to his face was almost worth the attack. He rushed towards her.

'Mom, are you okay? This is my mother. Could you all step back, please, give her some air. Mom?'

'Yes, I'm okay,' she said. She felt Tom holding her, putting his arm around her. He whispered, 'Hey, Mom, on the gin again.' She looked at him in gratitude and he winked at her.

She turned to the manager. 'Thank you for your help,' she said. 'My son here will see me to my car. Do you mind greatly if we do not proceed with the purchases? My name is Bourne. I will call to find out how much I owe for the damage done.'

'There is no need.'

'I do assure you, there most certainly is.'

In an oddly formal, old-fashioned gesture, the manager bent his head forward slightly at an angle and placed his fingertips together in affirmation of Gina's wishes, and with Tom at her side she left the supermarket, the girls he had been ogling parting before him. They looked at her, at him. He smiled at her and said to the girls, 'Hi there, how you going?' and kept on walking with her, strongly, confidently.

Where did I find this son? she asked in silent gratitude.

She cleaned up when she got home and heard Tom making a call. Jackie, probably. When she knew he might be going steady, Gina had sat him down and talked to him forcibly about condoms.

'Jackie and me are serious,' he said.

'Treat her serious now. Girls that age hurt real easy.'

'Boys that age hurt *really* easily, Mom,' he teased. 'Really easily. Where did you get your grammar from?'

'Where did I get you from?'

'Well if you don't know sure as hell beats me.'

Gina laughed, squeezing his arm in gratitude.

When she got out of the shower and dried herself she went downstairs. 'You going out?' she asked.

'Was. Changed my plans. I'm staying in and Jackie's coming over, do a bit of study together, okay?'

'Fine.' They looked each other in the eye, and her love for him nearly ate her where she stood.

CHAPTER TWENTY-THREE

When they told me they were going to increase my chemo, Doris, I told them I'd prefer to die. They're such bastards, they know how to play you. What about your son? said my specialist. Don't you want to see him grow? You can't be selfish here, you know. Bastard.

So. Get it right for Tom. Get it right for Tom. That's my mantra now.

If I'm dying, and I think I might just be, my ambitions are nothing, all nothing. I will vanish, I will leave these bones and this flesh rotting behind me and oh how the thought fills me with terror. And when I can push the fear to the back of my mind, then I feel guilty for being so selfish about my own health, and guilty because I fear I won't see Tom into adulthood, or even to his eighteenth birthday.

But this is stupid. This is speculating about the future. I have no future, only a series of presents, and my struggle is unbearable.

I look terrible, my hair is gone, I feel exhausted. My body isn't just fighting the cancer, it's fighting the after-effects of the chemo as well. My first session was awful. The rest were worse, and waiting for them perhaps worse still. I haven't abandoned my duties, though the Serbo-Croat is on hold. Warren is present but absent. I don't blame him.

Death looks at me in the face each morning of my life and I ask, Will I be the first of my generation to die, with so little achieved?

Doris, I am so frightened. What lies ahead for me? Me, the mother of Tom.

I lie awake and think of my flesh going cold and I feel

*ill with terror. I was reading only the other day of some
SS general, a cheerful, seasoned slaughterer, who is now
prospering in sunlit old age, surrounded by adoring
grandchildren, neighbours respectfully greeting him in
his Bavarian village: 'Guten morgen, Herr General,' and
the old man looks up from playing with his grandson
and waves a hand in acknowledgement. There is a smell
of cooking over the lawn. Birds sing in the trees. This
abominable old fiend who might have laid waste to half
of the Ukraine or Bosnia or herded all the Audreys,
Rebeccas, Ruths, Rachels of this world into cattle trucks,
survives into admired antiquity while I, under half his
age and undreamt of when he was spreading murder
across the steppes or in the woodlands of Poland, must
prepare for my death. Why? Why? It is so unfair. So
totally and completely unfair.*

And since Doris was in no condition to receive those letters,
still mourning her beloved Françoise, Gina placed them with
those she had written to Stefan.

*

Once again, she sat in the waiting area of the Boylan clinic,
sick with apprehension. Large potted palms drooped green
fronds beneath the clear glass roof. She often sat here
watching various maimed patients stomping around the
place. The through-put at Boylan was so high that people she
met once she hardly ever met again. The others vanished, got
better, died.

There were no mirrors in this waiting area; but there was a
forest of semi-plastic plant-forms which seemed to have been
specially bred for hospitals, some occasional glass-topped
tables with magazines, and a central abstract feature composed of coloured gravel, stainless steel, carved stone. Musak
chimed through the soft patter of water falling from the top
of the stainless font onto a pool below: hospital art, the
particular aesthetic which suggests survival without ruling
out its alternative.

She heard an enquiry: 'Now what in hell do you think that is?'

A strong-looking man in early middle age was gazing at the water feature. 'Search me,' she said.

The man smiled and raised a hand. 'George Floyd. Hi.'

'Gina Bourne. How you going?'

'Good.' His eyes lightly scanned her scalp as he started a no-holds cancer conversation. 'Where you got it?'

'Ovaries. You?'

'Testes. How're your antigens?'

'Still positive. But they're getting better each time. I'm not. That's the problem.'

'Ain't it though, God, ain't it. Shit, times I've woke up at home and said, no, goddamn it, I'll just stay here and die, better to die nice and simple, with a nice big cocktail of drugs inside you to ease the pain, than what these fucking ghouls do to you.'

'Yeah, but then you think, hold on one minute there, so what the hell has been the point of all those other sessions, all those months of nausea and agony, if I give in now? Makes nonsense of everything I've done, right?'

He laughed, and said, 'Right, you been there too.'

'I sure have. And back.' Gina looked at her companion more carefully. He had a full head of auburn hair, and a big broad face with a little net of smile lines around the eyes. He reminded her of Matt when she first knew him.

'You got a family?' he asked.

'A son. Tom. A fine boy.'

'I got my girls, BJ, Ellis, Dini, my two boys, Sam and Peter, five in all. They're what's keeping my going. My wife's dead, died five years ago, so it's been real hard.'

'Oh. I'm sorry to hear that.'

George smiled. 'Yeah. There you go. Hell, I'm fortunate, got a successful business, builder's supplies, my sister Charlotte's been good, real good now, and my wife's mother is a fine woman. But the stress, now, is something else. Boy, I'm telling you.'

Gina was almost relieved to hear a worse story than hers, and cheerfully joined him in sympathy. 'I can believe it. I thought I had it hard, just the one son, and a husband. And they're real good to me too, real good, yet it's been so hard to keep going. How've you managed?'

'Well I had to I guess, I had to. Life is everything. Hell, when I was a kid I'da said I'd rather die than lose my balls. Damn, now I know the truth. My reproductive days are well and truly over.'

'Mine were anyway. I had a hysterectomy after I lost a baby.'

'Shit. You sure have had one time of it.'

They were silent for a while. 'You see people round here with all sorts of things missing, and I reckon I'd rather lose my testicles than my jaw or my bowels.'

'Right,' said Gina.

'What time are you due?' he asked her.

'Half an hour ago. I'll be paged when they're ready. You?'

'I'm early. I always get here in good time, so I can feel relaxed when they give me my tests. Though relaxed don't quite fit the picture. If you take my meaning. Whatever, I want to stay alive for my kids.'

'Mind me asking, what happened to your wife?'

'Drunk driver near Gramercy, Louisiana. Hit her, drove her off the road, kept going, stopped by the highway patrol.'

'Gramercy, why that's no distance from where I live. I'm from Clapham, you know it?'

'You from Clapham? Course I know it. Sweet little town, and that's a real pretty little college you got there. I'm from Opelousas, my wife was going to visit her folks over at Hammond. It hurt me real bad, real bad.'

'What happened to the man who, you know – the drunk driver?'

'That's the bit that hurts almost as bad as my wife dying. A rookie cop made the arrest, not like the regular highway patrol at all, 'cause usually they're real good, but this kid screwed up, didn't read him his rights or something stupid and the guy walked. Nothing we can do. Nothing.'

'You mean he's walking free?'

'Yeah, he walked and he's walking free, but I can tell you, he won't be, ever I get the news that I'm outa luck. No, he'll go before me, that's for sure. I woulda seen to him myself by now, 'cept for the kids. No point in leaving them without a

Daddy, just for the sake of revenge, I mean. So while I still get good news, so does he, only he don't know it.'

'I'm sure he'll be punished one way or another, sooner or later. Don't you think?'

'If I thought that, I'd sleep easy. But life ain't like that, not in this world it ain't. No, the only justice you can be sure of in this world is one you find for yourself.'

'Guess you're right.'

The musak was interrupted as a monotonous voice recited Gina's name, asking her to reception. 'That's me. Time to go. Good luck.' She rose and shook George's hand.

'Been a real pleasure meeting you,' he said, and suddenly he leaned forward and kissed her on the cheek. She kissed him back.

'Good luck, George,' she said.

'Good luck, Gina – you did say Gina, didn't you? – good luck. Take care, you hear. Take care.'

They gazed at each other steadily in the eye, two people who instantly liked one another. Now the encounter was ending. For a moment Gina was tempted to ask for his address so as to stay in touch, but there was no point. Each had a war to fight.

She took his hand in both her hands, kissed him again and wished him godspeed.

Be of good cheer.

CHAPTER TWENTY-FOUR

Louisiana, 1992
A Dr Monash had broken the news to Gina: she appeared to be cured. The antigen count was zero. There were no secondaries, no weight loss, no pain. She looked and felt good; the Boylan Clinic had taken her through the gates of hell, but she had emerged at the other end.

My, but it was tough, Doris. And I had to mobilize all my resources to stay alive. Stefan was one of my resources – oh I used to write to him and talk to him about Serbo-Croat irregular verbs. He would visit me at night to coach me in dialect differences.

I think it was hope more than chemo which kept me alive. Death cannot conceivably be worse than the chemo treatment, which in the Galveston regimen is designed to be extreme. Other cancer patients I have spoken to – we recognize one another and talk in the street, you know – have not had nearly as terrible a regimen as I've had. Nothing like.

Time has done strange things. It seemed like I was on chemo for ever, but in that same period Tom grew up, and that seemed to happen overnight. He's in Yale now, doing Serbo-Croat, as he threatened he would. He inherited the full batch of linguistic genes from me, his Irish grandmother, his Irish great-grandfather. I don't know how good Stefan's father was at languages. Just a partisan war hero, I guess. Tom has picked up a good few scholarships, which removes most of the pain of college fees, though he'll have to work over the summer vacations, which is no bad thing. He now goes by the name of Tomas Djurdjev. He is very sweet and not a bit pompous and makes fun of himself for changing his name. He was worried that Warren might be upset.

I don't know whether Warren is or isn't. He leads his own life. I wish him well.

I have passed through the valley of death and am now overjoyed. Life lies ahead of me like a sunlit city full of fountains and cool marble courtyards, rich green orchards and streams with green trees along their banks, drooping into the water. I feel happiness pulse inside me like another living thing. All my sorrows are behind me . . .

Obviously there will be regular check-ups, just to make sure that everything is okay. And suddenly I have this extraordinary future ahead of me, one I never planned for. I feel almost lost, like I'm a child born unexpectedly, fully grown at birth. It is unnerving and wonderful. My heart is full of joy, but my mind is full of doubt.

Some things I really look forward to – like seeing Tom graduating. Learning about his true father seems to have motivated him amazingly.

On the other hand, where does this leave me? Living with cancer, your horizons are what you see. You concentrate your mind on special projects – like seeing Tom off to college. Nothing else counts in this world but the next project. But I'm not a project-planner any more, I'm back to being a member of the human race with the same horizons and the same time.

Hey, Doris, I might even have an affair.

That thought came to her only as she wrote it, and her heart gave a little surge at the thought. She remembered then the lowest moment in her sexual esteem, her anguish one evening nearly three years before, when Warren had rejected her despairing, pathetic advances. She thought then that sexual love for her was over. Now, she thought, touching her full head of hair, maybe not.

She looked at her watch. Since the war in Bosnia began she had been regularly listening to a Bosnian radio station which

broadcast in shortwave from New York. She turned on her
Sony radio-cassette, hitting the preset button nine, and heard
a report in the distinctive Mostar accent.

The phone. It was Roben. They had talked only briefly
since Gina had received her good news. Dave, Roben said
excitedly, had been offered a six-month scholarship in
Cambridge. They were due to leave in just a few days' time.
Wasn't that fantastic?

'I thought you hated all that Ivy League stuff,' said Gina
dubiously.

'Cambridge England, stupid,' cried Roben, delighted.
'Cambridge fucking England.'

Gina laughed while Roben outlined her plans, volubly and
at length. Gina gradually became aware of someone else
talking to her, but from the radio. Roben was telling her
about some failed seduction the night before.

The voice. It was familiar. It began to take form like a genie
from a bottle. She could no longer hear what Roben was
saying, but neither could she identify this vocal presence.

'Hush a minute,' she told Roben. She lowered the earpiece in
time to hear the last phrases of the voice from the radio. It was
too familiar. A trapdoor trembled beneath her. The voice was
talking in English: '. . . Sherb forches around Sharajevo,' it said.
'The Yugoshlav air forche—' She heard none of the details, just
the liquidized sibilants and a voice she could never forget.

The newsreader took over. 'Closer to home, Governor
Clinton of Arkansas has called for American intervention in
the crisis . . .' Gina heard, before the bulletin vanished in a
foam of white noise.

'Roben, I'll call you back,' Gina croaked in a borrowed
voice. 'Okay?'

She hung up and hurried over to the radio, racking back the
cassette for several moments and got the Mostar man. She
racked it forward and got the jingle for the news. The
newscaster started speaking about Bosnia, and Gina felt her
heart seize as the item moved, as it must, to the voice report
she had heard. Then there was a click. The tape ran out.

Jesus. She had put a half-used tape into the cassette.

No. I will not surrender now. I will not let myself be moved by events.

She played the cassette back. The station gave a number for volunteers who wished to help Bosnia. She dialled it, and a voice said, 'Hi, Jeff speaking, how may I help you?'

She started to explain her enquiry.

'Stop,' said Jeff. 'I got the guy's name here, Stefan Djurdjev. He's good, ain't he though? Funny accent. Those "S"s. He's in Dublin, Ireland. Trinity College Dublin. Thanks for the call. Say a prayer for Bosnia, y'hear? Stay tuned, why don't you? Have a nice day.'

*

Roben was so excited before leaving for Cambridge that Gina was sure she would forget her request – simply to put a British stamp on the envelope and to mail it over there.

'I will of course reimburse you when you get back, my dear, to the last farthing,' said Gina.

'If I get back. You never can tell, those Brits with those accents.'

She tucked the letter addressed to Dr Stefan Djurdjev in her shoulder bag, which generally carried everything from condoms to mousse, a Swiss Army knife, a bottle opener and a miniature of bourbon whiskey.

They kissed and Gina watched Roben walk towards the Toyota, carrying the first letter to Stefan in twenty years, though of course uncounted, unwritten letters lay in her brain and dozens more in her bureau.

My dear Stefan,

I heard your name on the radio just the other day and I thought I might write to you. My name is Georgina Cambell. Do you remember me? We knew each other briefly for a couple of weekends many years ago when I was a student in Ireland.

Hearing your voice, I thought it would be real nice just to write to you. It was funny hearing you on the radio, talking about Bosnia. I'd know that voice anywhere, sort of Irish and Slavic together, you know?

It seems that you move from one trouble spot to the

next. I hope you take care of yourself. I can only have a vague idea of the awfulness of that place. I pray it ends soon.

I guess you got to learn the language and visit the country and got to know the people the way you were threatening to. I'm real glad about that. It must be good to discover your true roots after all.

I do hope you don't mind me writing like this. It was just that hearing your voice happened to come at a particular time for me. I have had cancer, and have experienced a long and brutal course of chemotherapy at a special clinic in Galveston. The miracle is that though for a long time they thought I would not be cured, the news now is that I am. Totally.

They've still got to keep an eye on me but, generally speaking, everything is okay, and that's a great relief. For the first time in nearly five years I can foresee a complete future in front of me. It is the most wonderful feeling.

I should tell you I am very happily married. I have a son, Tom, who is at college. I just adore him. My husband Warren is a professor of linguistics. We met soon after I returned here from my wonderful time in Ireland, which I have never forgotten.

I just wanted to tell you that I have never forgotten you either. I hope that you keep warm memories of me as well. I often wonder if you ever got married and have children. You would be some great father. I remember the way you got on with that little girl I was minding all those years ago. You remember singing to her? She must be fully grown by now, older than I was then. Such things time does to us.

I won't send you my address. I don't live in the town I used to and just to ensure that the past is the past, you won't even find a useful postmark on this letter. A friend going to England is mailing it for me. I don't think that there would be any point in having a correspondence which complicates your life and mine. I just wanted to remind you that over here in the USA, somebody still regards you fondly.

I hope you are as happy as I am.
Your old friend, who often thinks of you,
Georgina (Cambell)

Gina watched the bearer of that letter drive away down Cody.
The Toyota paused at the intersection, a hand stuck out to
wave a farewell, and the car turned. The letter was gone.

Gina stood in the shade of the yellow poplar feeling the
curious vertigo of time. Her letter had gone into a bottle with
no return address. Nearly two decades had passed since she
made love to the man to whom she had sent it.

She looked around her, suddenly dizzy at the turns her life
had been taking. And not just hers: Tom and Warren had
spent the past couple of years preparing for her imminent
death, a near future which had now been cancelled. She
thought: Is that the way life is? What we learn might be of no
use to us; what we forget might be vital. Who can say? All our
futures are negotiable or even extinguishable, our pasts full of
causes with unseen consequences.

That evening she gave Eleanor a call, but the line was busy.
Too early for bed, she padded into the study and scanned the
bookshelves, ending up in the Ws: Wodehouse and Waugh
caught her eye, favourites of Noelly once upon a time.

A thought came to her. She would visit Ireland, and stay
with Matt and Maureen, just by herself, and see all the
Bracken kids again – adults, now, with Noelly married. Their
marriage effectively over, how could Warren mind her staying
a couple of weeks in Ireland with her oldest friends?

She went to bed, singing to herself, and never heard Warren
slip in beside her, never sensed his light goodnight kiss on her
brow, never detected the pang of sorrow within his heart. For
she was far off in Mayo, dreaming of the steel-grey waters of
Lough Conn, dreaming of the blue and brown heights of
Nephin Mountain, dreaming of the curlews' call through the
falling night, and dreaming of lying naked once again beneath
the lithe sinews of a handsome young Slav.

*

Šarac and the boy are lying in the sun beneath the cuckoos.

Šarac says, Look at those clouds over there. That wind. It's going to rain.

The boy glances and sees a weatherfront advancing darkly over the brown of the mountains miles away, can smell the wind changing. I know why poets write about nature, he says.

Why do they not write about my Type 53? It is so flawless, so poetical in its movement. Do you know about the movement of the Fifty-Three? It is exquisite. Each time the bolt goes forward there is a little stud, a movable stud, which strikes a little cam on the barrel extension, perfectly, every time – rat tat tat so fast it is a single noise. BRRRRRR. The most beautiful piece of machinery in the world. Hail to thee blithe spirit, he cries in English.

You are mad, says the boy.

Drivers used to love their steam locomotives. I love my Fifty-Three.

There is a difference. Your Fifty-Three kills. That looks like rain all right.

I touch the trigger and out come twenty rounds a second, each round just point zero five of a second behind the one in front, and travelling at a kilometre a second, faster than sound. Your enemy is alive, and then a thousandth of a second later dead. It is so beautiful, so humane – man's ingenuity at its most perfect. If only I could travel back through time to shake the hand of the man who devised it.

You have strange ambitions.

It is not strange to wish to meet genius. I love my gun. I love perfection.

They lie in silence until the boy hears Milošević's voice calling them.

What the fuck does he want? says Šarac.

Cunt, probably.

Milošević arrives, breathless. A moment, he gasps. A moment.

The two of them look at him, smiling, exchanging looks. The machine-gunner says, All those women have worn you out.

We're all to report back for duty. Now.

But . . .

I know, I know, it's not frontline stuff, internal security, there's a gang of Muslims loose around the place, they crossed over Croat lines north of Mostar, there's a ceasefire on there. Treacherous fucking Croats let them through. Oh to drop a Scud or two into Zagreb.

These men on foot or what?

No, they're in a bus, a fucking bus. Can you believe it?

A bus? What, on the roads? In a bus?

Yes, they were heading north near Bugojno, but the roads are down there – they'll probably cut over the logging tracks. Look at those clouds. Tomašević said it would rain. Right as always. Mountain-men know their rain.

What are we to do?

Stop them and kill them. Simple.

My fucking Fifty-Three is in the barracks.

You won't need it. There are spare FAZs in the police station. These are children, mere children. Lambs to the slaughter.

There are no lambs left in Bosnia, just wolves, says Šarac. We made sure of that.

Believe me, these are lambs. Tasty, tasty lambs, with tasty, tasty chops. You like lamb chops? I love lamb chops. Have you got your ponchos?

*

Maureen was of course delighted to hear Gina's news, and ecstatic at the prospect of an imminent visit. That phone call complete, Gina called a travel agent and booked her flights to Ireland. She phoned Eleanor to tell her of her plans, but Eleanor said, Stop: got to hear this in person. Come on over.

She was just beginning to discuss her forthcoming vacation when Douglas sauntered into the room, looking expensively casual. 'Mind if I turn on the news?' Eleanor flapped a hand in the direction of the seldom-used portable in the corner.

Douglas said, bending to the television set, 'I hear George Floyd's plane is missing.'

George Floyd. The name rang a bell, faintly, in Gina's memory. What was it? Douglas stood there watching, his hands inside his trouser pockets as a newscast began with a report of a plane crash that morning. Gina, her back to the screen, heard the newcaster's voice intone the tidings.

'Opelousas businessman George Floyd is believed to have

been the only fatality when his Beechcraft crashed not far from Clapham this a.m.'

Gina went rigid. Another voice, presumably an eyewitness, then spoke. 'Didn't seem there was nothing wrong with the plane, flying straight and true, then banked and dove straight into the ground, like one of them there kamikaze pilots.'

'Shit,' said Douglas. 'That's him. That's him. Shit.' He walked out of the room.

Her skin tingling, her mind in uproar, five orphans, she thought. But steady. There is more to come. This is a day you will never forget. This is like one of those telegram days which widows recall so perfectly decades later, the delivery boy paralysed by the weight of grief within that single little envelope.

The newsreader then whispered into Gina's ear of the other big local story of the day, the shooting of Clapham resident Greg Vasitch Senior at his home. Ah yes. The pieces fell into place. Vasitch, that drunk driver who nearly killed Gina and Tom and who had a hand in her mother's death. Vasitch must have killed George's wife.

There was speculation about the political possibilities of Vasitch's death; a well-known exile, he had been involved in Catholic right-wing anti-communist activities. The FBI had arrested and deported two men on suspicion of a conspiracy to murder Vasitch two years before.

Sorry guys. This time it wasn't political.

Now, Gina was totally focused on the newsreader's voice to the complete exclusion of everything around her. With a deep and certain intuition, she knew that the next bulletin was directed at her alone.

'A Natchez woman is one of the twelve people missing, presumed dead, after fire broke out in the Boylan Cancer Clinic in Galveston.'

'My God,' whispered Gina.

Eleanor looked at Gina. 'Are you okay? You know people there?'

'Only the staff, and why should I give a damn about those bastards?'

'They saved your life,' said Eleanor reprovingly.

At that moment, Gina knew they hadn't.

Part Four

CHAPTER TWENTY-FIVE

Louisiana, 1993
Three weeks later, Gina, key in one hand, coat and bag in the other, stepped into the fishtank silence of an empty house. She was alone. Warren was at a conference in Bloomington and Tom was up in Yale and there was no one to tell the most momentous news of her entire life to. Eleanor had been wrong. *You have cancer still. It is inoperable, untreatable and spreading. You have been grievously, shamefully misled. Now it is too late. We can offer you no hope.* 'Hello,' she called, to confirm her solitude. 'Hi there?'

Gina slipped off her shoes, put on the light casuals she kept by the door and padded through the house. Her footfall rose and perished in the silence and she heard the words of the Louisiana assistant state attorney, Henry Clomonso, who two weeks before had broken the news about the Boylan Clinic to her.

It was a fraud, a scam. You know that, don't you?

A roof beam way above her shifted in its bed like a sleeping torso, its crack resounding around her, the house disturbed in its foundations.

Once that madman O'Reilly inherited the place from his uncle, it became a weird experiment in mind over matter. Staff lied about antigen counts, falsified scans, even used computer-generated images to convince patients they were getting better.

The silence followed Gina around the house, stealthily keeping pace with her as she wandered from the kitchen back to the hall, into the study, out again.

The theory was that with massive blasts of chemo in vaguely the right direction so as to smash whatever was in the way, and a systematic programme of lying, patients could eliminate what their bodies did not want. I'm a Jew. Sort of familiar, you know?

She paced the corridors of her spiritless home, felt the drapes, gazed at the lampshades, ran her fingers over the sideboards and the coffee table.

He used disbarred doctors like Ancre. And the authority of the medical profession over the vulnerable ensured folks would believe any optimistic prognosis. Some of them had already been told the truth by MD Anderson just up the road. Didn't want to hear it, did they? Preferred lies.

Precisely. Now. How long to go? Weeks? Months? Weeks would be better. A sudden decline into the waiting arms of massive painkillers and a tranquil end, a slow going down of lights, until she could see and hear no more.

Never would have known but for that businessman in Opelousas, the guy who died in the plane crash. Smelt a rat and went to MD Anderson with his scans. Then told the authorities. Only some stupid clerk told O'Reilly and he tried to burn the records. He burnt a few patients too. Course he was used to doing that.

A noise at the door. She turned, expecting to hear the metallic enquiry of key. Nothing. Silence returned. There would be nothing new in this life, this world.

I took the liberty of checking you into MD Anderson in Houston. You'll get the truth there.

Now I have the truth. I knew this was a possibility. Always knew it. So why am I so devastated by what I now know?

Because you fought so long, that's why. Defeat in a few evil weeks is not as terrible as defeat after a long and brutal war. Surely nobody has fought a siege, a Leningrad, as long as you have, and lost.

She plugged in the kettle, and it began to murmur. Before the year was gone, this inanimate thing will have more life than I, she thought.

'Anybody home?' said a little voice behind her. Her neighbour, Sue Gray.

'Sue,' she said.

'Door's open,' said Sue brightly.

'Shouldn't be. I came in the front. I've been away.'

'I know. Saw you arriving in the cab. So what's the news?'

'Where's Ogden?' asked Gina abruptly.

'Work. I hope. Well it ain't Saturday, so it must be work. It ain't Saturday, Gina, is it? Now don't go telling me I done forgot what goddam fuckin' day it is.'

'No it's not Saturday, that's for sure, though I'm not sure what day it is – Wednesday? Thursday?'

'Ogden says I got the worst head for dates he ever come across. How you been? Okay?'

'So so,' said Gina. 'Kettle's on, want some coffee?'

'Thanks but no.' She rummaged through the kangaroo pouch in her dungaree front and produced an envelope. 'Here, new mailman, wrong box. From Galveston. Nosey little ol' me.'

'Thanks,' Gina intoned dully, taking the envelope.

'You okay?'

'Sure.'

'You don't look . . . Oh hell, I do believe that's ma fucking phone. Ain't that the goddamnest thing though. Listen, honey, be seein' ya.'

In a moment she was gone, the screen door tapping in her wake, the yard phone calling her imperiously through the silence of Clapham suburbia. Gina stared at the letter. What in the name of God had those murderous bastards in Galveston to say to her? It made no difference now. Houston had already told her. It's over: go home and die.

She looked at the envelope: government issue. Curiously, it used her full name, Georgina, though as a patient she had gone by her normal name, Gina. She opened it. Two letters fell out. One was from the FBI clerk who had been liaising with Henry Clemenso, Sidney Weizmann. It told her he had been instructed to forward the enclosed to her.

She lifted the other letter. It too was addressed to her by the name that only one person in the world had routinely called her since childhood, Georgina. She turned it over. On the back was the sender's name: Stefan Djurdjev.

*

Bosnia, 1993

The boy looks around at the men assembling at the police
station, and he thrills with pride at his race. Warriors of
Serbia. And he realizes, this is a huge mirror. What they are,
he is. What he is and does, they are and do. No need for
individual feelings here – no need for personal regret or
concern. Like that girl for example.

For this is a war and things happen in war. What happened
to the girl would no doubt in different circumstances have
been wrong – might even, indeed, have been a crime. But in a
war, with men like this around him, what can you expect?
Evil cannot be fought with velvet gloves on. They are fighting
for Serbia. Men must die, and women too. As it was, as it has
been, so it is and shall be.

He did not ordain this fate. Destiny had brought him to this
police station with these men as it had previously brought
him to the whimpering, wide-eyed girl.

Do not think of her, he says, but an image comes back to
him, of a look in her eyes he did not notice at the time but
is aware of now. She was twelve and now she is dead.
Forget it. She feels no pain now and felt little then. It had to
happen to her sometime in life. Her death lasted seconds.
She was lucky. Some men take hours to die. What was he to
do? Let her go off to breed fresh Muslims? Madness. Forget
her.

He looks at Šarac and smiles. Some bunch, eh?

I'd be happier if I had my fucking gun. Look at that fool
there with his Fifty-Three, oh just look how he carries it. And
look at this FAZ. When was it last cleaned?

Around them, men are standing in silence, transmitting
messages to one another; feral things, wordless communications about tracking, hunting, killing and, if need be,
dying. The boy thinks, I would fight and die alongside these
men, and they would do the same for me. My name doesn't
count. Only soldiers count. Section, platoon, company,
battalion, the uniform, the cause, the army. That sense of
common, anonymous purpose makes his heart thump.

Lorries arrive and the men file into the back of them,
squatting on their haunches, their guns beside them.

A captain leaps onto the back of their truck and tells them they are to make roadblocks outside Vranica. The vehicles move off, up alpine logging roads, and once in the open countryside they stop and the officer tells them to check their weapons. Šarac asks him for permission to test-fire.

Why?

Look, he replies, disgustedly raising his gun.

Quickly then.

Šarac points his rifle at a tree and squeezes the trigger. Nothing happens. Šarac ejects the round and aims again. Again there is a click. He ejects that round, and repeats the process. Five rounds go by. Finally, there is the sharp brutal crack of a 7.62 round being fired.

There are ironic cheers, and he empties the magazine into the same part of the tree. Brilliant, he observes mordantly, and then notices an elderly booted Serb, still wearing his dark wool hat in the heat, gazing at him unblinkingly from beside the truck.

He gets back onto the lorry and says, If I hadn't learned to ski, become an instructor, meet foreigners, I'd be like that man there, mad as a sheep in a storm – the lorry lurches off – oh for fuck's sake, take it fucking easy up there, Emerson Fittipaldi.

Can't imagine you without your Fifty-Three, says the boy.

You don't need to. Look at me here.

Yes, I mean in your ski-instructor days.

Good days too. Happy days. Before all this shit.

You're strange. When you have that Fifty-Three, you're Mr Silence. But now, you never stop talking.

Nerves. This bloody FAZ makes me ill.

The boy looks at it closely. That's not a FAZ, it's an AK, it's got no groove in the mag, he says.

What are you talking about? The only thing I know about is the Fifty-Three. Groove. What groove?

Look here, says the boy. At the top of the magazine in my gun there's this notch for working the bolt. AKs haven't got that. AK and FAZ magazines aren't interchangeable.

Christ – and what about these spare mags here?

FAZ, my friend. FAZ.
Perfect. Fucking perfect.
Relax. Nothing'll happen.

CHAPTER TWENTY-SIX

On the Aer Lingus flight to Dublin, Gina again read the letter which Stefan had miraculously sent to her and which had confirmed her decision to undertake the trip.

My dear Georgina,
Thanks for your wonderful letter. So much news in such a short note. I am so pleased, so very, very pleased, about the successful battle against cancer. That's the first thing to say.

The second is to wonder how you can ask whether I remember you. Remember you? A man doesn't forget the only girl who said he gave her the best fuck in all her life, even if he has not heard from her in a couple of decades. Are you surprised that I remember the words? Don't be. I don't remember the words. I don't need to. I kept your letter.

So much has happened since then. I think thanks to your prompting I finally stopped acting as a slavicist and became one. I'd inherited my mother's and my grandfather's ability with languages – once I set my mind to it, I discovered I was quite a linguist. A nice surprise. I work at Trinity College Dublin and with the Irish Government's Department of Foreign Affairs.

I know that weekend led me to my career, because of the things you said and how I felt afterwards. Those few days still shine through the years as something special. Everything I did with you and said to you then was authentic. My feelings were simple but true – simpler and truer than I realized at the time. Maybe the simplest feelings are the most powerful ones and the ones we should pay heed to more.

*But we do not know it – do not know it at the time –
because we're young and inexperienced and don't realize
the extraordinary uniqueness of what is happening. It
doesn't happen again. There's no way of knowing that
then. Doors close, and close for ever.*

*I look back to that section of my life and I see many
things, but from whatever angle I look I see you and
Wicklow, sunlight and cold streams, sex and love and
hot tea and scones beside a log fire.*

*You must be wondering how on earth I tracked you
down. Well I was determined to, one way or another.
Your letter didn't give much away – a British stamp and
a reference to a clinic in Galveston. But then there was a
fire there in which some people died – I suppose you
heard of that? – and the story made it to the newspapers
here. It was a tiny, one paragraph filler, the sort of stuff
which only gets in on a quiet day – FBI investigating
cancer-clinic fire.*

*I telephoned the FBI in Washington, saying that our
Department of Health needed to contact a Galveston
patient who'd been treated in Ireland. The FBI referred
me to the local FBI agent, a guy called Sidney Weizmann.
He wanted to be helpful, but my problem was your name
– what was it? Did you go by your married name? If you
did, I had no chance. Then, blindingly, I remember you
telling me your name was Du Pre, so I yelped at him, Du
Pre, her middle name is Du Pre! Surely that would be in
the computer.*

*It was. Weizmann said he couldn't give your address,
but he could certainly forward a letter.*

*And Georgina, since you're reading this, I presume my
ploy worked. And Weizmann, if you're reading this,
you've picked up some pretty damnable habits in your
line of work.*

*So what's happened to me? Well, I was married for a
while, to a Yugoslav woman named Mata who one day
metamorphosed into a Serb. We have a son. We split up
a long time ago and they've moved somewhere. I don't
know where. I'm single and unattached, as I was all*

those years ago, when the world was young.

So that is that. There's so much to tell you, but this has been enough for this first letter which ends with the reassurance, yet again, that far from forgetting you, I have always remembered you and the light you brought into my life two decades ago. And will do so always. Write to me again.

My love,
Stefan

Re-reading the letter on the flight to Dublin, she scratched an itch on her cheek and her fingertip came away wet, and she said, Oh God, why did you do this to me?

*

She had told the Brackens the news by letter, and suggested not making the promised trip to Ireland. Maureen had phoned back instantly. After the initial tears and worry about her Maureen said, 'Gina, my dearest love, what do you want to do?'

Gina choked back the obvious answer, and said, 'Oh I would so love to see you and Matt one more time.'

'Then do. Provided you're well enough,' said Maureen.

Only the Brackens knew what was happening to her. She could never have got Warren and Tom to consent peacefully to her vacation in Ireland. Tom was so busy in Yale, and Warren was so remote in her life that it was easy to keep him in ignorance.

Gina understood the absolute certainty of her fate when she saw Paula's eyes at Dublin airport. They searched and pitied her own eyes, her face, in a single moment. 'Hi,' she said to Paula, holding her. Paula hugged her in return. There was unnatural tension in the embrace, revealing more in its secrets than its open expression. Then they kissed and Paula said that she must be exhausted, holding her at arm's length and examining her while pretending not to.

In Paula's house in Rathfarnham, in the southern suburbs of Dublin, they drank tea, and after a while Gina said she needed a walk.

'I'll come with you,' said Paula.

Gina lied. 'No. I got to be alone.'

'Oh, I'm sorry. I'm so sorry,' whispered Paula.

Feeling unease for the calculated use of her illness, Gina walked into Rathfarnham village where she found a payphone. She was nervous, her fingers cascading coins over the floor. She twice forgot the number and had to consult the piece of paper she had scribbled it on. She dialled and waited.

'Yesh,' said Stefan's voice into her ear with sudden intimacy. She nearly dropped the phone.

'*Dobodan*,' she said breathlessly, meaning to speak Serbo-Croat. She stopped. 'It's me.'

'Welcome to Ireland, me.'

'Hi. Stupid, I should have said Georgina.'

'Oh I know who me is.'

He laughed, and her emotions turned upside down. His voice had hardly changed. As she'd heard on the radio, it had deepened by half an octave, and it contained that note of sceptical intelligence she had heard in other academic voices. Had he become just another university teacher?

They arranged to meet for coffee the next morning. Gina strolled back to Paula's, her mind dizzy with speculation and nerves. She went to her bedroom and, sitting on the bed, took out the old photograph of Stefan. He was so boyish then, how had he seemed so mature to her? She gazed into his eyes, and lying flat on the bed she took herself back twenty years, when she was young and lovely and life and all its infinite possibilities had lain before her.

*

Next morning Gina caught the bus to Trinity and beneath the grand arched entrance asked a uniformed security man for instructions to the Department of Slavic Studies. Within minutes she was standing in the Department secretary's office and asking for Stefan. Fool fool fool, she was reiterating inwardly. Let the past bury itself. Nothing can come of this. You are dying. Fool fool fool. This is stupid.

'I'm sorry, Stefan isn't here yet,' said the secretary, looking up from her computer. 'But Dr O Gallachóir says he should

be along any second. He really is so chaotic, he's impossible.'
She smiled at Gina, who, to her astonishment, heard an
absurd Vassar voice emerging from her mouth: 'That's Stefan
through and through. Pure chaos.'

Gina immediately stared hard at the ground, embarrassed
by her own phoniness.

'Hmm,' said the secretary looking up from her keyboard,
fingers dancing. 'Known him long?'

Gina felt the same absurd voice rising within her to declare,
'Absolutely yonks,' forestalling it with a non-committal 'Uh-
huh. You?'

'Years. Never changes.'

Gina stood there, her hands were cold and clammy, and her
heart was thumping solemnly. Inside her was this impostor,
ready to bray absurdities.

'His own worst enemy sometimes,' continued the secretary.
'Ah, here he comes now.'

There was the sound of heavy footsteps above them,
tumbling downwards like a delivery of logs just behind the
heavy oak door beyond the secretary. Gina waited, her
fingers resting on trembling lips.

The logs stopped with a final thump, the door burst
inwards, and Gina opened her mouth in welcome as a small
dishevelled fat man in his mid-thirties erupted into the office
as if ejected from beyond by bouncers. He skidded to a halt
by the secretary's desk, tugging on thin strands of fair hair.
'Jesus Mary and Joseph, Clare, this is great. I'm meeting the
Provost and I'm fucking late again, ach Jesus he'll be fucking
raging. Any calls, say I'm ach Jaysus, I don't know, whatever.
Regards to Mickie, by the way, glad he's better.'

He looked at Gina, nodded in an amiable, distracted way
and then charged out into the university square.

'That was Andreas O Gallachóir, Middle Slavonic expert,'
the secretary intoned without lifting her eyes from her typing.

'That's Middle Slavonia for you, every time,' said the
Vassar jerk-off inside Gina. Shut up, Gina commanded
inwardly.

'And I'm Clare Bardwell. You a Slavicist too?'

Gina shook her head. Her Vassar friend seemed to have

gone. 'A bit. Serbo-Croat. A couple of dialects. You know.'

'Well, Slavic studies is all the rage these days if your taste runs to burning cities and rape-camps,' said Clare. 'This place is getting to resemble Sarajevo, with missed appointments and mislaid files. Gets hectic, interviews, briefings, Department of Foreign Affairs looking for translations. Stefan's there three days a week normally. The Department, that is.'

There was a voice singing in the stairwell behind the oak door.

'That must be him now,' said Clare. 'And about time too.' She resumed her typing.

Gina felt her heart pacing, a prisoner in its ribcage cell. The oak door stayed closed; but behind her, the back door suddenly burst open and her heart nearly performed a back-flip.

Oh, she thought, half cried, her hand to her mouth, he's come round the back, and her heart suddenly went still on the cold stone slabs within her. She turned slowly to face Stefan, her mouth open.

'Christ have mercy on me and mine,' yelped the portly figure of Andreas O Gallachóir hurtling by. 'What have I done but only forgotten my bleeding paper on the cult of Seth.'

'The *what* of Seth?' asked Clare, an eyebrow arched.

'Very funny,' called his departing voice as he vanished through the oak door. Clare, her fingers still rippling over the keyboard, and the wry smile still on her lips, observed, 'It'll be the end of term soon and I'll be off to Bosnia for a bit of peace and quiet.'

The sound of Andreas's pounding footsteps diminished into the general noise of the building beyond.

'He's supposed to be meeting a professor from Sarajevo, the one the Serbs haven't shot, that is, and he's hoping to impress him and the Provost. Ha! By arriving an hour late and empty handed. He's actually very brilliant. And just as forgetful. Ah. Here he comes again, complete with paper on klephts, uskoks, Bogomils, Seth, et cetera. Entering stage left. Or is it right?'

There was a din of footsteps clattering down stairs, thundering around a landing and precipitating down the next flight. Gina braced herself for Andreas to come bursting through the door, while Clare sat there, eyes closed and hands to ears in mock readiness for the explosive entrance. There was none. The din died down and Clare, opening an eye asked, 'You ever see a Whitehall farce?'

Gina was about to shake her head when the oak door in front of her opened softly, tentatively, and a middle-aged, full-faced man, slightly less than medium height, donnish and balding, stood there gazing around bemusedly like a tourist at a crossroads. Gina, anxious to see the conclusion of the drama about the paper on the klephts, the uskoks and the cult of Seth, shifted her gaze beyond the newcomer back to the oak door, hoping to see tubby, distraught Andreas burst in again.

'Hello, Georgina,' said a familiar voice, and the strange man walked up and kissed her cheek. She stood there, Lot's wife, astonished, and heard her voice reply, a general noise, no more.

She blinked and tried to smile up at Stefan, beaming down at her. More thunder behind him, and Andreas burst through the oak door, crying, 'I couldn't find the shagging thing, couldn't bleeding find it. O God help me now.'

He exited, and the noise of him receded. Stefan and Clare were laughing and Gina felt an odd smile on her face, somebody else's smile, one you might find on a stone-age corpse dug out of a glacier in the French Alps, maybe, but not hers.

As Clare and Stefan were exchanging words, Gina frantically gathered her senses and looked at him.

She would have walked past him on a thousand occasions and not recognized him. The lithe athletic gait had been replaced by a middle-aged stockiness, the fair locks by thinning grey hair, the boyish face by a general imprint of age.

She could not speak, but felt this weak, stupid smile on her face.

Who was this man? Who was he? Could he possibly be the man she had once been almost ill with lust for?

Clare and Stefan were winding up their conversation.

'We're just off for coffee, be back in about forty minutes,

okay?' she heard Stefan say, and she thought, forty minutes? What will I have to say to this man for forty minutes? He's a stranger.

Stefan touched her shoulder and gestured her outside into the cobbled square gleaming in the spring downpour. The grass and stone reeked of ozone and the succulent electricity of the new season. Students lingered, flirted, kissed in the misty rain that tumbled the green emerging leaves of the broad chestnut trees, as Gina heard a voice inside her plead: Take me home.

CHAPTER TWENTY-SEVEN

Gina and Stefan remained silent as they walked up Grafton Street, their heads bowed in the rain. The crowds before them divided as they approached and closed behind as they passed, and Gina briefly reflected that they too must seem to others like currents parting around them.

Into the silence, Gina said, 'Nice woman, that secretary.'

'Clare? Desperate shame. Married to a gobshite, Mickie Bardwell. You women. The things you do. Why marry a drunk you've known all your life? It's in the blood, his mother was worse. She's worth ten of him and yet she adores him.'

Irritated and confused she followed him through the deep coffee aroma which suffused the air on Grafton Street into Bewley's Café and the hall of sweetness and heat beyond. Two parallel queues were formed at the self-service area. 'This one looks the shorter,' declared Stefan jovially, ushering her forwards. He gave no sign of realizing that this meeting was a very bad idea indeed.

'Have an almond bun,' he said. 'The famous Bewley's almond bun. All things have changed in Ireland, the sun rises in the west, and snows come from the south, all has changed but not the famous Bewley's almond bun.'

'Just coffee will be fine.' She suppressed a scowl which stayed simmering beneath her skin.

'You'd love an almond bun on a day like today, a cold wet day in May. Have an almond bun, Georgina.'

'Thanks, I'll stick to coffee.'

He laughed for no reason and said, 'Suit yourself, I'm having two.'

She looked away, wondering how she could end this purgatory. What is gone is gone. Leave the dead past alone.

The café hissed with simmering liquids, and the fragrance of fresh teas and coffees filled the air. Shiny silver vats with copper taps bubbled and spat hot water and issued that mysterious, nameless fragrance of steam. Opposite her another queue of damp, dripping people shuffled past the iced cakes and the scones and tarts and vast cream confections. She wished she were in that line, about to buy herself a coffee, to drink amid silence and pleasurable contemplation, and then to depart anonymously and for ever into the rain and cheery babble of Grafton Street. In that reverie, her mind drifted, vague and unconcentrated, her eyes scanning the second line, and suddenly her heart, a silent witness to all up to now, started, like a hovering fish over which a shadow falls.

She had just glimpsed a familiar face in the parallel line, but her eyes had passed on before recognition dawned. She looked back along the queue, her hand involuntarily raised an inch, her mouth open to say hello or even invite him over to dilute the torment of her present company. She scanned the line carefully, refocusing her eyes to where she thought she had seen him, but there was nobody there at all, just a vertical mirror running up a cake-stand and intersecting the opposite queue. She was about to look away, when she saw the familiar face again. It was a reflection of Stefan standing beside her, and in it she could glimpse flashes of the youngster of two decades before. Astonished, she stared again and this time saw a figure beside him, a thin and defeated female, weary and baffled.

Oh, she cried, and saw a hand go to the woman's mouth.

She was too stunned to switch her gaze as the man in the mirror turned his attention to his companion. Stefan was looking down at her. She could see him in the mirror, could see him smiling down at her head, and then he looked up towards the mirror and he saw her reflection, saw her looking at herself and at him.

'How are your old friends from long ago?' his voice said just above the real her, his Slavic face beaming cheerfully at her in the mirror. Then his image bent down and kissed the top of her head, and the thick tresses of hair on her scalp felt his lips. He said, 'Georgina, I've longed for this day more than you can imagine.'

She turned towards him, filled with shame, and in a reflex movement which she knew was right the moment it was done, put an arm through his, squeezed it, and then managed to say: 'In that case, I will let you buy me an almond bun. And thank you, my friends are fine.'

'Excellent,' he said, and she was about to tell him that he knew them when he turned to pay the bill. Embarrassment at her attitude still smouldered darkly within her and the Brackens left her memory.

They found a table and he unloaded the tray, sorting out the pot of Darjeeling tea and the coffee and the buns and the pats of butter.

She expected him to speak but he did not. Instead, he drank his tea, she sipped her coffee, confused, feeling tearful. Minutes passed before he sensed her distress. He grinned, and gave her a reassuring look.

'You jet-lagged?' he asked.

'No,' she said, and then added, 'I have something to tell you. I'm worse than I wrote.'

'Worse?'

'Much much worse.'

'I'm sorry, very sorry. After I wrote to you, Weizmann told me things weren't too good.'

'Oh! What do you know?' She drew a small draught of coffee into her mouth to hide her trembling lips. The coffee spilt from her mouth. She dabbed herself with a napkin, holding back tears.

'I know where there's life there's no cause to mourn.'

'No reason. None,' she said bleakly, 'save the undone years, the hopelessness.'

She was silent as she finished the rest of the words to herself: Whatever hope was yours, was my life also. Suddenly an incoherent emotion began to rise within her. Lost images of innocence flashed through her mind: a bare-legged boy on a river bank scouring rushes for wild birds' eggs.

She controlled her feelings with an effort, and yet again said silently to her body, oh fuck you, as her eye released a tear.

As naturally as he might remove a breadcrumb from his

lapel, Stefan reached over and trapped the trickling teardrop on a fingertip. 'Gina,' he said softly, leaning over and kissing her on her lips.

'What is this? What are you doing?'

'I'm not sure. What I want, I suppose.'

'Why would you want to kiss me like that?'

'Oh Georgina, what a question, what a question.'

They sat unspeaking till Gina said with a wholly bogus decisiveness, 'I'm going to get some more coffee. Want anything?'

He shook his head and smiled up at her as she rose. Their eyes met, and simultaneously she felt a surge pass through her entire body. She strode away with hurried steps.

Jesus, what is this, she demanded. What is this?

She busied herself with getting the coffee, repressing further speculation, feeling the beating in her chest subside. The middle-aged woman at the coffee counter looked at her in strange, piteous recognition, pointed at herself, and said, 'You can do it. I have. It's not over. Good luck now. Was it white you wanted, or black?'

How could she know . . .?

'You can do it. Trust me, trust me.'

'Me? How?'

The woman looked at her, and said, 'White or black?'

'White, please.' Gina returned carrying her coffee through the heat and teeming conviviality of a Dublin coffee shop. She saw Stefan cramming an almond bun into his mouth with schoolboy relish, a droplet of almond jelly sliding down his chin onto his tie.

She heard a laugh rise inside her, and Stefan looked up to smile at her approach. She bent down and kissed his chin, and tasted almond.

'Thank God I found you,' she said.

'I found you.'

'So you did.'

CHAPTER TWENTY-EIGHT

If I had my Fifty-Three I wouldn't mind this fucking rain in the least.

That's a pity, says the boy, because you certainly look fucking miserable at the moment.

There's a waterfall running down my back, my boots feel as if they're full of rocks, I have not eaten for twelve hours and probably will never eat again.

The two of them are crouched beside one of the small logging tracks that the bus containing the Bosnians might just come along. The rest of their section are covering other such tracks.

And you haven't got your Fifty-Three, the boys says, sensing that he is the stronger.

The machine-gunner muses for a while before speaking. At Vukova, I saw a line of Croats at five hundred metres. I lined up my sights so carefully, almost like a sniper, through the vee at the back, the barleycorn in the front. Oh they were so sweet, in line abreast, laughing, strolling casually, talking. A couple were armed.

He thinks for a moment. With FAZs, like these. The boy does not correct him.

I did a couple of traverses, mock traverses, and the bipod moved as easy as an armpit. The machine-gunner, his face suddenly alive with joy and humour, cries aloud in English, Hail to thee blithe bipod.

The boy opens his mouth to speak, but Šarac continues, You know that the Fifty-Three isn't for laying a field of fire blind over a hillside for some wretched bastards to wander into. That is contemptible. No. The Fifty-Three is an infantryman's weapon, with a sight and butt and a trigger. You see who you kill. You do what you intend to do. Real soldiering. Not blind slaughter but careful and intentional killing. Beautiful, so beautiful.

So it was this day with my little Croats. One sweep, my eyes down the sight, down they went, scythed down, one traverse.

Fuck, said Milošević – not that Milošević, the half-wit, another one, killed at oh wherewasit – you got the fucking lot. The fucking lot. Twelve, thirteen. Here, I'll take a couple of shots at them, see if they stir.

No no, I said, don't do that, they're dead, I know. Milošević said, Great, but how can we be sure? And I said, By feeling their pulses.

And I got up, with my Fifty-Three, and walked towards where the men were down, and Milošević was shouting, Get down you stupid, stupid . . . but I kept walking, slowly, because I knew the battlefield was mine. Not a thing on it moved without my permission. And I found my men, my line of Croats. I had fired about thirty rounds and thirteen men lay dead. The front one – I remember his teeth as he laughed – was telling a joke as he died. Odd, his mouth all blown to fuck, but his eyes still twinkled with laughter as he lay there. If there is such a thing as a nice Croat, he was it. I wish I knew what his joke was. It might serve me in a time when jests are few.

Šarac pauses. It was the most perfect sight, a thing to dream of in old age, when all else is failing in life, to recall the thirteen men I killed in under a second, in under half a second. So lucky.

Luck? It was good marksmanship.

No, not the shooting, not me, them, the men who died. Such lucky deaths. What have I spared them? Life, that's what. One second they were alive, the next they were dead, and their worries are over. No lingering death for them. No hideous old age. Just a soldier's death on a soldier's field. Perfect.

His voice drops further. So I probed through the bodies, lifting the wrists to feel if there was life. There was none, in not one of them. It was the most sublime thing I have done in my life – sweet and clean and neat. Heavy things dead bodies. I rolled them over, one by one, and looked them in the face, these dead Croats and oh how I envied them, to know that it is all over.

You're mad, says the boy.

Probably, says Šarac, looking up.

On his haunches beneath a dripping poncho, the boy hears something and turns and sees a bus tumbling towards them down the mountainside.

Shit, says the boy, this is it, this fucking bus.

And Šarac is suddenly up, crying Milošević, Obradović, Jovanović, captain, captain, captain, as this bus plummets down onto them, from up the mountain where it has no business being, yet there it is, a single wiper sweeping backwards and forwards in front of the straining white face of the driver. In a moment it's upon them, and the boy and Šarac are up, cocking their weapons, and the boy is flagging the bus down, but it keeps coming so he drops to one knee in the middle of the logging path, and he snaps the sight to his eye and fires one shot into the driver's forehead.

The bus skids and stops, even as the boy rolls sideways through the muck of pinebark and mud and tangled pine needles, off the log surface into a muddy pool. Šarac takes three steps to the passenger door, alert and lithe, just a couple of metres from it. The boy on the ground sees him switch to automatic, and flashing the boy the briefest of grins he turns to shoot into the bus.

His gun clicks. His smile is fading, and in one move he jerks out the magazine of his rifle and reaches for another which he slams into the housing, but it does not go.

There is the sound of metal meeting unyielding metal. He slams the magazine back into the housing again, but it doesn't click in as it should. He looks over at the boy and as their eyes meet they realize simultaneously that he is trying to put a FAZ magazine into an AK rifle.

Šarac spits, Fuck this.

They are his last words. He is shot twice in the face and he buckles and collapses. The boy, half up on one knee in the cold mud, is redirecting his gun back at the bus, but his limbs seem loath and cold. Even before his barrel is horizontal he is gazing suddenly into the aperture of a Koch and Heckler which has with shocking speed appeared from the side door of the bus.

And a voice says in accented Serbian, Drop the gun.

The boy sees Šarac's body prostrate in the rain suddenly settle; there is a sigh; the boy senses that light cargo of life leaving Šarac; the boy's FAZ begins to move upwards, as the voice says louder, Drop the fucking gun.

At that moment he can see right into the Koch and Heckler, through its barrel, up past the rifled groove, into the chamber where a bullet is a microsecond away from his brain.

A soldier with a UN helmet is standing on the top step of the bus.

The gun, on the ground or you die, he commands.

Metal hits the soft woodland soil as the boy lets his FAZ drop.

Walk into the woods, hands in the air, no, no leave your gun there, walk, my friend, walk, the UN soldier instructs him.

Rain drips from the trees onto the boy's head. He does not look back as he walks away from Šarac's body beside the muddy logging track.

Behind him he can hear the driver's dead body being hauled out of the seat, and thumping onto the floor of the bus. The bus engine starts, a gear changes, and the boy turns. The bus moves off with the UN soldier standing at the door. As it passes Šarac's body, the soldier blesses himself in the Roman style and then looks up straight at the boy. Their eyes meet. Croat bastard, thinks the boy. The bus vanishes into the mist.

*

She examined Stefan's face carefully. How his youth was gone. The facial structure was the same, yet different; the overall impression was of meeting a friend's father for the first time. He had gained stockiness without being fat and when he rose to get more tea, she saw his buttocks were firm and muscular, but his boyish figure was gone. As she watched him walk away, another shock came to her, a forgotten memory of him walking with the little girl, sloping; he walked identically now.

For a second she was back those two decades, the sweat from walking up the Wicklow Hills warm on her back, her breath heavy, Stefan before her, his slim tennis player's back ramrod straight. She paused in the winter sunlight to sweep her hair back from the dampness of her forehead. He was singing, his voice carried away in a breeze which had briefly risen as they breasted a slope, bracken falling away in brown, crusty waves towards the bottom of the hill. The girl was on his shoulders, her legs around his neck. A snatch of song drifted back. She felt a smile of pleasure on her face.

> *By banks of green willow, a maiden once strayed*
> *A soldier waylaid her, a compliment paid.*

'Smiley,' he said, suddenly back with her.

She started, blinking, inhaling the smell of coffee in Bewley's twenty years later. She realized then how much she had forgotten about him, for memory had been unable to store a record of his presence, his ready laughter. He was witty, his humour quick, light, refreshing. She kept sneaking glances at him, and every now and then would see mysteriously intact, buried in the older face, the youthful Stefan of a score of years before.

His features had not changed, detail by detail. The eyes were still grey, watchful, Balkan, the eyes of a wolf; his cheekbones were high, the nose strong and fine and so Slavic. Yet the whole was not the same.

'You know, I thought you were so *old* back then. You were the oldest boy I'd ever been with; everybody I'd had sex with was about my age, a student. It was a big age gap. Six years. That's big when you're nineteen.'

'Not as big as when you're forty.'

'Do you mind? Thirty-nine. November I'll be forty.'

'Well then,' he said. He smiled, toyed with a teaspoon, and said, 'So much to say.'

'You first. You told me you wanted to tell me things. Go on. Tell me things like how you learned Serbo-Croat, and what you have been doing, all the things that have changed so much, tell me about those things.'

He did and the forty-minute coffee break became lunch.
Later they walked through St Stephen's Green as the sun
dried up the rain and the tulips glowed in the fresh light of a
new glorious spring day.

'Nothing in life prepares you for life,' he said. 'That's so
obvious that it is hardly worth saying. Yet it is true. We're
warned about the things for which we need no warning, but
we're not told to prepare for loss, confusion, accidents, the
consequences of other people's deeds pursuing you through
life. We begin chapters without knowing it and end them
while we think we are in the middle. We make decisions
based on falsehoods, lies, rumour, legend. Nothing is
permanent. Nothing. Then we die. That is it. As simple as
that.'

He sat down on a bench beside a bronze bust, and dried a
place beside him for her.

'You don't mind getting wet?' she asked.

'You get wet, you get dry. He got wet. And cold.' He was
looking at the bust beside him. 'Poor bastard.'

She turned round also. 'Why poor bastard?' she asked.
'Who was he?' She looked at the inscription beneath the bust
– 'Poet and Patriot, Killed Ginchy, 1916'. 'Was he shot by the
British? Where's Ginchy?'

'France. He wasn't killed by the British at all. He was
wearing a British uniform, Royal Dublin Fusiliers. He was
killed by the Big Bang that made and shaped me, this, us,
everything. The Big Bang. This is a microsecond after the Big
Bang.'

She tentatively tucked her arm into his, concerned that he
might be discomfited by close contact with the dying. Instead,
he smiled at her.

'If he was a patriot, how come he was wearing a British
uniform?' she asked.

'Because of the Big Bang. Everything comes from it. This
state was made in that bang. So was Northern Ireland. So was
the Europe we know today. There isn't a border march, not a
frontier line, which wasn't shaped and reshaped by the thing
which caused him to go and die in France. Communism,
fascism, gas chambers, genocide, interplanetary rockets, the

twentieth century, began with a few gunshots on a Bosnian street corner. That day – you know? – the killing range of mankind was at maximum twenty miles, a naval gun, say, the target unseen. Planes were powered kites. There were despotisms, but petty things compared with what was to come. It's hard to imagine. Totalitarianism was utterly unknown. The worst of the tsars maybe disposed of a couple of score humans a year. And people had beliefs about gallantry and patriotism and duty and honour.

'Just four years later – Christ, four years, say the time between "I Want to Hold Your Hand" and "Sergeant Pepper" – the British had four-engine bombers which could fly a thousand miles and drop a ton of bombs on Berlin. Gallantry was dead. So were forty million people. Lenin had mastered the art of totalitarian state-seizure. In four years. A twenty-year armistice, more war, the same war, and everything that we take for granted was invented in the same period which elapsed between oh, say *Rocky* and *Rocky III* – holocausts, genocides, the nuclear age, supersonic flight, intercontinental rockets, computers, electronics.'

He went silent before looking around again at the handsome bust beside him.

'This is a lie, of course. Poor Tom Kettle was overweight, an alcoholic, not the fine and poetic beauty you see here. This statue is simply legendizing, unsuccessfully, as it happens. I suppose we keep doing this, falsifying so as to make palatable, to make endurable what is unendurable.'

He paused and sniffed and said, 'World events aren't history, not any more. They're a branch of astrophysics, blended with the magic of myth, most of it outside our conscious control.'

'The things you forget,' said Gina.

'Like what?'

'Like you can be such a windbag.'

He laughed. 'Maybe. Don't you ever feel like an asteroid?'

'An asteroid? I'd forgotten this part of you too. What time you got to be back in St Patrick's hospital?'

'You know about St Pat's?'

'Sure I know about St Pat's. Little guys with white coats,

sure I know about them. I even visited an old guy there once.'

'Good. Then he probably told you. We're all asteroids. The asteroid typically thinks it's the biggest, most important item of material in the entire universe as it turns about its orbit. But it also orbits the earth, which turns. The earth orbits the sun. The entire solar system turns about several axes. It belongs to a galaxy which turns and spins. Galaxy wheels about galaxy. Systems of galaxies have their own dance to perform. Somewhere in the middle of all this is our asteroid, proudly turning, very pleased with itself and its independent ways, shouting, Look at me, I'm free, I'm free. Ha. We're all whirling debris from the Big Bang.'

'For Europeans, maybe. Not America.'

'Really? Two world wars, one cold war. Korea, Vietnam, the Middle East, thousands of missile heads and your submarines slinking on the ocean bed. All from the Big Bang. No Big Bang, no totalitarianism, no nuclear weapons, no Israel even. Not the US, eh?'

'Okay then, not me.'

He sat back on the bench for some time before speaking. 'Who am I?' he asked her, and she told him of what she remembered, of the Yugoslav father, the former partisan who had died when Stefan was a baby.

'And I have a son,' he said, 'to whom I told these very things.'

He bent forward and looked at the ground beneath his feet.

'Next to that statue there – look, can you see? – is a garden for the blind. A garden of touch and smell. A garden for us all. You know, everything I told you and Milenko.'

'His name? Milenko?'

'Yes, yes,' he said impatiently. 'You remember how I told the Community Relations people in the North a few lies all those years ago. Little did I know. Nothing about me is what I said it was.'

He looked at her quite seriously, his grey eyes glinting in the spring sunlight. His voice had the grave tone of a doctor bearing the worst news. Gina felt nausea warring in her stomach.

'Tell me,' he said, 'do you like my Slavic features?'

Puzzled, she nodded cautiously and said, 'Of course.'

He said nothing but looked down at his knees and silently she observed his profile, and through the chaos in her brain she thought, he is so handsome. The Balkan blood, of course, the Balkan blood.

CHAPTER TWENTY-NINE

'Listen to this story of mine,' said Stefan. 'Bear with me.' He took her hand in his and told her again of his mother, Sorcha, who had been studying in Cambridge in 1939 at the outbreak of war. Though from an ardently nationalist Irish family she had volunteered to serve with the British intelligence.

'She was fluent in so many languages – French, German, Russian – and she was put into this cloak-and-dagger crowd, Special Operations Executive, who put her into F-section and a couple of years later flew her into occupied France from Gibraltar Farm in Buckinghamshire.

'F-Section, Gibraltar Farm. Why should I remember that? But I do. I forget almost all my friends in national school, but I remember that. Anyway, her network was soon rounded up by the Germans, tortured, murdered. My mother was lucky. The leader of her group, an American woman, incidentally, got my mother out in time. If she hadn't, no us. No coffee this morning.'

Gina, anxious to hear what Stefan was coming to, said, 'Go on.'

'Mum was then trained for operations in Yugoslavia. Well she had Russian, you see, just a hop and a skip from Serbo-Croat. Hop one away, skip the other, Serbs love the Russians, Croats hate them. Oh that place. Did you but know.'

He stretched back and paused, smiling wryly.

'You only understand the lunatic desperations of war when you see that someone like my mother, about five foot five of innocent niceness, except on the tennis court mind, oh that forehand drive, was trained in the black arts of killing. The things that happen in war.

'She was parachuted into Yugoslavia in 1943 to be radio operator, translator and courier with a column of communist partisans in central Bosnia. She soon discovered how the heroic volunteers against fascism were recruited.

'She was with a column of partisans who went into a Croat village in western Bosnia. All the young men there were simply conscripted into the column. There weren't many. The Ustase, the Croat pro-fascists, had been there the week before and had collared all the men they could find. One of the few lads that the Ustase had missed had been off tending goats at the time. His brother wasn't so lucky and was abducted. But the second brother was in the village when the communist partisans arrived a few days later. He was invited to join up at gunpoint – welcome to the freedom-loving partisans, comrade.'

The new recruit, said Stefan, was unusual. He spoke a smattering of English and German, and Stefan's mother became quite friendly with him. He told her about life in the Croat village, about the mixed peoples of the valley – Serbs here, Muslims there, Croats here and there.

The Serbs were an uncouth people, he joked. He should know. His grandmother was a Serb. The Muslims were arrogant and ignorant, strutting bumpkins. He should know. His granduncle was a Muslim. The Croats were jumped-up mongrels. He should know. His grandfather was a Croat.

The column was joined by two British guerrilla experts, SAS men, who had been parachuted in. A few days later the column attacked a group of about fifty Ustases seen camped in a defile. The Ustases were apparently quite amazingly incompetent. No sentries, nothing. Many of them were drunk.

'A few shots were fired, a handful of Ustases killed, and the rest surrendered. They were pathetic. My mother talked to a few of them just after surrender – they were all country boys who'd been abducted, just like her friend and his brother.

'Her friend had taken his pin out of his grenade during that attack, but had never had the chance to use it. Maybe he'd forgotten about it. Who can say? Who can ever say about these things? Anyway, he saw his brother in the crowd of prisoners and shouted out – well, according to my mother and who can say if she was telling the truth? – Pavel, Pavel.

'Pavel turned and waved, and his brother waved back and my mother thought that in the excitement of seeing his brother still alive he simple let go the grenade without even realizing what he was doing. Christ, he'd only been press-ganged the week before. Boom.

'He blew himself up and one of the SAS men. And in revenge for this oh so dastardly deed the partisans murdered all their prisoners. Cowering boys, some drunk, all incompetent, none fascist, not really. Murdered. The lot. But . . . the funny thing was, the man who dropped the grenade survived. Appallingly injured but alive.

'So my mother and the uninjured soldier – Harrison – and some partisans, carried the two men some huge distance to a partisan field hospital. The injured soldier – O'Rourke, was it? – didn't make it and they buried him somewhere. The other bloke, a real tough bastard, survived. His name was Milenko Djurdjev.'

Gina looked up at him from the trance the story had lulled her into. She had not caught many of the details of Stefan's tale. Now, suddenly, the narrative had an immediate relevance.

Stefan continued. 'My mother got to know the surviving SAS man. Harrison was from Ballymena, in Northern Ireland. His father was a Presbyterian minister. Harrison,' added Stefan reflectively, 'was probably a little mad.

'My mother got dysentery soon afterwards, and she met Milenko again, in a British military hospital in Bari, in Italy. His family was dead, and he detested the communists. The war was over. He had nowhere to go. She invited him to come and stay in Ireland. The only way he could get an entry visa to Ireland – Ireland was passionately anti-communist and poor Milenko counted as a communist, God help us – was by my mother marrying him. So they married, though of course the marriage couldn't be consummated, even if they'd wanted to. His injuries were, well . . .

'My mother got a job at University College Dublin. She and Milenko bought a little house in Hatch Street.'

'Hatch Street? Isn't that where we met?'

'Did we meet in Hatch Street? I couldn't remember where. In that house, was it? Fancy that. Mum rented it out for years.'

Gina looked at him closely. Was he joking? He didn't remember where they'd met? She was about to remind him of Josey, but he kept talking.

'About a year after the war, there was a regimental reunion of the Royal Ulster Rifles in the Shelbourne in Dublin and Harrison came down for it. Stayed with Mum and Milenko, and I was conceived, whether by rape, seduction, lust, I don't know and never will. My mother refused to tell me. The one truth of my existence is the truth forever concealed from me.

'Milenko, apparently, didn't mind a bit. Harrison after all had saved his life. In fact, I think he was quite delighted – if you'd gone through what he'd gone through, a spot of unauthorized sex didn't count. It did with my mother, of course, being Irish. Not great at adultery, us Irish. Well, not in those days. Milenko was just happy to see his name on a baptismal certificate. Then he died. Toxaemia. Well he was mostly grenade anyway. So I was brought up believing I was his son, and I have, accordingly, spent my entire life, consciously and otherwise, being a Yugoslav. I am nothing of the kind. I am a son of the manse. A son of the Ulster Protestant manse.'

'When did you hear all this?' Gina asked softly, astonished, postponing questions about Josey. 'You've always seemed so Slavic to me. It's part of your character, part of what you are. It makes no sense that you're not what I've always known you to be. I mean, Christ, Stefan. How'd you discover all this?'

'I found out last year. My mother was dying and she thought I should be told the truth. So she told me.'

'Oh, I'm real sorry to hear about your mother. What did she . . .?'

'Heart.'

'Oh.'

Gina searched around for something to say before coming

up with the pathetic: 'Are you glad she told you?'

He inhaled deeply and said, 'You know the strangest thing? I don't even know Milenko's real name. That was a war name. My mother died without telling me who he really was. But Milenko Djurdjev was probably a fiction. A complete fiction.'

Gina sat on the bench in amazement.

Tom. Tomas Djurdjev. Milenko Djurdjev, Senior and Junior. All fictions.

Gina replied numbly, 'Shouldn't people keep the truth to themselves? I mean in circumstances like that?'

'Yeah, maybe, if you know when you're telling the truth. But for the love of the divine Jesus, what is the bloody truth? I've told the truth all my life and ended up telling nothing but lies.'

'Bunbury,' she whispered.

'Bunbury,' he agreed.

He paused.

'I have a son who thinks his father is a Slav. Somewhere out there. A Serbian son.'

Not one son, said Gina to herself. Not one.

'So. Here in a park named after Stephen, I have to tell you that I am not Stefan of the southern Slavs but Stephen of Dublin and Ballymena.'

Then he fell silent. Birds were foraging in the hedges, and a robin sang on a tree beside them.

'So the real name should be Stephen Harrison?'

He looked puzzled before a smile came to his face. 'No, sorry that was stupid of me. No, Harrison was my father's first name – that would have been his mother's maiden name, Harrison. That's the way they do things in the North. Harrison was his Christian name. Or Harry, as he was called. No, my real name should be McCambridge.'

'McCambridge,' repeated Gina. 'McCambridge. Not Djurdjev.'

Twenty years had passed since she first heard the outline of this story, of how war had meant death for Rory O'Reilly and survival, of a kind, for Harrison McCambridge. Neither version was correct; no accurate account existed or exists, for the solemn duty of memory is both to mutilate and to forget, and not know the difference.

Gina's memory had discharged its duty splendidly.

Part Five

CHAPTER THIRTY

Gina had taken a deep breath to tell Stefan about Tom but her mouth was unable to shape the words. The truth remained untellable, beyond the captivity of language.

And truth remained elusive as she and Paula ate together that night. They spoke of Noelly, the ornament of the family, a linguist and a brilliant army officer. 'Loads of girlfriends too in his day,' mused Paula. 'Amazing, isn't it? Sure what would girls see in our Noelly? No point in asking you, sure you wouldn't have a clue either.'

Gina blinked in feigned mystification. Paula laughed. 'Look at the face on you. You still think of him as a little boy from the wilds of Mayo. We might just be culchies, but we've got hormones too.'

'Well all you Brackens had to come from somewhere, I guess.'

'You can't imagine your parents doing it, can you? Funny, that. The one act which makes you is the one act you can't bear to think of. And God, sex education when I was a kid, sure it was barely above the birds and the bees, even though Mam and Dad were, by the standards of those days, what you'd call progressive. Scabies taught me more about sex than they ever did.'

'Scabies?' said Gina. 'The skin infection? Come on.'

'No really. Went through the school like a dose of salts when I was, what, thirteen, and I thought I'd go mad with the itching. One night I was scratching away, and hey presto, I was so frightened, I thought the devil had come to me in my bed. Stupid, isn't it, but that's the nuns for you. But it didn't stop me scratching my scabies.'

Gina gazed at Paula in silence. 'I never would have

guessed,' she said, wonderingly. 'You always seemed so, well . . .'

'Sexless? Thanks,' Paula laughed. 'It all comes to human nature, Gina, and I'm human too. How was your friend?'

'Stefan? He's fine.'

'Stefan? Is that his name? You're joking me. Sure there was a Stefan once who stayed with us when Mam was doing the B and B. Mad about him I was, mad about him entirely. He kissed me and I thought I was going to come. Well, not really, but you know what I mean.'

'He kissed you?'

'Saying goodbye, on the platform. Oh I nearly died, and mam and dad beside me.'

Gina looked in amazement at her friend, and then, her mind sent in a certain direction, asked, 'Will I be able to see Noelly?'

'Who knows? He's in Vienna the last we heard, but Eilis was saying he should be back any day now.'

'I'd love to see him again.'

'Next time, maybe,' said Paula. She inhaled sharply. 'Oh Gina,' she said. 'Forgive me.' They fell silent, their hands touching.

The next morning she caught the train to Mayo. The vast expanse of sedgeland and lake and the small, malnourished woodlands of the central plain of Ireland passed by her, a whirl of waders wheeling from a bogland pool in a white arc as the train thundered on, a thin blue smear of hills resting remotely on the horizon. The carriage passed over points and adjusted itself like a dancer to a new rhythm. The clicks transported her back to her other journeys on this line, the bogs unchanging, the birds foolishly scattering, the habits of curlew, track and train unaltered and unaltering, no matter what happened to her.

When she first travelled on this line on her way to Mayo, she was beginning her young adult life. A future ahead of her as secret, as promising as the landscape which had rested before her then. Others of her age would live for two score more years, would see grandchildren and great-grandchildren romp and revel, generations following generations. To the sound of the rhythm of the track, she could hear a voice inside her uttering goodbye, goodbye.

Her heart lurched for the thousandth time at the thought of Tom. Stefan's revelations had troubled her, and she had been strongly tempted to call her son in Yale. But this was not news for the telephone, for it would undermine everything he had made of himself. He was now a respected expert on Bosnia – impassioned, articulate, sensible, even though he had never been there. Nobody disputed the passion of this defence of Bosnia by a son of Bosnia, especially as the news had come out about the mass rapes, of the ethnic cleansing, the murders.

Her eyes scanned the dreary and featureless expanses, their monotony broken by the odd cottage, the skirl of wading birds, and gazing, untroubled cattle. Rain swept against the window, steaming up the inside panes. Countless memories of water against glass in Ireland, of mist forming, of droplets dribbling against a vast forlornness beyond, formed in Gina's mind.

At the otherwise deserted station stood the Brackens – Maureen, grey and silent, her lip trembling, and Matt beside her, braced with the austere heroism of a man before the firing squad. Gina stepped down from the train, her overnight bag slapping against her thigh. 'Oh Gina,' said Maureen, taking her in her arms.

'I'm fine,' said Gina, embracing her. Matt touched Gina, and cleared his throat. The three of them stood mute on the cold grey stone of the platform, a wind tugging at their coats, until a sob ended the silence.

'This is inexcusable,' declared Matt. 'And we had promised to be so strong, and here we are . . .'

'It's all right,' said Gina. 'Please, it's all right.'

'Gina, I'm sorry, forgive me, forgive us both, oh we swore – didn't we? – we wouldn't . . .' sobbed Maureen, '. . . but then I saw you coming towards me, and oh it was just like you were a young girl again all those years ago, and something inside me broke. Oh Gina, forgive me, us, and you with all your worries . . . Matt! What are you doing, take her bag, what are you up to, standing there gawking? Get on with you now, get on with you.'

They turned and walked off the platform. Silently they got into the car. They drove to the house, past the telephone booth from which she had once telephoned Stefan all those years ago. The old kiosk was gone, replaced by an aluminium and glass structure from which you could telephone anywhere in the world, courtesy of satellites lofted into space by the descendants of V2 technology.

Maureen made tea and Matt chatted with distracted energy about the family, the twins in New York, Noelly, married, two girls – oh you should see them – and him the fastest rising officer in the Irish Army. Then he fell silent and appeared to embark on a long and anxious hunt through his brain for something to say before Maureen came in with the tea tray. 'A fine pair you are, all this time apart and not a word for one another.'

'I've words enough,' said Matt wanly. 'I don't know which ones to start with.'

Gina smiled at him. 'You don't have to say anything, truly you don't.'

'Oh yes I do,' he said, and sat down. 'I don't understand it.'

'I don't understand it either. But that's the way it is. I can kid myself they'll come up with some new therapy, but I know they won't. The funny thing is I feel so well. Nobody tells you that, do they, that you can feel well when you're not. Well I do, and sometimes I feel I'm going to live for ever. But I'm on medication to kill the pain. It's good. No real side effects at the moment. But it doesn't change the reality. Life ends. It's part of the deal.'

Matt nodded his head, and said, 'Oh sure I know this. Part of me knows it's part of the deal. The rest of me's unable to make any sense of it at all, at all.'

Maureen had been standing saying nothing, the tea tray in her hands. 'Here, Gina love, sit down over there on the couch so I can sit beside you. Oh I forgot the blessed seed cake. Would you like a bit of seed cake?'

'Have the seed cake, Gina, it's delicious,' said Matt, in a firm show of steadiness under fire. 'I'll get it. Is it in the cake tin, dearest?'

'It is, where the bloody else would it be for the love of the divine Jesus,' said Maureen, putting the tray down. 'Oh Gina,' she said in a low voice once Matt was gone. 'I've many things inside me, things in the heart which speech has no words for and the brain can't divine. I know what God does is for the best, and that we'll meet again in the next world, and it'll be a happier one than this.'

'But it won't have seed cake like this, you can be sure,' announced Matt as he came back in. 'The devil had a hand in this cake, it's that good.'

'Well, I guess I might just be eating it for all eternity,' said Gina. They allowed themselves small tight smiles and then busied themselves with the tea, the cake, the diverting enterprise of teaspoons.

Gina said finally, 'I had this feeling before, sitting in this room with you, all those years ago. You didn't have central heating, and it was always cold, my God so cold, always, and you didn't have a telephone, and everybody had a bath once a week, well maybe, and you had a fried breakfast every morning and you never ate fruit. I'd been feeling a little sick with apprehension, that poor girl who was meant to be staying here cancelling because her brother had been killed in Vietnam, me not knowing what to say. But now we know. We don't have to say anything. Only this. You have been my family, my real family.'

She picked her words carefully, to avoid melodrama or distress. 'As for what's happening to me. Listen, I'm lucky. I will know what's happening to me. I will know my death. It will be the most vital part of my entire life. What I don't know is what follows. Maybe nothing.'

'Do you believe that, Gina? About knowing your death?' asked Matt, softly.

'Maybe. Sometimes I don't know, sometimes I do. We treat death as unfair. Being born is the unfairness. Death isn't the mystery. It's the natural conclusion to the original injustice, that's all. Accept it. I can, I think.'

Matt rose from his armchair, a large if baffled smile on his face, walked over to Gina, took her teacup from her, raised her to her feet, put his free arm around her and kissed her. He said, 'Oh my dearest creature. God love you for your strength.'

She said, 'Matt, it'll be fine, I promise you, it'll be just fine.' She leaned forward and kissed his ageing face.

'Go on,' said Maureen, 'help yourself to my husband, why don't you.'

'I did. And very tasty too. Now I'll help his wife clear up.'

'And I've got some paperwork I must sort out today or I'm a ruined man,' said Matt, scratching his head, bemused, and he moved to put down Gina's cup.

Maureen cried, 'Matt, don't you put your cup down on that table without the saucer, not if you value your life – Matt! – how many times, I don't know.'

Matt shuffled off apologetically and Maureen and Gina were alone.

Maureen peered out of the window. 'Will you look at it now, it's a grand day, thank God, it'd be lovely to go for a bit of a spin.'

'Is there any chance of seeing Noelly?'

'Oh Gina, I don't know. Look, we'll see.'

'I'll just get my coat and be with you in a second,' said Gina. Suddenly, their eyes met and flickered ferally, communicating wordless things that are known. In silence they left the room and another shutter came down on her life.

CHAPTER THIRTY-ONE

Passing through Bewley's lobby, Gina examined herself in the mirror from whose depths she had not long before conjured the image of the young Stefan. She looked happy. She looked well. She laughed.

Stefan was on his way from Trinity, and she felt a thrill to the pit of her stomach when he joined her.

'How are you, you bogus Bosnian?' she said as he arrived with his tray.

'Not as well as you, by the look of things.' He sat down. 'You look great. Get lucky last night?'

'Maybe. You expecting company?' she said, looking at his full tray.

'I found it. Almond buns, cherry buns and tea for me and coffee for you.'

'You don't put on much weight, do you? How heavy are you?'

'A ton. You should see me without any clothes on.'

She smiled at him but he was too busy eating. He looked up and said, 'Sausages, I should have had the sausages. They're good here.'

'As good as Haffner's?'

'Good God. How did you ever hear of them?'

'It just came back to me. An old man in a bed and breakfast that first time told me about them.'

'Here,' muttered Stefan, puzzled. 'Where's my tea?'

'What?'

'Where's my tea? Stupid, left it at the counter. Mad, I'm mad.'

'Where's my tea,' Gina said aloud, another, fainter memory spinning back towards her, lingering and then fading. She felt the presence of recollection tapping insistently on some inner door, as if memory, renewal, were working strangely within her. It gave her power, an odd mastery.

'We have so much to talk about. Bosnia, for example,' she said when Stefan sat down. She was smiling at him.

'Yes, I know that.' He poured himself some tea.

He said nothing for a while, and then spoke. 'Have you heard of Gorazde, Serbenica? Terrible places. Sarajevo, of course, you know. My first trips were simply to help the Bosnians. More recently with UN or Irish Government accreditation.'

He was silent as he stirred his cup. 'The soul of evil lives there. Geologically, it is the crash zone of Europe, Africa and Asia. The collision threw up the Balkans and the Dinaric Alps, this vast range of mountains, ravines, crevasses, gorges. They divide everything, brother from brother, neighbour from neighbour, tribe from tribe, empire from empire. Everything collides there – east and west, Islam and Christianity, Orthodox and Rome, laws and cultures, even alphabets clash. What I felt was certain there was the ubiquity of death. That was what was so frightening.'

'And I know how,' said Gina. 'Do not feel sorry for me, ever, in this. I know how. I have seen Tom to adulthood. I have seen my life, and it is good.'

They left Bewley's and began to walk down the quays and smelt the Liffey smells of the tide and wrack and hops. Red mullet loitered beneath the Ha'penny Bridge, begging in the sunlight. They continued to the Phoenix Park, and there they sat while animals hooted and wailed in the zoo.

'You know there's a stone plaque there to commemorate the massacre I was telling you about? To the heroic victory – heroic, that's the word they use – of the partisans over fascist forces. Eighty fascists were killed, and no partisans, just one allied soldier. Which rings true. There are plaques all over Bosnia to commemorate heroic partisan victories. This one just has the details right.'

He was silent, clearly working on something in his mind.

'The last time I was in Bosnia, I was asked to mediate on the return of some Bosnian bodies outside Sarajevo. The library was burning. Like the Four Courts here in Dublin in

1922. A nation's stories in flames. Christ, I couldn't believe it. I loved that bloody place, and here it was, its books falling in ashes all around us, as they were here, right here, just over seventy years ago, only this time falling on all the recently dead. There was an eyebrow sticking up through the soil. Sorry, this is dreadful talk.'

'No, just honest talk. It doesn't scare me, nor revolt me.'

He bowed his head in assent. The supermarket manager bowing his head in assent, fingers steepled, shimmered briefly in her memory and was gone.

'There was a Canadian Serb woman there being photographed beside the eyebrow, grinning, fingers in a v-sign. Twenty-eight young men beneath her feet, they'd been alive when she left Ottawa, now there they were rotting just beneath her, till finally she said, "Phew, guys, these Muslim babes sure do fucking stink."

'And I wondered then and I wonder now about those men she was walking on, laughing, the men whose stench I could smell. Men. Boys. How did their killers feel when they had done this? All this flesh under my feet.'

He stayed silent then, abstracted, until she said softly, 'This is the first you've spoken about going to Bosnia. I'd have thought you'd have been talking non-stop about it.'

'There's too much to say. Confession time.' He looked at her and inhaled deeply.

'The bodies were returned to Sarajevo for burial, and the Serbs bombarded the funerals, probably from where I'd been standing, killing half a dozen of the mourners. With that signal achievement behind me, I headed off to Split.'

Close to sunset, he told her, he saw a Croat soldier on the roadside. He stopped, they talked, and the Croat invited him to join his unit for the night.

'There were four of them. Two from Zagreb, two from near Knin. My friend had a picture of the Virgin Mary on his rifle-butt. His parents had been killed in their home near Knin by Serbs. His name was Miles Vasic, a nice lad. When the war was over, he said, he was to join his uncle Gregor in America. A very important man, he said.

'I went off to sleep in my car. The Croats became

poisonously, insanely drunk. They started arguing. I could just make out what the argument was over. All along they'd had a Serb prisoner. The Zagreb men wanted to keep him prisoner. The Knin men wanted to kill him. I heard their arguments. They had a fight. That ended. Then I heard them torturing him.

'Once, just once, I went out to stop it. Miles pointed his gun at me, cocked it, and told me to get back in my car. His look was, well, I'll shoot you or maybe not. It didn't matter to him either way. I went back to my car.

'At first light and with everything silent, I returned. The Croats were comatose. The two Zagreb men had been beaten unconscious, and the Knin men were drunk. Empty bottles of slivovitz everywhere. The Chetnik was still alive. Blind, castrated, his tongue cut out, his ears chewed off, God knows what else. So I took a gun and I shot him through the head. Nobody woke up. I went to Bosnia to bring peace, and ended up orchestrating death or even inflicting it. The rule of Seth.'

Gina looked steadfastly at his face before asking, 'Seth? The secretary back at Trinity mentioned Seth. What is he?'

He told her of the twin gods of Egyptian myth. Plutarch had mentioned them. Seth is the god of war and death. He kills Osiris, his brother, the god of the Nile and tides and of harvests. Like Jesus Christ, after his death he was resurrected, and with each harvest is resurrected again. But without death there is no resurrection. So both are vital. Within the value system which embraces the brothers, Seth renews. Seth revitalizes. Murder must have its season, as it had with him, and as it had, unknown to him, with the boy who had ended the life of a similarly mutilated enemy.

'Some think that the cult of Seth remained long after the Pharaohs. Manichaeism seems to have spread from Egypt to the Balkans in the third century, and never quite vanished. The Bogomil heresy in Bosnia a thousand years later certainly suggests it survived. Both Bogomils and Manichaeans were dualists. Andreas O Gallachóir has been working on a thesis about the cult of Seth and Osiris remaining invisibly in the religious cultures of Bosnia.'

'Is he right?'

'Didn't I end up killing someone there?'

'But you had no choice.'

'Precisely. Those who follow Seth believe they have no choice. It is not merely a right but a duty to kill. But this sense of duty is part of a subculture which uses opaque and coded language. Words have meanings you cannot find in dictionaries and the unspoken speaks loudest of all. Outsiders who say they know the place are merely declaring the depth of their ignorance. That's all.'

Tom, she thought. Poor Tom.

She touched his hand with a single finger and they looked at each other steadily and with knowledge, and at that moment she felt a wellspring of loss bubble darkly. For a fraction of a second she could not distinguish between the worlds of her memory and the bewildering present.

He sensed something stirring within her, and said, 'What?'

Her treacherous eyes had misted again, and she said, 'Nothing.' Then, 'Don't you understand anything about me? There's nothing you could do that I would disapprove of.'

She wiped her nose and put away her handkerchief. He was sitting back on the bench looking at her, troubled, and she knew she would remember this moment until the last seconds before life departs – him, gazing at her solemnly, his muscular legs stretched out in the sunlight before him and crossed at the ankle, his green socks and black shoes and light charcoal trousers and green shirt and his fair hair streaked with grey, speaking of his journey from Sarajevo.

Oh I love you, she thought.

CHAPTER THIRTY-TWO

Stefan collected her the next morning. Gina had decided overnight that she must this morning tell him about Tom, but her courage failed her. Instead, she asked about his wife. 'You know you've hardly said a word about Mata.'

'Mata was a mistake. Full of the woes of the Serbs, which are infinite,' he said as they drove off.

'Do you hate her?'

'No, I don't hate her. We just got it wrong.'

'How?'

'Even when people used to pretend to be Yugoslav, she didn't. She belonged to her tribe. My tribe, right or wrong. Now she and little Milenko have vanished into the heart of her bloody tribe.'

'Where are they, do you think?'

'God knows. She had family everywhere. Her family's from Banja Luka, she has one aunt there and another in the mountains near Pale, both her brothers live in Belgrade, one of them a millionaire. Cars. I wrote to most of them, asking if they knew what had happened to Mata and Milenko. The aunt near Pale replied. She understood about separation – both her sons were in the army. She didn't know, she said, but she wished me well, in an old-fashioned Serbian way. Typically gracious, typically courteous, typically Serb. For all that's said about them, a lovely people. There's been no serious fighting where she is, thank God. And she did at least write to me. Why didn't you?'

'What?'

'Why didn't you write?'

'Why didn't I what?'

'When you went to the States, why didn't you write to me? Why didn't you reply to my letters? I kept writing to you.'

Gina was speechless, instantly reproaching herself for not preparing for this the most obvious of questions.

'I don't know,' she said hesitantly. 'I met Warren, and you know, it seemed kind of stupid to keep . . .' she fell silent, the weight of her falsehoods and her cowardly evasions too great to manage.

'Well it's good to see that you're a poor liar. Why didn't you write? You're not going to hurt me now.'

Now. He continued, gently. 'I even telephoned you, but your mother said you'd told her not to take any calls from Ireland.'

A waterfall sounded in Gina's ears, obliterating thought. She was silent for several minutes before she spoke, and even then she didn't know what she was going to say before she said it.

'I'll tell you why I didn't write, but I don't want to do it while we're driving. Can we stop somewhere? I'll tell you then.'

'Sure,' said Stefan, looking at her amiably. He put on some music, Fauré's Requiem, which Gina knew well and loved, and realized that for the moment he had forgotten her condition. They listened to it, to its conclusion and then Stefan changed cassettes, and a piece of music she had never heard before began to play; intense melody, nostalgia, innocence or innocence lost – she wasn't sure.

'What is it?' asked Gina. 'I don't know it.'

'Butterworth. The Banks of Green Willow.'

'Very English. Oh very Englishy English. Is it innocent, or is it nostalgia for lost innocence?'

'Both, actually. He was part of that dangerous thing called a folksong revival.'

'Dangerous? Why dangerous? Folksong has to be good, doesn't it?'

He listened to a few bars, humming along, before saying, 'It is in a way. The problem is – listen to this bit . . . lovely, isn't it? – people start off listening to the music of their ancestors and pretty soon start getting insanely proud, discovering their race and, often enough, all sorts of past injustices as well. We owned this land. We had that civilization. Stolen from us, et cetera, et cetera. A lot of the most wonderful European music is about the tribe. Just think. Elgar, Dvořák, Rimsky-Korsakov, Canteloube . . .'

'Grieg, Bartók, Sibelius,' she added.

'All very grand, then you get one crowd of folk music enthusiasts saying our music's nicer than yours, and our history's been rottener to us, and while we're about it, that there land is ours too. There was a revival of music in Ireland before the troubles began. Happened in Yugoslavia too. So much "folk music" is achingly beautiful, because it reminds us of a mythical stolen past. That's Butterworth. The past that never was. Here, I'll put it on again.'

She listened.

'I don't know his name at all. Did he write much?'

'Very little. He died young.'

Gina said nothing. 'Younger than me?' she said finally.

'Much.'

They drove on, the car windows open and the sun pouring in as the music filled them with melancholy pleasure. The lanes grew winding, deep hedgerows covered in walls of brilliant blossom rising to obscure the small fields and pastures. They rounded a bend on a hilltop and below them they could see a churchyard.

'Oh isn't that sweet?' cried Gina, realizing instantly that she sounded just like an American tourist. 'So beautiful,' she finished self-consciously.

She spoke as if she had never seen the church before, but she had. Twenty years before they had been down this road, and she had glimpsed the freshly cut soil and heaped clay of the little graveyard. She had forgotten it all. That day had been a crowded day in a crowded weekend; and all a long time ago.

Stefan drove towards the church gate and stopped the car. Inside the churchyard an elderly man was standing in long grass and looking with regret at a scythe. He turned to look as the car stopped beside the church wall.

'If it's help you've come to offer, the offer's accepted,' he said agreeably. 'Sure would you look at that bloody grass now.'

Stefan laughed obligingly and spoke through the open window. 'Not this time. I once tried the scythe myself and made a complete eejit of myself.'

''Tis easy to do that all right. Takes a knack,' agreed the man. 'Are you looking for something?'

'Tomnaskela. It's a while since I've been here and I've lost track of myself.'

Gina looked hard at Stefan.

'Sure you're doing grand. Keep on going, 'tis marked on your right a couple of miles down the road.'

'That's a lovely old church. Can we see inside?'

'Not now, but at six, say, of course you can.'

'Thanks. Good luck now with the grass.'

'Ah. The bloody old grass has me heart broke.'

They drove on, cow dung drying on the road, its sweetness filling the air, before Gina said, 'Tomnaskela, Stefan, please, what are you doing?'

He smiled at her and said, 'Revisiting old sites. Any objections?'

'No. None.' Something within her pulsed. 'You must know that . . .'

'Shhh.'

Tomnaskela. Tomnaskela. Breathing deeply as the car drove through the embanked road, Gina found that long-stored memories jostled with her present sensations and were almost indistinguishable. The hedgerows closed in on the road which then rose up so that soon great green valleys stretched behind and beneath them and the road petered into barely more than a track.

Finally Stefan slowed and eased the car off the road through an unfenced gap in a stone wall. He said, 'Okay, from here we walk. Okay?'

'Sure.'

The pasture rising before them was covered in a carpet of little wild flowers. She inhaled the giddy fragrance of the meadow as larks yammered in the blue above, and strode up the hill, long paces through the tresses of grass. Insects were spurred by their movement, and they leapt before these figures on a landscape like hand-cast grain.

Stefan walked beside her. She put her arm through his and he kissed her softly, and she thought, do not let this get out of control.

She looked up at him and said, 'Stefan.'

He kissed her again and she felt despair. They walked on in silence, the clear, clean sunlight warm on their faces, a breeze from the south-west carrying memories of the ozone of the ocean. Gina asked herself: How come I never felt happier in my entire life than I do right now?

They came to the breast of a hill and the valley opened up before them. A waterfall, silent and remote, twinkled against the green and blue of heather.

'Oh,' said Gina.

He said, 'Do you remember? This is where it was.'

She turned to him as he stood looking down on her, his eyes smiling, saying yes to her, and she said, 'I remember.'

She sat down. 'So why didn't I write? Because my mother was a madwoman. She's dead now. If she weren't I'd go back to her now and make sure that she was. I didn't get your ten letters.'

Stefan looked puzzled, still standing there, looking down at her.

'Sit down,' Gina commanded.

He sat down and Gina said, 'I found them. Years and years later, when my mother died and we were clearing out a bureau in her house, we came across a stash of letters. Your letters. They'd never even been opened. Goddam madwoman.'

Stefan was silent beneath the aerial choir of skylarks.

'I didn't ask her to say that I didn't want any phone calls from Ireland. The opposite was true. I wanted to hear from you, hoped to hear from you, fucking longed to hear from you, you understand?'

'No.'

He sat there shaking his head, and finally said, 'It's my fault. I should have known. How we blunder through life. The wonder is, how we ever manage to get things right. If only I'd known, I'd have got on a plane and flown over to you.'

'Oh please, please don't say that. I can't bear it. Hell you were, oh, twenty-five or something, fucking loads of young women in your life, you wouldn't have flown over just for me.'

'Why wouldn't I? Anyway, what difference would it have made? You had your Warren.'

'No,' said Gina in a weak voice. 'No. Hush. For a moment.' She lay back and they were silent for a long time.

'What a mess we make of things,' said Stefan. 'The moment we achieve a passing symmetry, and we're congratulating ourselves, hairy savages slouch in through the city gates, and start warming themselves with burning manuscripts.'

'Don't get philosophical on me now. Smell the soil,' said Gina.

He bent towards the grass and inhaled deeply. She did the same, her eyes closed, and then she felt his tongue in her ear, and she lay there while he kissed her. Her toes curled. In the pit of her stomach, at the base of her pelvic bone, she felt something move, stir, open.

'I want to hold you,' she said.

'Do,' he said.

He took the fingers of her right hand and licking them softly said, 'I love you.'

She bent forward and kissed him on the lips. 'Shhh,' she said.

They lay back in the long grass as the cuckoos called across the Wicklow Hills.

CHAPTER THIRTY-THREE

Gina woke, felt Stefan looking at her and she opened her eyes. He asked, 'Are you happy?'

'Never happier, in my entire life.' She watched him, lying there smiling, his shirt open to his waist, and she saw that he understood her meaning. He bent down and kissed her, and as their tongues met, she put her hand on his bare chest and part of her wilted yet again.

He asked, 'May I be serious?' She assented silently. 'Are these cancers pre-ordained, was it in your genes?'

'I don't know. My own doctor was away and I got this old quack who did nothing for about a year. I reckon otherwise the tumours could have been dealt with. Thank you, Rigman,' she finished, unaware of her error.

'Who's he, your doctor?'

'No.' She fumbled around in her mind trying to analyse events. She couldn't and allowed herself to laugh dryly. 'What can I do? This is my life, the one I've had, not the one I might have had. Would we be here now if things had been different? Right now, whatever condition I'm in and whatever future I have, I don't want to be anywhere else in the world.'

Then the truth erupted.

'Listen,' her voice declared. 'That weekend, the best weekend of my entire fucking life, I got pregnant. Pregnant.'

'What?'

Gina looked into his baffled eyes and he said softly, 'Tom.'

Gina nodded.

He was silent, his face containing so much distress that Gina was unable to say anything which might ease the pain.

She reached out to him, and he, taking her fingers, coiled them around his own, and he began to weep, softly.

'I'm sorry,' she said.

He shook his head, smiling ruefully. 'Such a cliché. Lost love, son born, father doesn't know, oldest mythic trick in the book. Cronus and Zeus. Nothing new in this world. And as always in these things, you, I, are not to blame.' He cocked his head. 'Oh will you listen to the cuckoos.'

Gina did, not merely because it gave her time to order her emotions, but because their birdsong demanded it. After a while she replied, 'Nothing new because we never learn, huh? Thing is, I wrote so often and you never replied.'

'I never got them. Everyone I knew, I thought including you, had my address in Belgrade.'

'I wrote to that government agency you worked for too.'

'Them. Christ.'

They were silent for a long time.

'Asteroids,' he said at last, 'fucking asteroids.'

Gina leaned forward and kissed him and saw fresh tears welling in his eyes and was silent. He inhaled, a half sob, controlled himself, and said, 'What a fucking fuck-up.'

Later still, he asked, 'What does he know about me?'

Gina told him. 'But I have to tell you he was more interested in his ancestry than in just you.'

'Ungrateful cur!' Stefan laughed. 'What man isn't more interested in his forefathers than his father? Fathers are mere flesh and blood parents. Thoroughly boring. But forefathers are ancestor and legend.'

'Not so much his forefathers as his forefather. He's fascinated by his grandfather, or rather the man he thought was his grandfather.'

'Why his grandfather in particular?'

'War hero, that kind of thing.'

'War heroes. Boys.'

'Listen, this isn't just a boys' thing. He's changed his name to Tomas Djurdjev, he's just about the most active supporter of the Bosnian cause in America. He speaks fluent Serbo-Croat. He is Serbo-Croat, Bosnian, whatever. He *is*.'

Stefan's face was filled with incredulity and a dawning comprehension.

'Oh Jesus,' he said in a low voice. 'I've seen his name in news-sheets. Is that him? Only nineteen or twenty-something? God, I thought he was older. When I saw his name I was tempted to write to him. Writes beautifully. I was wondering who he was. Same name, et cetera. Now I fucking know. And this explains his naivety. His American naivety.'

Gina said, 'He's proud, real proud of being Bosnian.'

'Which is what he's not.'

'Does it make any difference? He's got a cause, isn't that something?'

'A cause. Listen, this isn't stamp collecting. Being Bosnian isn't so much a nationality as a state of mind more complex, more simple, more deadly than anything the ordinary American child can understand.'

'He's real smart.'

'Than any outsider can understand. These are loyalties transmitted in code, and they are the codes of Seth. Seth who killed his brother. Seth is Baal. Seth is war. Seth is the devil. And Seth is worshipped. Outsiders blunder in there and cannot possibly know the codes. They are beyond ordinary language. Beyond the understanding of Tom. What does he know of how these people behave?'

'He's sided with the Bosnians. Aren't they more tolerant than the Serbs?'

'Some are. Others aren't. The Black Swan are Bosnian Muslims and perfectly vile. Where is he?'

'Relax. Yale. The genius of the year.'

'How does he feel about you being here as ill as you are?'

'He doesn't know. Nor does Warren. Look, they thought I was dying for so long. Then they thought I wasn't going to, that I was cured. So now the cure isn't a cure but a respite. I just haven't got the heart to put them through all that waiting and uncertainty again. I'll tell them closer to the end.'

'Georgina, love, you've got a lot to tell them. Far too much in fact. Not just your condition, but about my father as well, and so much more.'

And then some fresh catharsis seized and held her as she began to choke with a sense of loss. That part of her mind reserved for grief, which had not emerged since her mother's death, began to speak, and it overwhelmed all other faculties.

And a corner of her mind observed Stefan take her into his arms, kissing her through her hair and murmuring to her, and registered the slow diminuendo of her anguish, spiralling gently through keys and chords to a strange silence in which they were coiled together, limb upon limb, his lips touching her ear.

And then the torment was past, and she was aware of her tears dying on his skin, their bodies neatly stacked together according to some ancient design. She felt a happiness grow within her until it was an ecstasy which filled her as totally as the grief which it had replaced.

*

'We're not going to burn, are we? Back home we'd be toast.'

'We'll go soon. Should have brought sun stuff. Stupid.'

'Irish weather,' she said. A wet day, a cancelled tour of Dublin, suddenly flickered in her memory, and was then gone.

She was filled with a peace unlike anything she had ever known, and she knew that it was composed in part of the certainty of what was to come. Her life's business had ordered itself into a conclusion, and that conclusion was fine. She felt free.

They exchanged looks. They knew that a part of their lives was coming to an end. There could be no repeating these last few hours. She would never again feel such joy, nor weep as she had done there.

She had told him of their son and together they had stood on the shores of a continent of loss, which had defined so much of their lives and their identities. They had seen a vast firmament of untaken, irrecoverable opportunities stretching forward from a score of years ago to this point and to this hillside, and glimpsed only as a traveller looking over his shoulder might on the horizon see a country which had been blanketed in fog throughout this now completed journey, a land he had been searching for from the outset, and which was now, with its stands of weeping riverside trees, finally vanishing for all time.

They walked in silence down towards the car, knowing that however often they returned to this place, they could never come this way again.

CHAPTER THIRTY-FOUR

'We must make sense of this,' Stefan said as they belted themselves in the car. 'We could have got married and you could have been a career-academic and neglected me while I stayed at home baking scones, *or* you would have been a drunk and a husband-beater and we could have been thoroughly miserable.'

Gina smiled at him. 'Sure. You kind of guessed about my violent streak.'

'A shrewd observer can *always* detect these things.'

'My, you are so sharp. Too sharp for me.' He released the handbrake and turned the car.

'We don't know anything about one another. We've never even had a chance to disagree,' he said as he pointed the car away from the hill and their shared past.

She let out a huge belly laugh. 'Listen, fuck, I love you, I adore you. Fuck you and your disagreements, we're never going to have any, okay?'

'You didn't seem all that taken with me when we met again.'

'Forget that. I was being an asshole. You've matured, grown bigger and better and cleverer, and it shows in your physique, in your eyes, in your bearing. You don't want to look like a twenty-five-year-old.'

'Who fucking doesn't?'

'You fucking don't,' she laughed.

'Well you wouldn't mind looking like a twenty-five-year-old.'

'I have looked like a twenty-five-year-old. What I want is to look like a forty-five-year-old and a fifty-five-year-old and a sixty-five-year-old, that's what I want to look like, with you beside me each morning of my life as I wake, and beside me each night as I fall asleep. That's what I want.'

He was silent for a while before he replied. 'I'm sorry. That was idiocy of me to say that. May God forgive me for doing so.' He paused, then said, 'Look. Let's be realistic. Passions like this can't and wouldn't have survived the humdrum of domestic duty, putting out the garbage and empty toothpaste tubes, and bad breath in the morning, and finding yourself inevitably attracted to other people, and flirting at parties and drinking too much, and raising children and cleaning children and seeing them off to school and having periods and going off one another and secretly masturbating and farting in bed and being just plain bored with one another.'

'Okay, nothing secret about that, I fart and I masturbate. Wouldn't do without. Hell, they're the plus side of marriage.' He looked closely at her. She was smiling a smile. 'Marriage has its minuses too, you know.'

'Don't I know.'

Then, looking steadily at him and in a clear and certain voice, she said, 'I know I made the mistake of my life not staying with you. I could have seized my destiny, except I didn't know it was my destiny. I was young, I was unsure, shy, cleverer than I realized, sexier than I knew, prettier than I suspected. I didn't know what I was until I wasn't. I was weak. But listen, wonderman, how could I be sure back then that I wasn't just another one of scores of flings for you? How could I be?'

'You couldn't be. That's the terrible truth about life.'

They drove in silence for a while before he illuminated her with such a smile that the catch in her throat almost stopped her breathing.

She smiled back, coughed and said, 'Put on that music again,' and so he did. They drove through the tiny lanes of Wicklow, past the clusters of hedgerow and thicket, dense with birds and birdsong, rich fluting melodies which entered the open car windows and mingled with the tune within.

They breasted a rise and once again they saw the little church, its spire peeping above a surrounding cluster of beech and ash trees. As the road wound through the small valley and their perspective altered, they could see their friend of that morning working with the scythe through the long grass growing amongst the headstones.

Neither Gina nor Stefan said anything as they drew up outside the lych gate. Stefan stopped the car and they listened to the last bars of the music.

Stefan looked at her and said, 'Something's happening.'

'What do you mean?'

'I've had this feeling before. It's the glimpse through the trees. Something's happening.'

They got out and Stefan's brief mood of gravity evaporated as he called cheerfully, 'How are you again?' to the man, who looked up as he cut and nodded, before continuing his sweep alongside a line of lichen-covered gravestones.

This time Gina looked more closely at the man. He was about sixty, white-haired, wiry, his face lined and brown. He smiled at them as he finished his sweep.

'I should have done this last week or before, sure 'tis easier to postpone work than it is to do it.'

'It is,' said Stefan. 'It is indeed. You've noticed that too. I thought it was just me. Tell me now, what would be the name of this church?'

Looking relieved to be able to rest on his scythe, the man gave a full and measured reply: ''Tis the church of Rathmall, after the village, though 'tis a church no more in the full ecclesiastical sense. I was sexton there and my father before me. It is properly known as St Mael's church, or some call it Cloncawell church, this being the townland of Cloncawell.'

'It's not used any more?' said Gina, peering up at the spire and confused with the surfeit of information. Jackdaws circled and disputed in its old stone, vying for admission through belfry apertures.

'Barely. Once a year. Sure there's no congregation, barring me and my father behind ye there.'

Gina and Stefan turned, surprised, and there sitting on the gate-wall was a very elderly man, concealed from the road by a large hollybush.

The man nodded his head and grunted in greeting.

'If it's his father you are, then you are looking well indeed,' said Stefan with a careful decorousness which reminded Gina of what a bullshitter he could be.

''Tis his father I am,' agreed the old man, offering a hand like gnarled oak-roots to shake.

'Is it possible to see inside the church?' said Gina, her hand in the oak-roots.

The son behind her spoke up. 'It is. My father there has the key. Father, you have the key? He has the key.'

'How old is the church?' asked Stefan.

'No more than two hundred and fifty years old, though of course the Victorians had their say in it, as was their way,' said the son.

'And what happened to the congregation that it's hardly ever open?' asked Gina.

'You are an American? You have an American accent. It is pleasing to the ear, so it is, pleasing to the ear. Being an American, so, you might not guess the truth about this church, though an Irish person would know to look at it. This is a Protestant church, and sure most of the Protestants around here has died out.'

'Oh.'

'Died out. Father, can you find that key now, can you?'

'I have it here, Ernest, I have it here, don't be impatient.'

The son laid down his scythe and took the heavy, ornate key from his father. 'Come with me.'

They followed him to the large oaken door, beside which clumps of grass grew luscious and uncut up the sides of the lichen-green stone.

The door opened slowly and a sweet smell of damp and of diligent rot filled the bare-walled echoing church within. It was cold. Whatever light there was came through dark and dirty windows.

'We've had the occasional vandal, but little enough trouble here. Sure we're not worth bothering about here any more. We're gone, just about, gone, 'tis the pity of it all.'

Slowly the features inside the church emerged from the dim depths. An altar, a side chapel, a pulpit, some wallhangings, family memorials alongside the old pews.

In the murk, Gina caught sight of a large marble wall plaque with names on it, and she scanned it. Her heart leapt. Her own name, Cambell, with her spelling, was there twice.

'Look,' she said. 'My name!'

'Is it your name, is it?'

'Yes, yes, the only time I've seen that spelling,' she said excitedly.

A voice behind them boomed through the dark confines of the church. 'Me two brothers are there, Harry and Jack,' said the old man. 'Harry and Jack. Would have been there myself, only too bloody young.'

He coughed a soft liquid rattle.

''Tis too dark for me in here, too dark entirely,' and he turned and walked slowly out into the bright sunshine beyond the darkness of the church.

Gina looked at the plaque, marked Our Heroic Dead – 1914–1918. 'So many names,' she breathed finally.

'Too many. 'Twas the death of us Protestants around here,' said Ernest. 'My own children now, and I have five, are Catholic. I'm still a Protestant, but I married a Catholic. After this,' he gestured at the awful stone tablet, 'there was nothing for many of the girls in the area to do but leave, and they did, for Belfast or Glasgow or Canada.'

'Why so many? Why?' asked Gina, wonderingly, looking at the tablet.

'Foolishness mainly. Or courage. Or loyalty to the King. Much the same thing,' said the old man's voice from the door.

Gina heard him shuffling back to the churchyard, and peered at the list of names. Seeing two more the same, she turned to the sexton.

'Mr Bould, that is your name?' she said.

He inclined his head in confirmation.

'What happened here?'

'Begod, I haven't a clue. My father saw them off – he was mad to join himself, so he says, mad to join, but they wouldn't let him – and he saw them back. The few what come back. But sure it's never talked about these days, ancient history.'

Gina looked at Stefan. He was gazing at the names, in a reverie.

'Who were the Cambells?' she asked.

'The Cambells? I don't know.' He moved back to the doorway.

'Father,' he called. 'Father,' and stepped into the yard. Gina
followed him to the door and stood in the half light.

'The lady here was asking who were the Cambells.'

Old Mr Bould blinked, raised his head, took off his cap and
ran his gnarled fingers through thin wisps of white hair. He
coughed as he thought for a while.

'The Cambells, a quare crowd altogether. No "p" in their
name because they renounced popery. So it was said. Had
been Catholic but renounced popery. The family fortune was
squandered, in the way of them families. The son and heir
vanished, who knows where, England, Australia, America.
His younger brother was the grandfather of the two lads you
seen listed there. Nice boys. Fierce smart, they were, oh fierce.
But long gone, long gone. They were the last of the breed.'

'Oh,' said Gina, smiling politely. 'Thank you. And the
Cambell who disappeared, what was his name?'

'Cloowan. The name ran in the family. Cloowan Cambell.'

Gina turned over in her mind what she knew about her
family history before saying disappointedly, 'I think my
family's been in Louisiana longer than that. My Cambells
must have come from somewhere else. And there are no
Cambells left?'

'Sure there's no anybodies left. The last burial we had here
is that one there, and him a stranger and not even a stone to
mark it,' said Ernest amiably. 'Isn't it the shame of the world,
an unmarked grave?'

'Them lads in there could tell you a thing or two about
that,' grunted his father.

Gina looked at the plot Ernest had just nodded at and he
looked back at her helpfully. 'The rector said he'd put a stone
up for your man there, his name's in the register inside, but
sure didn't the rector himself die soon afterwards, and he's
buried back up north where his family's from.'

Stefan, just now appearing from within the church, picked up
these last words and said, 'This is the last grave here? Who is it?'

'He's just told us he doesn't know,' said Gina. 'Mr Scatter-
brain.'

'There!' cried Stefan triumphantly. 'I warned you. Fighting
already.'

'You,' she said, drawing close to him and putting her hand through his arm.

'It's no real mystery,' said Ernest, 'just no headstone.'

'There!' repeated Stefan. 'Pay attention.'

She punched him in his ribcage and he smiled down at her.

''Twasn't a local man,' Ernest continued, almost unheeded. 'And there was but one mourner, and not a bit mournful either, though a nice enough elderly gentleman who tipped me a couple of bob. I remember it well, the last I ever done.'

Gina was thinking impatiently about the Cambell connection and did not notice as Ernest's father said to nobody, 'O'Reilly, it was O'Reilly what gev him the few bob,' and then closed his eyes. 'O'Reilly.' He fell instantly asleep.

'Whisht, Father, whisht. So that there was the last grave I dug, though there's space enough for more. If you're interested, sure I can get the name for you, 'twill be no problem. Would you like to see the name? A Northern name, if I remember.'

There was a pause, broken by a snoring sound from the father. The three of them stood in the little chuchyard amid the leaning stones, warmed by the sun, and inhaling the aroma of freshly cut grass. Above them jackdaws continued their disagreements about tenancy of the steeple and pigeons called their soft chant from the beech trees.

Stefan stepped towards the unmarked grave and Gina turned to the sexton.

'What do you think about the Cambells? Would anybody round here know anything about them?'

'Sure I could look your man's name up in a moment, 'twould be no trouble,' he said in answer to a question in his own mind. Gina, a little irked at her failure to get him to attend, said a little sharply, 'I wonder if there's any way of knowing if my Cambells came from here, you know, way back?'

Old Mr Bould snored in the shade and Stefan, turning from the graveside to his son, said, 'You know nothing about the Cambells yourself?'

'Not a thing. I never even heard of them till you asked the question, and I never bothered looking at the old memorial thing.' Gina stared back and forth at the pair of them in frustration.

'Ah well,' said Stefan. 'You've been very good but we're keeping you from your work. We must be going.'

'You're welcome to keep me from my work at this time of year. What with the sun and rain, I can hear the grass grow up behind me. I can tell you there're days when I'd give my right arm to be a Catholic and not be worrying about this old graveyard and its dead Protestants and bloody old weeds, blast them to hell and back. And would you listen to me now, it's blaspheming I am, beside the Lord's house.'

He laughed and Gina, abandoning hope of hearing anything of use, cursorily offered her hand to him. His hand was like his father's – all knuckle and hard hide – yet he held her fingers gently and then offered his hand to Stefan.

'Thank you,' said Gina, a little curtly.

'It was a pleasure meeting you. You sure you wouldn't like me to check on that name? It wouldn't take a moment. Ah well. If you come again and I'm around I'll get you the name. If you like. We should erect something in his memory, if only a modest little stone.'

'Goodbye now, goodbye,' said Stefan. 'Pleasure meeting you, a pleasure indeed.'

'Bye,' said Gina. 'Bye.'

They drove unknowingly yet no less richly away from the point of conjunction of their two histories, from where Gina's family had come and where Stefan's father lay buried.

'Disappointing,' said Stefan. 'I thought we were going to get a glimpse through the trees, to the forest clearing. Ah well.'

Part Six

CHAPTER THIRTY-FIVE

What is that? his mother said, her heart starting with terror.

The boy looked up sleepily from his book. Nothing, he said. There is nothing to be frightened of.

But there is. So much. I feel it within me. I feel fear, sickness, everything falling apart.

Of course things are difficult. But you must relax.

I have relaxed in the past. What good did it do me, you, us?

He looked at his mother fondly. All will be well, he said.

All will be well, she jested. All will be well.

*

'What's Tom like?' Stefan had asked, his look of earnestness making Gina laugh. She was drinking cocoa, he had a large whiskey, his third. An extraordinary contentment lay in the pit of Gina's stomach.

'What's our son like? Well, he sure isn't Warren's son. He's got your build. Slight. Like a dancer.'

'Ha. Those were the days.'

'Come on. You look good. Anyways, we're going to have to tell this boy of ours the truth, the whole truth and nothing but the truth about himself, that he's not what he thinks he is. Kind of hard on a boy. Third time in his life that he's learned about his ancestry. And it sure won't be easy, with him being so darned proud of being a Bosnian patriot, you know.'

'Bosnian patriot. Djurdjev isn't his name, neither is it his father's, it's not even his supposed grandfather's. It's nobody's name.'

'Poor Tom. Can he make himself a Bosnian?'

'Whatever that is.'

'Poor Tom. Poor, poor Tom.'

'Ring him,' said Stefan. 'Right now. Tell him the truth. He's a typical American mongrel. Tell him now.'

He lifted the phone and offered it to her, but she waved it away, Stefan grinning mockingly at her.

'You know I can't tell him that kind of news over the phone,' she whispered, returning his smile. 'But I like your nerve, I surely do. Typical American mongrel, huh? Leastways, *I* always knew who my parents were.'

'And so have I! They just kept changing every few years or so, that's all. Look, at least ring Paula, tell her you're staying.'

She dialled Paula, but the line was busy.

Now Tom's father lay sleeping beside her and she felt both pleasure at his proximity and guilt that she had not telephoned. In the warmth of the bed she decided. She would call Tom at midday. He'd just be waking up. As her mind cherished the idea of the coming phone call, she realized she had not managed to call Paula either. She should have done that.

No matter. All was well. She turned and snuggled beside Stefan. He murmured in his sleep. She smiled, her heart filled with joy. She could not remember going to bed, and here she was, naked beside him, and he naked beside her. He must have undressed her and put her to bed, and she was exultant at the thought of that secret intimacy. She lightly caressed his back and ran the fingers of her left hand down his spine to his buttocks, then round his front so that she could cup his genitals, her other hand on her own as she flagrantly declared, so loud that the entire world inside her could hear: I love you. She rejoiced as she descended into sleep.

*

'Stately, plump Buck Mulligan came from the stairhead bearing a bowel of lather, I'm sorry did I say bowel of lather?'

Stefan was standing before her, smiling, a glass in his hand. 'Forgive me. A bowl of lather. Some would dispute the term plump. Friends would. Some would say I have an uncommonly genteel figure. And it is not even lather. Just orange juice.'

She lay with her head on the pillow, taking in the smile, the glass, the orange juice, but not quite making sense of them. She forced out a little laugh, and said with feigned good cheer, 'You're wonderful. You're not in the least plump.' As she lay in bed, the world wobbled slightly on its axis.

Bravery commanded that she smile at him, and she said, 'My,' realizing suddenly that she felt very weak. She took the orange juice and put it on the bedside table and added, 'I'll drink that in a minute, I've got to go to the bathroom.'

She rose and felt dizzy and mumbled about getting up too quickly. When she returned to the bedroom she felt dizzier still and sat down abruptly on the bed.

'Are you okay?' asked Stefan.

Gina nodded sleepily. 'Still tired.'

Stefan was dressed, she naked still. He sat down beside her. 'You must ring Paula. We should have done it last night. It's not fair. We can't have her worrying.'

'You know you've met Paula?'

'No, I don't think so.'

'You have, you have, oh there's been so much to tell you I forgot. You stayed with her family for a weekend, oh, a zillion years ago, eighteen years ago anyway, outside Ballina, and she fell in love with you.'

He smiled. 'Fell in love with me, of course.' He paused. 'Eighteen years ago. That's a long time, you know.'

'Not as long as twenty-one.'

'You mathematical genius, how do you do it? In so little time too. So I stayed in her home. Why?'

'I can't remember. It was shortly before I stayed there, when I came back.'

'You came back? You never mentioned that.'

Gina felt the narrative slipping out of her control. She had not told him about the time she locked the door of the railway carriage at Ballina station – indeed, had actually forgotten it in another act of sub-conscious elision, and now she must tell him the other truth, of that other time she had excluded him.

After she had finished her tale, she asked, 'You remember that awful day?'

He shook his head bemusedly. 'Not really.'

'Don't tease. You must remember that.'

He laughed and said, 'No.'

'But you must, you must, you must.'

He looked at her, wryly, mystified, and shook his head. 'No. Why do you say it was me? I'm always missing trains. Now if you'd told me there was a train I was on time for, I'd remember that, oh yes, by God I'd remember that, I would most definitely. But you tell me I missed a train. No doubt. As distinctive a memory as buying a pint of Guinness.'

'You don't remember that? You truly don't?' said Gina, half offended, half incredulous; how was this possible, that the event which had tormented her for years had gone unnoticed by him? Her head was swimming. She sipped her orange juice and began to analyse what was happening to her. It did not take long for her to recognize the ultimate truth, that the attack for which she had so long been preparing herself was now at hand.

But oh, despite the warnings, she realized that she wasn't ready.

Through her fear, she groped for words, ending limply, 'That was the second time I walked away from you.'

He laughed. 'There, it's what I've said all my life. Merlin had it right. We should be living backwards. It's not reasonable to expect all the right decisions to be made by people who're too young to make them. Middle-aged people have to live with the consequences of deeds done by rash post-adolescents. It's so stupid.'

Merlin, she thought; and Apollinaire's mysterious dialogue between the magician and nymph Viviane came back to her, as the author's fate shimmered and vanished. 'You're not mad at me?' Her brain was doing small somersaults.

'How can I be mad at you? Yesterday was the best day in my entire life. All the decisions you've made in your life, all the idiocies and all the strokes of genius, were needed for you to assemble that rickety structure you call your life to reach that point on the hillside. Deed upon deed, consequence upon consequence, all of them imponderable, all of them with incalculable outcomes, all of them necessary to make our lives what they are.'

He thought for a while before speaking. 'What is, is, you know this. You know it. Do I regret you didn't open the carriage door? Yes, that way we might have spent the rest of our lives together in wedded bliss. Or we might be divorced, hating one another, me paying you alimony, who knows. There is no promised land which we just missed. Only romantic nationalists or fascists think like that.'

She shook her head, her glass of orange juice cold upon her thigh, as she tried to impose her will on a mind straining to be free. Struggling, she had to search for the words, which finally emerged: 'No, divorce, alimony, hating one another. That would never have been. You can go on about consequence and unpredictability and all that man's talk about romantic nationalists or fascists as much as you like, but I do know, I know as much as I know I'm dying, that I was made for you and you were made for me, and foolishness and bad luck and cowardice kept us apart.'

He took the glass from her thigh and raised her naked to her feet and standing there in his shirt and trousers he enfolded her in his arms and kissed the side of her forehead. 'Which doesn't get away from the fact that you must ring Paula, whether I've met her before or not. Man's talk.' He laughed, shaking his head. 'Man's talk, indeed.'

She laughed uneasily with him, because she still felt so dizzy and frightened, then she lay down again. He passed her the phone and she dialled Paula. Stefan walked out of the room.

'Hi,' said Gina. 'Sorry. I should have called.'

'You should have,' said Paula in a voice Gina had never heard before. 'Tom telephoned last night looking for you. He left a number for you to ring. Last night, for you to ring, *last night*. I think he'll have gone by now. What time is it in Connecticut? Five hours behind us. Yes he'll have gone. Gina, you should've been here, or phoned.'

'I tried. The line was busy. What is it?' said Gina in a low voice which fetched Stefan back from where he had retreated to.

'It was busy because he was endlessly trying to make contact with you. He's flying to Bosnia, with a group of Americans and Bosnian exiles, to join the Bosnian army.'

'Give me the number,' said Gina. 'Now, give it to me now, I'll call him, maybe he hasn't left.'

It was Tom's number in New Haven, the one she hadn't telephoned the night before. There was no answer from it. She rang Warren. The answerphone. She rang Sue. Sue, yanked from the depths of complete slumber, took a few moments to collect her thoughts, then said, 'Warren's gone off, shit I don't know, I got to feed the dogs, Christ Gina, what's the fucking time? Son of a bitch. You know what time it is? He went off some place. Smokies, was it? It's four o fucking clock, Gina, ten off. What is this, hey? I mean what the *fuck*.'

Gina put the phone down, her heart thumping in terror. She had not told Warren or Tom of her condition in order to protect them. Warren had even mentioned that he might go to the Smokies while she was away, but in her stress she had forgotten it. Both husband and son were now unobtainable because of the ignorance she had created, with, worst of all, Tom now embarked on pure lunacy.

Stefan asked, 'What is it?'

She told him, and he nodded, and said, 'Right, get dressed, use my toothbrush. Oh, and don't worry. It'll be okay.'

*

Gina felt herself begin to spiral downward as Stefan talked. Her brain was uncertain, uncoordinated. Something important within her, beneath her diaphragm, seemed loose, like a boat drifting from its moorings, and a strange, unexpressed pain, an agony yearning to be free, rested taut, ready to be unleashed in her stomach. She listened, half hearing, as Stefan spoke to her.

'There are any number of flights he could be on out of Boston, New York, Washington. He's untraceable.'

It was now mid-morning. Stefan had spent the past two hours telephoning people in Washington, Dublin, Zagreb, Vienna, Split, even talking by satellite phone to an army friend near Sarajevo.

'Sarajevo. He couldn't fly into Sarajevo?' asked Gina, forcing herself to be intelligent. 'Could he?'

'No. Mick Geary on Mount Igman said no, absolutely not.'

Gina, through her confusion, said, 'Igman?'

'Georgina, there's so much we don't know. Like how volunteers and arms get into Bosnia, but they do.'

'What does this mean?' she managed to ask.

'Are you okay? You look terrible.'

'I'm fine. I'm fine. I just need to know what to do about Tom. What can we do?'

Gina knew he could tell she was lying. She felt unbelievably ill. Some fierce destructive power was working inside her, unlike anything she had ever felt before. There was a completeness about what was occurring, as if since she had fallen asleep, vibrant and happy, some deadly army had been released within her, overwhelming her thin, enfeebled defences after a long and ruinous siege. Had death, she wondered, finally arrived?

A noise. She looked. Stefan speaking. She gazed at him dimly, idiotically, focusing hard on the movements of his lips so that her eyes could guide her ears towards an agreed version of what he was saying; yet his words sailed right by her.

She assembled the simplest question she could think of. 'What are we going to do?'

'There'll be a duty officer on the Bosnia desk in Washington at this time, but he'd just be a gofer.'

She stared hard at him, urging herself to focus. Stefan was looking back at her. He continued speaking, his eye unwavering, searching.

'It's six in the morning there, Georgina. Are you all right? We can only do something when we know something. And we know nothing. Are you okay?'

'Mm,' she said, bobbing her head. 'Fine.'

He said nothing but walked out of the room. She was sitting, gazing through the window overlooking Dublin Bay, which was now glowing blue and brilliant. Beyond, south, was Wicklow. She found she was humming a tune to drown the pain.

What is that tune?

She could hear him telephoning from the bedroom. Her head drooped. She hummed to herself with increasing loudness. Louder and louder and the melody filled her mind, lush and pastoral, and her eye saw a valley, a broad green valley, a church steeple, a river bank, and along its length, a line of weeping trees.

CHAPTER THIRTY-SIX

Listen, there are these strange meetings. I have heard them. So have you. Night after night. Look what happened to the Ibrahimovićes.

The Ibrahimovićes. You go on and on about Muslim invaders, but then you help them escape.

We are Serbs. Not Nazis. And Izzet was a friend of yours.

Not really. Only sort of. And you gave them money, though we had none, not after Banja Luka. You spent it all at that stupid hotel.

I didn't spend it all. It was a nice hotel, and anyway, if we'd found your cousin there, it would have been worth it. Mr Yugo himself could have spared us a few thousand dinar, and now we'd be rolling in it.

But we didn't and we're not. Is that your foot making that noise?

And the Ibrahimovićes are safe now in Sarajevo. What noise?

It was nothing. While we're here in the middle of nowhere, no money, nothing. There! Did you hear that?

Stop. You are being stupid. We both are, we're simply managing to scare one another. We have no enemies.

Serbs always have enemies. You taught me that.

I meant us. As individuals, like the Ibrahimovićes were individuals. Hush. There! Did you hear that?

I heard nothing. Do you want me to check outside?

No. Stay here.

Nobody is going to attack this village. Everybody here is a Serb and we are armed. We are safe. Even Mujo and Suljo are not stupid enough to attack us here.

What is that noise?

A nightjar, he said. Whirr.

Hush! Footsteps! There! Footsteps, hurrying!

You and your imagination. Footsteps. Ha.

*

A hand touched her shoulder. She snapped her head up.

'Hi,' she said brightly to the owner of the hand, not sure who it could be. Tom? Stefan? Her mother? Warren? She arranged a smile on her face and turned it towards the person standing beside her. It was a stranger.

'Georgina, this is Peter Burke, he's a doctor and a friend of mine,' said Stefan's voice. 'Georgina, listen to me, you're unwell, you need to be examined.'

Gina protested, like a drunk. 'What about Tom? That's much more important. Much.' She felt sleep stealing up on her again, and she jerked herself awake. 'Much more important, much, much.' She sat up and tried to look adamant.

Peter looked at her steadily and smiled, and said, 'Georgina, how are you? I'm afraid I'm your favourite kind of doctor. An oncologist.'

'Great,' said Gina, feeling her wits scatter like cockroaches.

'Georgina, what time is it?'

Gina smiled pluckily and said, 'Oh you know.'

'It's three in the afternoon. Georgina, you passed out, okay? Georgina, listen to me, I need to examine you, do you mind?'

She replied simply, 'No, examine away,' before examining her own condition. She found she was lying on a bed. Stefan was nearby. So was his friend Peter, who then spoke.

'May I open your shirt here? I want to feel your tummy. Good.'

He probed his fingers into the area of her liver, and felt the soft tissue of her abdomen. He took her blood pressure, her pulse, her temperature. He looked into her eyes. He smiled at her again, and said, 'Georgina, tell me truthfully, how are you feeling?'

'Oh, you know.' She paused, and then sobbed and was silent while she rallied herself. 'Truthfully, doctor, I feel like

I'm dying.' Her voice was squeaky. She coughed softly. A small amount of liquid arrived in her mouth.

'Are you in pain?'

'Yes, in my stomach, where I usually get it, you know? But it's okay, I can ignore it. I feel a little short of breath. Is this it, doctor? This is it, now?'

'You're very ill, Georgina. Sure you know that, anyway, don't you? Would you make it Peter? I'd feel happier. We met before. You don't remember. I remember those eyes.'

'The eyes. We met? Good memory. Sure, Peter it is. Is this it?'

'We met the first time you were here. You don't remember. I do. Not necessarily *it*. Look, these things have ways of developing and stabilising, maybe sometimes even reversing completely, a patient who looks as if he's finished one day is running four-minute miles the next, so to speak.'

'Me, I don't think so.'

Peter placed his hand on her. 'I don't want you to do anything. Just stay here. We're going to put you in hospital and an ambulance is coming.'

'Tom,' she choked. She was about to explain the importance of the crisis, but a mere whimper emerged from her lips instead. She heard Stefan's voice, saying, 'Georgina, there's nothing we can do at the moment, you'll be better off in hospital. Believe me.'

Helplessness and fatigue rose within her and filled her, and she felt herself falling into a deep pool of sleep. There were voices. She smiled. Something was put in her arm. At one point somebody kissed her lips – Stefan, she knew – and then she plummeted into a dreamless dark.

*

She awoke and Stefan was sitting beside her.

'Hi,' said a voice from within her ribcage, and it was strange and high, as if it were someone else's. Her hand was on the outside of the blanket and she lifted it to wave, but it did not move. She waggled a couple of fingers instead. Her weakness filled her with foreboding. She spoke, 'Oh Stefan, is this it? Not now, with Tom up to his ears in madness, not now . . .'

But then, even as she talked, she slept again, and in that sleep perceived death, an annihilation of everything in history. In its place was an utterly all-consuming evil. There had been no Creation, no universe, no her. She knew total emptiness. Is this death? She sensed it was, advancing to claim her.

Then she was wide awake. Peter was beside her, wearing a white coat. He looked at her and he smiled. She tried to sit up but was unable to. In her bed she felt weak, pathetic, and tried to raise herself again.

'Don't do that,' said Peter. 'Take it easy.'

Gina, her mind waking, and astonished, said, 'I'm alive.'

'You are. You are incredibly strong. I thought we'd lost you. Look, Georgina, I work on the simple basis of telling the truth. I won't lie to you, okay? Don't ask me direct questions you don't want direct answers to, is that a deal?'

Gina nodded. 'There's no recovery, no remission possible from here on, is there?'

'The tumours are very advanced in both lungs and the liver. But I can't tell you that no recovery is possible, nor can I say there'll be no remission. I've read of both but only in the rarest and most clinically improbable circumstances, and I have never witnessed it with tumours as advanced as yours. So, it would be wrong of me to hold out hope.'

'Well then?' said Gina emptily.

'Look, I think I'll call Stefan in, okay? He can explain things for you.'

Gina felt panic pass through her as Stefan came up to her and kissed her.

'How are you, my love?' he asked gently.

'Dying, I think,' she said.

'You've been doing that for a long time and you're still not dead.'

She paused before she felt able to say, 'I've never been this bad. I never felt this bad.'

'Yes, but you're not feeling as bad as you were last week, are you?'

'Last week? What day is it?'

'It's Thursday.'

'Thursday? Oh no, that can't be, it can't, what's happened

to all that time, what about Tom? Do you know where he is? Does Warren?'

'No, I don't. If Warren's party's in the Great Smokies, they don't seem to have registered with the rangers in Gatlinburg. And as for Tom, we don't know. Your State Department simply knows nothing about a party of Bosnians leaving for Bosnia.'

'Can't you just ask them, government to government, what happened to him? Did anybody of that name fly out of the US on that day?'

'Georgina, he's an American citizen. We can't ask the US government for information about the movements of US citizens. Do you even know what name he's travelling under? Does his passport say Bourne or Djurdjev?'

Gina shook her head, feeling despair and then courage well up within her. She braced herself and said, 'Okay, where does this leave us?'

'There are two issues here,' said Stefan. 'One is you, the other Tom. Let's deal with you, okay?' He nodded at Peter who cleared his throat.

'This is complicated, and unpleasant. This is a bed for the treatment of cancer. You have untreatable, inoperable cancer. Do you hear me? You can stay here for a few more days, but after that we're going to have to move you. I'm sorry, but I have no choice. We have people on a waiting list for this bed. I'm sorry.'

Gina heard the words fall upon her.

'But I'm dying, am I not?'

'If you're simply dying, you stay,' said Peter. 'But you are terminally ill, and you've just come back from an impossibly profound coma. I know why you're fighting the way you are, and I sympathize. My guess is you're going to keep on fighting. I need this bed to treat and possibly save other patients. Do you understand this?'

'I understand this. What I don't understand is, what can I do?' She felt bitterness. 'Is there a park bench you can just dump me on? Or a beach, maybe?'

'No, you're coming home with me,' said Stefan.

CHAPTER THIRTY-SEVEN

Gina's mind, resting sideways on the pillow and confused by sunlight seeping under the drapes and onto the carpet, fumbled numbly with events. She was in Stefan's home.

In the clinic she had said, 'I can't let you do that, I can't be a burden on you. I can't.'

Stefan had said, 'No, no, you don't understand. I'm being selfish. Do you understand that? You don't. Listen, soon you might be gone from me. I want what's left.'

'Please, please.'

'Hush.'

He'd sat there, his hand folded over hers, and said, 'Don't worry.'

'I'm a burden.'

'Burden,' he'd said, shaking his head. 'Listen, it's for me. I need to be with you. I need to be beside you.'

She had still murmured dissent.

'And whenever news comes from Tom, I'll be the first to know.'

That afternoon an ambulance had taken her to Stefan's.

Visitors came, treading with the silken footfall of those who attend the dying, as the last days of life and the first of death began to assemble in her room.

Inwardly, in one of many private communications she heard a voice chant, Hear my cry, Hear my cry. She remembered: Doris crooning to Tom at her breast all those years ago, a memory stored then and recalled only now.

*

When Maureen arrived, Gina told her the truth about Tom and Stefan, about the stolen weekend which had changed her life. 'My mystery girl,' said Maureen admiringly. 'And I thought I knew you all these years. Oh begod you're the quare one.'

Gina murmured, 'Do you know, I thought you'd be real pissed off with me, lying like that.'

'God, what is youth for but to deceive those older than you?'

Yes, said Gina, thinking of Tom.

*

Matt arrived while she slept, and she felt his wordless urge: Be Strong. He sat in almost unmoving silence for hours.

*

Stefan was whispering. 'Good news at last. Tom's safe. UN troops stopped a busload of returned Bosnian exiles and some American volunteers near Tientiste. They're being escorted back to the Bosnian border. The whole lot. With a UN armed guard.'

Gina's heart rocketed within her deep slumber and, once the immediate relief was passed, it still thumped with a steady and uplifting joy as he repeated to her, 'The UN have them. They're safe.'

When finally she woke she found she was looking across Dublin Bay to the Wicklow Hills beyond, where for her it had all begun, at Tomnaskela, the mound of the storytellers, more than two decades ago. Now she scanned the purple distance where such secrets rested – a hillside, a stream, a small church, a graveyard, their clandestinity still intact, and she wondered: What of the men called from the glens of Wicklow to vanish heirlessly and forgotten, leaving behind an empty church and unpeopled, neglected fields?

I am so much luckier than them, she thought.

Her mind stored that memory, like freshly ironed sheets in a linen cupboard. Before her, large vessels ploughed towards Dublin Port, past the red and white column of Poolbeg lighthouse in the middle of the bay, their wakes spreading, meeting, bouncing around one another like children at a fair.

'All those people, making all those journeys,' she said aloud.

'"*Heureux qui comme Ulysse a fait un beau voyage,*"' said an aged voice behind her.

'Doris! Oh Doris, oh Doris!'

'"*Ou comme celui-là qui conquit la toison,*
    Et puis est retourné, plein d'usage et raison
    Vivre entre ses parents le reste son âge."

'Forgive me sitting here, that damned chair beside the bed is too uncomfortable for my old bones, so I just sat on this nice easy chair, and I'm ashamed to say I fell asleep.'

'Come here, Doris, let me look at you.'

Doris rose groaningly, unseen, and came into view. She looked remarkably well.

'So I finally got to meet your young man. Tracked me down like he tracked you down. But for him and his seed, what kind of scholar might you have turned out to be?'

'Oh Doris, Doris.'

They spoke volubly, ramblingly, and finally Gina told her of Tom, once missing and now saved, of his parentage and of the myths of his life. Doris murmured, 'The same ghosts haunt us all.'

They wept for a while. Their words had far fewer meanings than the emotions which formed them. Finally they sat in silence, their hands entwined.

*

'Where's Doris?' Gina asked.

'She's not well enough to travel. She calls you Gina.'

'Everybody calls me Gina,' she said. No Doris. Ah.

'Oh, I . . . She's sending you the letters.'

'Destroy them,' said Gina.

'No.'

'The past is past.'

'It never is.'

Her voice suddenly strong, Gina declared, 'Give me a time machine, and I'd take you back to the past we did not have, and, oh Stefan, such things we would do, I would ravish you in a thousand fields, and in the rain and the sun, on our loins and skin and flesh. We could undo those wasted years, the undone years.'

'Yes.'

They were silent, then Gina slept.

*

Gina knew she needed the toilet. 'Who is here?' she asked.

'Us. Maureen's gone into town.'

'Where's the nurse?'

'Esmerelda? I sent her home. She was tired. We've got enough people here.'

'Stefan, I need to go to the bathroom. And it's not just my bladder.' A sob escaped her. 'And I can't hold on.'

She moved her legs to ease herself, and felt the resistance of the summer quilt confining her feeble limbs. She was so weak. She looked down at the hand on the sheet. Her wrist was thin, bony.

'How terrible I look.'

He said, honestly, 'You look as if you have cancer.'

She lifted her eyes from her vanishing frame and her departing flesh, and she said, 'Stefan, do you mind very much if you help me, do you?

He pulled out the commode from under the bed and removing the quilt, pulled up her nightdress, raised her hips, and rested her on it. He said into her ear: 'Do you want me to leave?'

'No. No. Stay. My mother did it for me, I've done this for Tom, I'd do it for you. Somebody else one day will do it for you. I wish it could be me.'

'What odd ambitions you have.'

She laughed, and his presence beside her was comforting. 'Finished,' she whispered.

He lifted her off the commode and turning her sideways, he cleaned her. He took the commode away and returned. His voice outside her vision said, 'Would you like me to bath you?'

'Yes,' she said.

As she heard the bathwater running, she felt suffused with a childlike happiness. Stefan returned and smiled when he

saw her face. Kissing her, he removed her nightdress. He
carried her into the bathroom. He lowered her assembly of
bones into the water, then he gently soaped her all over while
she lay immobile, her limbs rocking gently in the moving
water. He kissed her forehead and ran his fingers through her
luxuriant hair.

'Shall I wash it?' he asked.

A memory flickered of an old man declaring, Hair a sign of
good health.

'Please,' she said. He kissed her again.

He rubbed shampoo into her hair, and massaged the lather,
his fingers lingering with a forceful delicacy over her scalp.
Another bath, another place, another life, another pleasure
came spiralling back. Once again, he washed the shampoo
from her hair.

He put toothpaste on a toothbrush, opened her mouth
and cleaned her teeth as carefully as a parent with a child.
Then he gave her mouthwash, which she spat into the bathwater as he lifted her out. He carried her to the bedroom and
placed her on towels on the bed. He dried her, then covered
her with talcum powder. He dressed her in a white cotton
nightdress, limb by limb, easing it down her fragile spine,
and then laid her on the bed again, drawing the quilt over
her frame.

She said, 'I feel so happy. I have no secrets from you.
Everything I am is yours. When I am gone I will love you from
wherever I am. I thank God that we met. I adore you, Stefan,
I adore you.'

He kissed her lips and she felt an echo of all those
sensations which had brought her so much pleasure over the
years. His hand lay on the quilt, and she covered it with her
hand.

She said, 'Oh how is it possible that I love you as much as
I do? How? You feed me, you put me on the toilet, you bathe
me, or bath me as you say,' she laughed, tears springing from
her eyes, 'you dry me, you even make me feel sexy, here in all
my illness and my disease, oh my dearest, dearest man. Kiss
me.'

He kissed her again.

'Come. Lie beside me. Naked.'

He undressed and lay beside her. She murmured, 'Oh you, oh you,' to the skin of his chest, inhaling his fragrance, his body protectively enfolding her.

'If people knew they would not understand,' she whispered.

Tucked up like students in the single bed, they slept.

CHAPTER THIRTY-EIGHT

Dreams filled her with new realities, fresh possibilities, yet then they vanished, leaving no trace. Had Stefan bathed her, had she once again felt that radiant warmth below? Had she invented it?

She was back in Mrs Ryan's one December morning two decades before, awake in her bed, rain lashing at the windows, as she said silently, I'll stay in bed, I'll stay in bed.

She felt warm in bed, so warm. She closed her eyes again, gave herself an orgasm and drifted off to sleep.

'Gina, stay in bed if you like, but will you let me know if you'd like a hot breakfast? Only I've got to visit a friend,' Mrs Ryan's voice broke through her dreams, through her bedroom door.

'I'm coming,' cried Gina, lying. I just did, she thought.

'Take your time, I'll be down in the kitchen.'

Gina rose, and went to the toilet. When she was done, she washed her hands, then her face and brushed her teeth. No shower in the house, and baths cost extra. It was so cold. With ice crystals forming in her bone marrow, she dressed and went downstairs.

'Good morning to you young lady,' said an elderly gentleman passing through the hall. 'A shocking day, quite shocking.' He doffed his trilby at her and opened the front door. A gust of cold wet wind barged into the hall and accosted her. As she fled from it, Gina briefly observed the man's departing figure, head bowed in deference to the weather, his hand over his trilby. The door closed behind him as she walked into a now empty dining room. She chose a table beside the fire.

Mrs Ryan scurried in. 'Would you like porridge, what you Americans call oats?'

The room was chill and dead and the words fell emptily around her. 'Anything to warm me up.'

'The porridge it is so,' said Mrs Ryan.

After breakfast Gina watched the rain trickle down the windows of the drawing room while draughts tugged at her ankles like playful dogs.

'I'm going back to Mayo,' said Gina to Mrs Ryan. 'I miss my friends.'

'Whatever you like, dear. You can leave the money on the hall table, we'll call it a pound, is that all right?'

She returned to Mayo alone, happy to be returning to the Brackens.

*

Stefan was beside her and he said, 'I'm sorry. Tom and his group have been abandoned by the UN.'

'What do you mean, abandoned?'

'The UN escort was withdrawn after Serbs kidnapped some UN personnel and demanded that protection for the people on the bus be withdrawn. The UN headquarters in Zagreb said okay.'

'The UN said okay? And the UN soldiers agreed to the deal? What kind of soldiers are they?'

'The modern kind it seems. But one of them is of the old-fashioned variety. He disobeyed UN orders and stayed with them. At least they're still free, somewhere in Bosnia, presumably heading for the frontier. They'll be fine, I'm sure.'

What did all that mean? For the moment it barely mattered. Her mind began to plummet, into confused war-like depths where she knew nothing. She saw ramparts stormed and defenders massacred. What was dream and what life?

Her dreams would make her free.

So her mind became its own master. Liberated of the dominion of her body, it stole from her room and from her sleep and roamed abroad with velvet tread. It came to know the little house well, lifting books and eavesdropping on the sculleried whispers beside the bread bin and the butter dish, as knives deftly made sandwiches and heads shook in consultation.

In her bedroom, beams of sunlight stalked the carpet, inch by inch as she, unobserved, decoded the mimed and murmured bed-end language of her friends. Finally, she could understand all. Nothing now was beyond her ken, no star beyond her seeing. New powers had come to her; through the din of approaching death, she could hear so much.

But where was Tom? She had a son to save. There was so much to do. A television set in some distant corner of the cottage whispered beyond walls impenetrable to the human ear, and she learnt the truth.

Tom was taken by the enemy, a murderous and evil enemy.

Stefan came to tell her the news, but of course she knew it. Hush, she said. I must concentrate. And so she began to focus intently through a deepening night, until finally the imprisoned voices came to her, whispering of Bosnia, of the trenchworks and pickets on violently disputed slopes and valleys and plains of Sarajevo, Igman and Vogosca.

She heard of the fall of an enclave. Was this a foretaste of her own future?

Storytellers came to whisper to her their tales, which they told with wild eyes and restraining hands on her shoulder. Listen, observe, hissed a part of her mind to her protesting self. Learn this much. These are the stories of our tribes, the stories of our race, our century. Pay attention to this news at last. *Listen. Here it is. It is unspeakable. It is Seth's truth.*

Cowering men are herded together, their elbows to their faces. They are made to undress. Guns are cocked. The youngsters grovel and howl as they die.

These conscript boys now lie in heaps, their skin white and gleaming. There is horseplay. The living jestingly turn the torsos of the dead with their feet. And amongst those angular bones she looked for Tom. Here? There? So many as far as the eye can see.

Duty bids her bear the unbearable, so, slowly she probes through the cumbrous potato-sacks of dead young men, heaving the corpses aside. Their limb joints are leaden. Sunlight falls onto lolling heads, onto parched tongues, onto teeth varnished with stale saliva. She pauses in her work to wipe cascading sweat from her brow, and sees in their eyes only the unglinting lacquer on sightless corneas, brittle as cellophane in the scorching sun. One by one, she Belsen-tugs the bodies aside, looking for Tom's soft fair curls, those delicate little bones of nose and cheek and chin.

Beneath the young corpses are older ones, forgotten ones, in countless numbers. O'Reillys and Boulds and Butterworths and Apollinaires and Alain-Fourniers and so many others, all of them bearing the same news, endlessly repeated through the century, pulsing from the same street corner in the same capital. She sees all; it is a panorama before her eyes, and she scans it for detail.

There! A hand, a brave hand, an American hand, plucking Stefan's mother from imminent death in France and dispatching her ultimately to motherhood in Ireland. And look – there she is, the hand's owner, Audrey Weinstein, smiling, waving, before unflinchingly going to the guillotine in Dachau.

Doris was right. So lovely, she thought, so lovely. There it was. As Stefan had said: contingency and consequence governing all.

CHAPTER THIRTY-NINE

The boy awakes. Milošević is sniggering, into his ear, We got them, the entire squad of Bosnians, so easy, right into our hands like that.

The boy is awake. What?

Thirty, forty Bosnians. Soldiers. We've captured the lot. And the UN murderer who killed Šarac.

The boy pulls back the blanket. Good.

Milošević laughs. I was nothing before this war. Nothing. Now I am free.

They walk swiftly out of the hut, Milošević's flashlight leading the way, towards three lorries standing with their engines idling, their headlights on full. The prisoners are gathered in full light, naked from the waist down, their trousers around their ankles, their hands joined behind their heads.

*

Gina woke. Maureen and Doris were there, in communion but saying nothing. She began to speak, to report what she knew about Audrey Weinstein, but instead slept again.

Peter came in and examined her abdomen. She smiled thinly at him, and said, 'What news doctor?'

'Do you know I think the tumour here is diminishing in size. Incredible.'

She slept again and when she awoke she did not know whether she had dreamt of Peter's visit or not. 'Did Peter come?' she asked Stefan as he washed her face and her armpits with warm water and a face flannel.

'Yes.'

She inhaled the fragrance of flannel and soap and warm water, steeped in the molecules of infancy; even amid her tormented confusion, those scents were still reassuring. She asked, 'What did he say?'

'To me?'

'To me.'

'I don't know. I stayed outside.'

'Oh.'

She was fed, eating little but chewing joylessly, for her duty was to eat to stay alive, to feed her tumour, to nourish it and care for it. Her mind spoke to it and soothed its angers, urging it: Be patient. Its time was not yet come. *But it will.* Hush now.

Every day Stefan rubbed oils into her thinning back, her wasting hips, her elbows which were now just pauper's knuckles covered in drumskin. She could feel where the flesh faded, could feel the bones pressing out towards the open air, could sense her body vanishing as her tenancy expired.

She awoke and said to him, 'What's happening?'

Stefan looked curiously at her, and said, 'I don't know. Your voice is back.'

'What do you mean?'

'You had lost your voice. It had gone squeaky. Cancer makes it squeaky, Peter was explaining to me. The squeakiness is gone.'

She slept again and did not know whether she had invented Stefan's words. And she dreamt of Tom, of his thin and passionate frame, those keen eyes, Stefan's eyes, those once-Slavic eyes which were now no longer Slavic, his long, soft fair hair. In her dream he was walking through banks of green willows.

When she awoke, Stefan was beside her, holding her hand. She sensed an electricity in his touch. She awoke fully. 'How's Tom?' she asked, her heart paused within her, alert, listening.

'Alive,' he said. 'That much we know. He's being held in a car factory at Vogosca, outside Sarajevo.'

'Vogosca.' *Of course*, she thought. 'And they're shooting prisoners.'

'Yes.'

She spoke with surprising strength, and her voice suddenly filled the room. 'But he's alive.'

'We think so.'

'Oh yes he is. My boy is alive.'

For a moment she slept, and then asked again in her clear strong voice, 'What will happen to them?'

'I was speaking to one of our lads, Mick Geary. He says UN troops are not far away.'

'The UN!' she managed to cry in derision.

'Listen, Mick says they're good. Canadians. The best in the region. No one fucks with Canadians. Believe me, this time, no hand-overs, not from Canadians.'

'What is there to hand over if my son is dead?'

'Our son.'

*

A haunted silence filled the sleep which followed, the silence of keening grasslands beneath which the slain lie without stone or cross, their bones jumbled purposelessly. Tom came to her and held her hand. She awoke and wept, and wondered again, what is a dream and what is not? Is this all a dream?

Peter was beside her, speaking to her, feeling her stomach, listening to her lungs, getting her to blow into a little device, and, after touching her hand, he left. When he was gone Gina asked, was that a dream as well?

*

A Serb soldier is examining a Bosnian's penis. Its owner stares straight ahead. This is too big, the Serb announces, lifting the organ with a pistol barrel. Look. Far, far too big. Muslims have no need for pricks this size. They do not need to fuck their women, we do that for them. Here you, come here, he says to another Muslim.

That Muslim hesitates, half lowering an arm to indicate, who, me?

The Serb raises his gun and shoots him through the testicles and he falls.

You and you, pick him up and tie him against the lamp standard there.

Two Muslims hurry to obey, looking unwaveringly at the Serb, knowing what even an untoward flicker of any eyelid might cost them. The Serb watches in silence while the Bosnian is bound upright with barbed wire.

Now, says the Serb pleasantly, looking at one of the two Bosnians, what I want you to do, please, is to bite this other gentleman's balls off. Now. If you please.

There is no movement.

What, he says incredulously. What? You do not understand me. Here, I want you, sir, to get down on your knees and bite off the testicles of this man, sir. You do not understand me, no? Ah well.

The Serb shoots one of the two Bosnians in the stomach. The Bosnian collapses, howling. The Serb looks at his audience, puzzled in the headlights. Respect, he says. That is the problem with the modern world. There is no respect for authority. None. Now shut up, he says, raising his voice. There are decent Serb soldiers over there who are trying to get a decent night's sleep, that's all, after a hard day slaving over hot Muslim cunt. And here you are, screaming your guts out, yes, screaming your guts out – look, I can see them there on the ground – as if you don't care about them. It's a disgrace. You should be ashamed of yourselves, yes, ashamed of yourselves.

CHAPTER FORTY

It's not my imagination, she said. Things are bad in Bihać, Bratunac, everywhere. People are being killed. Innocents slaughtered.

We are safe, he replied. There is nothing. We've been hearing things.

She spoke her final words in English, emphatically, clearly. You're right. Everything is okay. She looked at him and he saw her smile, radiant by the fire.

He grinned back at her in the flickering light. He reached out to touch her hand. She looked at him gratefully, and he echoed what she had said: Everything is okay. They were the last words she and he were to utter before the Black Swan arrived.

*

One night, she understood things with a delirious clarity. The unconnected filaments of her life connected. Words which had been forgotten or barely heard were retrieved and revived.

Now things made sense. There was a unity to it all. She was the asteroid. She had met old Con O'Reilly and all else followed – his brother, old Harry McCambridge in the ward in St Patrick's, Josey O'Flaherty, Stefan, the Boylan clinic, run by Con's nephew. In her mind, she could even see Ann Gemeti writhing under the lithe limbs of a tall blond ski instructor on Mount Igman. Ah yes, even he fitted into the narrative of her life. So who does not?

For the power of Princip had pulled them all to this new destiny, as it had her grandfather, and had in 1918 old Con's father before him. She saw the torpedo strike the sorting room in the mailship the *Leinster* in the bay above which she now lay, and through the window she heard, amidst the scream of hundreds of others, the sounds of a young father of three from Wicklow perishing. When, she wondered, did the hand of Sarajevo first touch her? But then she reproved herself for her stupidity. There had never been a second since that day of the Archduke's death when it had not reached out and guided the lives of virtually everyone on this planet.

But even as she received that truth, she dreamt again, and the secret was whispered to her of that unnamed grave deepsunk in the churchyard called Cloncawell.

Cloncawell, said a voice, echoing a knowledge first heard and last heard some decades before. Cluan, meadow, du Pre, meadow, Cawell, Cambell.

She smiled in her sleep. So obvious. The knowledge brought peace of a kind, and she resolved to tell Stefan of all she knew of his father's grave. Such priceless knowledge! Why do we remember some things and forget others when they are of equal importance, equal insignificance? *This,* God, I will remember. A bugle sounded through her mind, lingering on a breeze from some sad shire far away.

When she awoke she had forgotten it all, and she was puzzled. Her brain in its loss felt uneasy, yet she did not know why, for she had even forgotten that there was something to remember, something to forget. She slept again.

She sensed Paula beside her, sensed her grief and unhappiness, and though asleep, in her acute condition could hear the tears running down her cheeks, could taste the sorrow in that good soul.

She was aware of Maureen and Matt joining Paula, of the three of them praying in silence; and she dropped deep into a coma. Through this vigil she could hear her heart pulse its liquid duty, a solitary sentry in a windswept courtyard, his footsteps ringing on the cold wet flagstones through the longest and darkest watch of a midwinter night. Like my sentry, I will keep going, she told her waiting soul, until dawn brings me the news that I must hear.

*

'Where's Noelly?' she asked.

'Away,' said Maureen's voice.

Then Karen and Eleanor and Roben were in the room.

'I'm sorry I'm so late,' said Eleanor.

'Yes,' said Gina.

Karen merely said, 'Gina.'

'It's good to see you all,' whispered Gina. 'You're looking good.'

Roben laughed and said, ''At's my girl.'

Gina woke and Stefan was beside her, and she said, 'Did I dream of Karen and Eleanor and Roben?'

'Karen's here, this second. The others phoned. They're coming.'

Gina smiled, 'Are we alone?'

Stefan said, 'Yes.'

'You know,' said Gina, with a sudden level of energy, 'I think I almost once went to bed with Eleanor. For a moment, it just might have been, just might have been. The only woman I could ever have, you know? You remember that? I wrote you.'

'Did you?'

'Yes. Didn't you get my letter?'

Her mind went back to the swimming pool, the warmth, the sensuality of that Louisiana afternoon. She smiled at the thought. Young people, sunshine, so long ago. Vanquished years, vanquished flesh. She sensed Stefan smile.

Gina felt tears on her cheek but made no move to wipe them off. They dried there. Stefan kissed her closed eyelids as she lay in the bed.

*

Have you ever been shot in the knee, he continues in a lower, more solicitous voice to the man on the ground. Very painful. The Irish do it a lot. Bobby Sands. Great man. Have you ever. Been shot. In the knee? No? He fires. A moment's pause before he intones to the shrieking man on the ground: Welcome, to a new experience.

Who is he? asks the boy in wonder.

Račić, one of Arkan's boys. He can cook too. What a man. Right, continues Račić. The first prisoner to chew off somebody else's scrotum gets to keep his balls. Is that a fair deal?

There is a long silence. What? comes the incredulous cry. Come now. Is that a fair deal or what?

Answer him, says Miloš, walking forward.

Thank you my friend, says Račić. Thank you. I was beginning to believe I was all alone here. Anybody else out there? Any other Serb who is not afraid of being a Serb?

Me, says the boy stepping forward into the light. And me. And me. Volunteers step out of the shadows.

Oh dear me, little Muslims, my little Mehmets. Now, any volunteers? No.

He walks to a Muslim who stands weeping. I suppose you miss your wife. Ah well. She is probably dead. My friend, join her.

The shot enters the Bosnian soldier's right eye and exits through the back of his skull, a scarlet fountain briefly cascading over the captives lined behind him.

Now. Where is our UN friend?

I am here, says a voice in accented Serbian.

Alone here in the middle of Serbian Bosnia, and speaking so strangely too.

He is not alone, says one of the Bosnians.

Really. Another odd accent.

CHAPTER FORTY-ONE

Peter, she feels, is beside her. She hears him say, 'This is Dr
Potoriek from America. You remember him? He's come to
see you.'

She thought, Dr Potoriek?

She lay naked on the bed, her eyes closed, while they
probed her stomach, listened to her lungs, examined her eyes,
touched her skin, and the feeling was so real that she was
certain she was not dreaming.

'How do you feel?' Dr Potoriek asked in a gentle voice. 'I
fear I might have underestimated you.'

'Terrible,' she said.

'You should be dead. Do you know your tumours appear
to be receding?'

The doctors withdrew, and her mind followed them,
bending an ear. Potoriek whispered, 'That is incredible.
Never in my life . . .'

'How can . . . ?'

'Exactly . . .'

'Medical history . . .'

'Quite . . .'

'Fuck medical history. Where's my son?' she cried, but was
unheard, and, blinking, found she was alone.

*

Well my little UN man, says Račić, who do you think you are,
coming to Serbian Bosnia, killing our soldiers?

The UN man says nothing.

I know this man, says the Bosnian alongside him. He is a
UN soldier. He was doing his duty.

Fuck you all, says Račić.

Račić, chimes in Milošević, listening through a radio

earpiece, we must hurry, the Canadians are on their way. Don't mess with Canadians, Račić. Please. They kill people who mess with them.

This is madness, urges the Bosnian. This is a UN soldier. You can't harm him. The Canadians are coming.

He killed one of our men, one of our best men.

Milošević, who is still listening to the radio, urges, The Canadians are coming, Račić, we must be quick. Kill this man now if you must, but NOW.

Račić says, So what happened to all your other big brave UN men, UN man?

The others fled, says the Bosnian with the strange accent. They were UNPROFOR. He is a UN Military Observer. There is a difference. He refused to go.

Račić, hisses Miloš, there's a Canadian APC at the factory gate. We must hurry. The Canadians are not Ukrainians, Račić, for God's sake.

Račić says, A UN observer who shoots Serbs in their homeland. He has no right to carry arms. Then to the Bosnian, smiling, he adds, Listen here, my little Mehmet, who are you, talking to me like this, telling me about UN this and UN that? Has this man got a tongue in his mouth?

The Bosnian says, He is not the same as us. Nor is he some illiterate private from Kiev. He is important. Very important.

Račić says, Important, ha. Nobody is important when they are dead.

Milošević, close to panic, urges, Listen, Račić, we must hurry. Let him go. Those fucking Canadians are madmen.

The Bosnian with the accent asks, Račić, who do you trust here? The Canadians are at the gate. Do you trust him or him or him? Kill us, nobody will mind. But killing the UNMO is different. Listen. Listen carefully. The Canadians are outside. Take them seriously.

The UN officer, cool and persuasive, suddenly says, Be wise. Hand us over to the Canadians.

The boy thinks, now here are two men I would love to kill: this Muslim slime and the man who killed Mihail. Both. A barrel each. He inhales deeply at the thought and takes out his

Remington Derringer, fingering it meaningfully in the sight of the Bosnian.

Their eyes meet. The boy nods his head slowly, twice, mouthing, yes, yes. An American point 41, 10 mm, the boy whispers. It will make a nice hole in your head.

It will, agrees Račić. Show the gentleman what you mean.

The boy points the gun at the Bosnian.

No, fool, says Račić, how can you show him a hole in his own head? Show him a hole in somebody else's.

He points to a small battered man in the front rank of prisoners. An ear is missing and his nose is broken.

Come here, little fellow. Come here.

The man shuffles forward. Please, he whispers through clenched teeth. I'm American.

They broke your teeth too, the bastards, observes Račić, shocked. Those lovely American teeth. Mark me well. I will have some sharp words with whoever did that.

Račić smiles at the man and reaches out to pat his head. Never you worry, little man. All will be well. Now, he says, nodding to the boy.

Mom, oh Mom, says the American through his broken teeth as the boy raises the pistol and in a single movement shoots him through the temple.

*

Gina awoke, unaware that she had been asleep. She felt very weak. Stefan was beside her looking tired.

'Was Dr Potoriek here from Anderson?' she asked, before instantly returning to her dreams. She was again in Wicklow, in the graveyard at St Mael's, and Ernest Bould had a long-handled spade.

Will you bury me there beside the mystery man?

It is no mystery man.

I know. Will you bury me there? Stefan can visit us together there.

I will of course. But what if you outlive me?

She awoke again. She wanted to tell Stefan about her discovery, but he wasn't there, and she had forgotten what it was. In that second, she realized the meaning of Tomnascela:

it was not simply mound but *burial* mound of the storyteller. What a name to give a boy: and then she forgot that too.

*

Warren was standing nervously at the end of the bed, Stefan beside him.

'Tom?' she said.

'The Canadians have found his party. They're preparing to go in if the prisoners aren't released,' said Stefan.

Odd, she thought. The Cajuns had come from Canada. Something Doris said echoed and died.

She felt stronger. Halfway through the egg and toast her nurse was feeding her, she took the spoon and fed herself. Bring Tom to me, she whispered to Esmerelda's departing back before she suddenly plunged into a lightless void.

Strange noises entered her ears, intruded upon the vast darkness within her mind. They were visitors, gazing, waiting. She was in a deep coma on the threshold of death. She knew this.

She saw Tom walking in a meadow, long wild grasses blowing around his knees and a carpet of wild flowers stretching as far as the eye could see. He was smiling and he said, Mom, don't worry.

She awoke. Warren and Stefan were sitting beside her. 'Anything?' she whispered, her lips paper-thin beside the crisp sheets.

'Nothing,' said Stefan softly. She knew he lied, for her vagrant mind had discovered that a renegade called Račić was in charge, and that killings were now almost uncontrolled. Gina turned her eyes to Stefan. He looked seventy. Beside him Warren watched on. She said, 'Let us sleep now.'

*

Oh Christ, says Milošević.

Račić is looking down at the body of the dead man. It is making the tiny movements of those just slain. He shifts it with his boot.

Dead, says Račić. Good. You have done this sort of work before. What age are you?

Sixteen.
Sixteen. You like killing cold?
Killing cold is better.
Račić inhales deeply in agreement.
Milošević cries, The Canadians.

*

Dreaming, Gina said, Let me die, God, but let my son have
children and grandchildren, God, please, let him discover
who he is, let him know the truth, what truth there is amid
the din of myth and storytelling, but do not take him away
before you take me.

When she felt the gentle hands of physicians probing her
body, she asked, Am I near death? Or am I instead to live
after all?

*

Now, my friend, says Račić to the Bosnian, you were
commenting, I believe, upon the reliability of these, my
men.

Let me kill him, says the boy. Račić, Račić, let me kill him.
He is mine. Let me kill them both, this Bosnian fool and this
UN murderer.

Yes, if I think it right.

Račić. Give them to me.

The Bosnian says, You might trust the boy here. Do you
trust every other man who can see what is going on?

Račić! cries Milošević despairingly, as gunfire erupts from
the main gates, the fucking Canadians.

Your accent is funny, Mehmet, says Račić, unperturbed.
Where are you from?

My name is not Mehmet.

Where are you from?

The Geneva Convention states that—

The Geneva Convention! screams the boy in delight.

Račić looks at the Bosnian closely. You are out of your
fucking mind, Mehmet. Where the fuck are you from,
Mehmet, talking such fucking shit? Here, kill him, he says to
the boy.

And the UN officer says, You can't kill this man. Tom, tell them, you are American.

He is an American who wishes to be a Bosnian, chuckles Račić. Very well. Then let him die like a Bosnian.

Tom's face registers the imminence of his fate. He lowers his head and murmurs the suddenly remembered words, *Introibo ad altare Dei*, which means, I will go the altar of God.

And the UN soldier whispers in reply, *Ad Deum qui laetificat juventutem meum*, which means, To God, the giver of youth and happiness.

And Tom says, *Judica me, Deus, et discerne causam mean de gente non sancta: ab homine iniquo at doloso erue me*, which means, Oh God, sustain my cause; give me redress against a race which knows no piety; save me from a treacherous foe and cruel.

What the fuck is that, Mehmet? Are you speaking Turkish gibberish at me? Or is it the Koran? God, fucking Arabic shit.

A din of gunfire erupts on the outskirts of the factory grounds.

Emitte lucem tuam, et veritatem taum: ipsa me deduxerunt, et adduxerunt in montem sanctum tuum, et in tabernacula tua, whispers the UN officer, his voice unwavering – The light of thy presence, the fulfilment of thy promise, let these be my escort, bringing me safe to thy holy mountain, to the tabernacle where thou dwellest.

Račić is smiling.

Even in the din of gunfire, he says to the young Bosnian, And now, Mehmet, the end approaches.

My name is not Mehmet, says the Bosnian with a sudden strength, looking directly at Račić.

What is it? asks Račić, smiling, indifferent.

It is Djurdjev, says the Bosnian.

The boy laughs. Miraculous. What a coincidence. And what is your name, Mr UN man, as he opens his little Remington Derringer, ejects the used cartridge with his thumbnail and reaches for a fresh 10 mm round in his little ammunition pouch.

It is empty.

The man he has spoken to replies strongly and in Serbian.

I am a serving officer of the United Nations. My name is Bracken, Commandant Noel Bracken, a major in the Army of The Irish Republic.

Irish, sniffs the boy, good. He snaps his Derringer shut with only one bullet in the chamber. He says, in English, My father was Irish, and a sheep; but I am, thank God, a Serb.

*

Gina slumbers thoughtlessly and insensate, the tiny ampage of her cells commanding her to survive, though part of her is seduced by the prospect of death. Yet even as she begins to capitulate, she suddenly senses Stefan's arrival beside her. She knows crisis is to hand, but she is too weak to act or speak.

She hears herself asking, Where will I go? And in the dark, a voice whispers, Hear my cry.

*

There are shouts from nearby, the circle around the captured Bosnians breaks up, some men firing in panic into the darkness towards the advancing Canadians. The boy raises his voice above the gunfire, You killed my friend, he says. And you are Irish. So it will be my pleasure to kill you. And as for you, ridiculous American, my new friend here is right – if he wants to live like a Bosnian, he can die like one. Who first?

He lifts the Derringer. He looks at Noelly and Tom. There is a click as he cocks the little pistol, just as Canadian gunfire begins to cut down the Serbians. Milošević chokes and falls. The boy swiftly points his gun towards a forehead as automatic gunfire scythes through the group. Bodies collapse, flailing, and his finger instantly closes on the trigger.

*

And now Gina is fully awake, blinking, the sun shining through uncurtained windows, high over the blue expanse of Dublin Bay, and silhouetting the verdant osiers weeping beyond in the mythic, steepled glen of Rathmall. Her heart hardly beating, she looks at the quiet estuarial waters at their ebb, and finally comes to understand something of Seth and Osiris.

Her knowledge fills her with a dark and terrible serenity. Finally wisdom is hers and she has mastered mystery.

But more than this, for Tom, her Tom, her lovely smiling Tom – oh see how handsome he is: see his young, lithe good looks, so Bosnian, so true – is standing beside her, his hand in hers, and bending gently to her he whispers good news at last from Sarajevo.